Alongside Night

J. Neil Schulman's
Alongside Night

PULPLESS.com
150 S. Highway 160, Suite C-8, #234
Pahrump, NV 89048, U.S.A.
(775) 751-0770
http://www.pulpless.com
Inquiries to jneil@pulpless.com

Originally published by Crown Publishers, October 16, 1979
First Pulpless.Com HTML edition: November 3, 1996
First Pulpless.ComTM Edition August, 1999
30th Anniversary PDF Edition: June 16, 2009

Library of Congress Catalog Card Number: 99-062027
30th Anniversary PDF edition ISBN: 1-58445-201-3
Book designed by Samuel Edward Konkin III
Cover Illustration by Billy Tackett,
Billy Tackett Studios
http://www.BillyTackett.com

Author's Note

The Independent Arbitration Group is an actual organization founded by attorney Ralph Fucetola, and the author thanks him for permission to quote from his organization's General Submission to Arbitration agreement. Though the Independent Arbitration Group pioneered the General Submission service contract, all other references to the organization within the body of this novel, or to its clients, are purely fictional.

God Here And Now: An Introduction to Gloamingerism by Reverend Virgil Moore; and *The Last, True Hope* by Bishop Alam Kimar Whyte are included with the Pulpless.Com[tm] Inc., edition courtesy of the Church of the Human God.

Excepting the above, the characters, organizations, and firms portrayed in this novel are fictional, any similarity to actual persons, organizations, or firms, past or present, being purely coincidental. Though the names of some actual locations, institutions, and businesses have been included as cultural referents, this should not be construed as reflecting in any way upon past or present owners or management.

In particular, let me make clear that there is no correspondence between the Dr. Martin Vreeland of my novel and the real-life Milton Friedman, though Dr. Friedman was kind enough to read my novel's manuscript to critique it for me. In fact the first draft manuscript of my novel awarded the Nobel Prize in economics to Dr. Vreeland over a year before Dr. Friedman well-deservedly received his ...

Any reference to actual government bureaus, agencies, departments, or protectees is purely malicious.　　　　—J.N.S.

Acknowledgements

I would like to thank those who generously lent me ideas, criticisms, reactions, technical expertise, encouragement, discouragement, and other valuable considerations throughout the various stages of this effort. A listing of this kind can never be quite complete, but particular thanks go to Steven Axelrod, Don Balluck, Nikki Carlino, Oscar Collier, Charles Curley, Dan Deckert, John Douglas, David Friedman, Milton Friedman, Joel Gotler, Drew Hart, David Hartwell, Virginia Heinlein, Victor Koman, Samuel Edward Konkin III, Robert LeFevre, Mark Merlino, John J. Pierce, Jerry Pournelle, Murray Rothbard, Gloria Rotunno, Thomas Scozzafava, Thomas Szasz, Andy Thornton, and my sister, Marggy.

Most of all, I thank the most generous Mr. and Mrs. Herman Geller; and with love, my parents.

The final product is, of course, solely my responsibility.

J.N.S.

To Samuel Edward Konkin III
Mentor, Co-conspirator, and Friend

Table of Contents

CHAPTER   PAGE

Part One 13

1 15

2 23

3 29

4 37

5 43

6 53

7 63

8 73

9 81

Part Two 87

10 89

11 97

12 109

13 123

14 133

15 141

16 151

17 163

18 171

Part Three 179

19 181

20 189

21 199

22 209

23 219

24 231

25 237

26 245

27 253

"Are We *Alongside Night?*" by J. Neil Schulman (1979) 257

"How Far *Alongside Night?*" by Samuel Edward Konkin III
(1987) 271

"Pulling *Alongside Night*: The Enabling Technology is Here"
by J. Kent Hastings (1999) 277

"Remarks Upon Acceptance into the Prometheus Hall of
Fame for *Alongside Night*" by J. Neil Schulman (1989) ..291

"God Here And Now: An Introduction to Gloamingerism" by
Reverend Virgil Moore 295

and "The Last True Hope" by Bishop Alam Kimar Whyte,
Church of the Human God. 299

About the Author 301

Alongside Night
Parallel day
By fearful flight
In garish gray
Will dawn alight
And not decay
Alongside night?

Part One

The result was that on February 28, 1793, at eight o'clock in the evening, a mob of men and women in disguise began plundering the stores and shops of Paris. At first they demanded only bread; soon they insisted on coffee and rice and sugar; at last they seized everything on which they could lay their hands—cloth, clothing, groceries, and luxuries of every kind. Two hundred such places were plundered. This was endured for six hours, and finally order was restored only by a grant of seven million francs to buy off the mob. The new political economy was beginning to bear its fruits luxuriantly.

—Andrew Dickson White
Fiat Money Inflation in France

In afternoon developments, the Bank of America is reported to have been closing all of its Los Angeles branch banks and moving money to safer locations, away from the chaos that is spreading through various neighborhoods. Other businesses are said to be closing and boarding up their windows in an attempt to prevent future looting. Reports were received that the crowds of looters were said to be moving into an area on Hollywood Blvd. and that thievery seems to be spreading as the day progresses....Entire families were seen working together to steal from stores in their own neighborhoods. Often, what was being stolen was not of any necessity, but rather luxury items such as designer gym shoes, radios, and starter jackets. Frequently, it just appeared that it was those "without" were taking from those "with," because they could.... —*EmergencyNet News Service*, May 1, 1992, reporting on the Los Angeles riots

The ruling ideas of each age have ever been the ideas of its ruling class.

—Karl Marx
Manifesto of the Communist Party

Tzigane – Maurice Ravel

Chapter 1

Elliot Vreeland felt uneasy the moment he entered his classroom.

Everything seemed perfectly normal. Though in an old brownstone building, the classroom held several late-model teaching systems including a video wallscreen that was also used as an intercom; but it also contained a traditional chalkboard, teacher's front desk, and a dozen tablet armchairs. All but one of Elliot's seven classmates had attended Ansonia Preparatory with him since freshman year; by this February in his final semester their faces were loathsomely familiar.

The exception was at the window, gazing out to Central Park West, New York.

The two did not look as if they should have had anything in common—at least by the standards of previous generations. Son of the Nobel-laureate economist, Elliot Vreeland was archetypically Aryan—tall, blond, and blue-eyed—though with the slightest facial softening that precluded stereotyped Aryan imperiousness. Phillip Gross, shorter than Elliot, wirier, with black hair and silent eyes, had emigrated to Israel from the United States as an infant, being shipped back to an uncle in New York when four years later his parents had been machine-gunned by Palestinian guerrillas. The two boys had been close friends since Phillip had enrolled at Ansonia in their junior year.

Phillip spoke without turning as soon as Elliot drew near. "You didn't do it, did you, Ell?"

"I told you I wouldn't."

Phillip faced his friend. "Well, you just may get away with it."

Before Elliot could inquire further, the assistant headmaster entered the room.

Benjamin Harper dropped an attaché case onto the teacher's desk, then began erasing the chalkboard while the students, for lack of any other ideas, took their seats. "Tobias is out sick?" Elliot whispered to Phillip as they took seats in the back. Phillip smiled secretively but did not answer.

"I have several announcements to make," said Harper, shelving the eraser. He was a thin-boned, impeccably attired black man in his late thirties, sporting mustache, short au naturel hair, and glasses. Waiting for the students to quiet, he continued: "First. Mrs. Tobias has left Ansonia permanently. Consequently, she will no longer be teaching Contemporary Civilization."

Elliot glanced at Phillip sharply. "You saw her walking out?" he whispered. Phillip shrugged noncommittally.

"Second," the assistant head went on, "as it is too late in the term for Dr. Fischer and me to hire a replacement, I personally will be taking over this class."

"I'll bet Tobias was canned," Elliot stage-whispered to Phillip. Several students giggled.

Mr. Harper eyed Elliot sharply. "'Dismissed,' 'discharged,' 'fired,' 'removed,' 'let go'—perhaps even 'ousted.' But not 'canned,' Mr. Vreeland. I dislike hearing the language maltreated." Elliot flushed slightly. "Shall we continue?"

Mason Langley, the one-in-every-class teacher's pet, raised his hand. Harper recognized him. "Mrs. Tobias assigned us a three-hundred-word essay last week," he said in a nasal voice. "It's due today. Do you want it turned in?"

Several students groaned, looked disgusted, and blew raspberries at Langley, who seemed to gain great satisfaction from all this negative attention. Elliot glared at Langley and thought, I'll kill him. Harper looked as if he shared the students' opinions but seemed to control his feelings. "What was the assigned topic?" he asked.

"The Self-Destruction of the Capitalist System," said Langley.

Harper unsuccessfully concealed his disgust at the propagandistic title. "Very well. Pass them forward."

As each student—with the single exception of Elliot—passed forward a composition, it became evident to Harper why Elliot had looked more angrily at Langley than had all the others.

After collecting seven essays, Harper said, "Your essay, Mr. Vreeland?"

Elliot answered resignedly, "I didn't do one, Mr. Harper."

"Surely you must have some feelings on the topic?"

Elliot nodded. "I disagree with the premise."

"Did you express this disagreement to Mrs. Tobias when she assigned the topic?" Elliot nodded again. "What was her reply?"

"She said that I can start handing out the topics when *I* become a teacher."

"I see," Harper said slowly. "All right. You may present your rebuttal in a composition due the day after tomorrow—this Friday. Let's make it a thousand words. Is that satisfactory?"

"I guess so. If I can manage a thousand words."

"I myself have that problem," Harper said brightly. "Few editorial pages will buy anything longer."

Releasing spring latches, Harper opened his attaché case and removed a *New York Times*, which he waved in front of the class. "Enough time wasted," he continued. "We have few enough weeks until graduation and—heaven help you—you'll need them. I assume you're all expecting to start college this fall?" He did not wait for replies. "Of course you are, or you wouldn't be here. Well, here's some advance warning: *Don't count on it*. There's the extreme possibility that there won't even be necessities this fall, much less operating colleges."

All of the students—with the exception of an attractive friend of Elliot's, Marilyn Danforth—were now turning their eyes intently forward. Harper was a good dramatist, a good teacher.

Harper waved the newspaper again. "Top of page one, today's paper. Let's just see what we find.

> WASHINGTON, Feb. 20—The President today vowed, in a televised address at 8:30 E.T. this evening that he will order the Federal Reserve Bank to keep the printing presses running day and night, if necessary, to ease the shortage of New Dollars.
> The President further stated that the country's present economic difficulties are well within the government's ability to control, charging, 'They stem from loss of confidence in our governmental institutions due to the reckless predictions of socially irresponsible, doomsday economists.'

Elliot noticed several students looking at him pointedly, during the reference to economists, but he pretended not to notice. Harper did notice, however, and quickly discarded the first section of the newspaper. "All right, on to the financial page," he continued. "This dateline is official from the Office of Public Information:

> WASHINGTON, Feb. 21, (OPI)—The cost-of-living index rose 2012 percent in the final quarter of last year, the Bureau of Labor Statistics revealed today.

Mr. Harper chuckled. "Good of them to let us in on the secret." He set the paper down. "Now, I realize this must sound rather dry, but I cannot stress too strongly how such events affect your daily lives. We are looking at a crisis that will make the Great Depression look tame by comparison. I assume Mrs. Tobias had started discussing this in class?" There were several murmured affirmatives and a nod or two. "Good. Marilyn Danforth."

"Huh?" The class joined in laughter as the pretty brunette was roused from her daydream.

"Please describe for us the antecedents of inflation."

"Uh—do you mean what Mrs. Tobias told us?"

"If you have nothing original to say," Harper said backhandedly, "yes."

"Well," she started hesitantly. "Uh—inflation—you know—has a lot of different causes, depending, you know, on just when you're talking about. F'rinstance, you might have a war somewhere and that will cause inflation, and just when you're expecting it's over, there might be a crop failure, you know?" She looked thoughtful for a moment. "At least I _think_ that's what she said."

"I'm certain you remembered it perfectly. Does anyone wish to add anything?"

He recognized Mason Langley. "She left out about the greedy businessmen."

"We mustn't miss that, Mr. Langley. Proceed."

"Inflation," Langley said, drawing himself up, "is caused by greedy businessmen who force higher prices by producing less than consumer demand. They also create artificial demand by planning obsolescence into their manufactured goods so they have to be prematurely replaced." He smiled smugly.

Harper ignored him and answered politely. "Thank you. Anyone else?"

Cal Ackerman, the class yahoo, raised his hand. Harper called on him. Looking backward directly at Elliot, Ackerman made each word a deliberate insult: "I agree with what the President said last night. All our troubles are caused by brownies"—he almost tasted the word—"following economists like Elliot Vreeland's old man."

Elliot's eyes flared at Ackerman. Mr. Harper intervened quickly before a fight could start. "I think you owe Elliot an apology, Cal. Dr Vreeland's views—while admittedly radical—are respected in many quarters. Aside from that, I do not allow name-calling in my classes."

Ackerman stayed mute.

Elliot said, "That's okay, Mr. Harper. Ackerman is much too fascistic to have read any of my father's books."

"Now stop this, both of you," Harper said. "Elliot, do you

have anything constructive to add?"

"Nothing I haven't said a million times before."

"Very well." Harper noticed—gratefully—Bernard Rothman's hand was raised. "Yes, Mr. Rothman?"

"I don't understand *any* of this, Mr. Harper."

Before Harper could reply, the video wallscreen activated with its speaker crackling. A petite but imposing woman in her sixties—silver-haired with large, piercing eyes—appeared on the screen. "Excuse me, Mr. Harper." She spoke with a polyglot European accent. "Is Elliot Vreeland there?"

Elliot raised his head as he heard his name.

"Yes, Dr. Fischer," Harper answered the screen.

"Would you please have him report to my office immediately?"

"He's on his way."

The screen cleared. Mr. Harper waved Elliot to the door with an underhand gesture.

Elliot picked up his books—nodding to Phillip Gross and Marilyn Danforth on his way out—and traced the 45-degree bend around the still-busy school cafeteria on his route to the stairs; the headmaster's office was on the first floor, a flight down. He wondered what could be important enough for Dr. Fischer to pull him out of class. Perhaps his college applications?

He did not have to wait long before finding out. When Elliot entered the headmaster's reception area, he found his sister seated inside with Dr. Fischer. Denise Vreeland was sixteen, a year younger than Elliot, with a strong resemblance, only at the moment she looked even younger and extremely vulnerable. Her strawberry-blonde hair was disarrayed; she looked as if she had been crying. Dr. Fischer was sitting next to her— frowning.

"Denise, what's wrong? What are you doing here? Why aren't you at school?"

Dr. Fischer stood. "Elliot," she said softly, "you must leave with your sister immediately."

"What for?" he asked. "What's all this about?"

Denise took a sharp intake of breath, looked Elliot straight in the eye, then whispered:

"Daddy's dead."

Chapter 2

The New York wind was damply chill as Elliot and Denise Vreeland left Ansonia's five-story brownstone at 90 Central Park West, but Elliot's thoughts were not with his surroundings. That his father was not alive seemed impossibly foreign to his entire orientation, to his entire life. Certainly he had expected that Martin Vreeland would die someday—but *some day*, not when Elliot still needed him.

At once he felt like slapping himself: Was that all he thought of his father? Just someone he "needed"? Somebody to provide him with the material artifacts of life: a bed, binoculars, books, camera, computer, trip to Europe? No. His needs were for things less tangible but nonetheless real. Teaching him to defend himself. Staying up with him one night when he was vomiting. Answering any question openly and intelligently. Or just being the kind of man who took time to teach him viable principles, living them himself without evasion.

Even though his father had not been stingy with the free time he had had, there had never been enough of it, so far as Elliot was concerned. During the academic year, Dr. Vreeland had worked a demanding teaching schedule, while his summers—spent with his family at their New Hampshire lodge—resultantly became his only chance for research, contemplation, and fulfilling publishing commitments.

Elliot reflected that the two of them had not been close in the stereotypical father-son sense. They had never gone camping together, played touch football in Central Park, or eaten hot dogs at Shea Stadium. Moreover, his father's Viennese upbringing had restrained him from any open displays of affection. But Elliot now recalled sharply that, in Boston four years earlier, Dr. Vreeland had been dissatisfied with every preparatory school to which he had considered sending him. Then, while addressing a monetary symposium in New Orleans, he had met Dr. Fischer and found her adhering to an academic philosophy identical to his own. After returning north and visiting Ansonia, Dr. Vreeland—a department head at Harvard who had not yet won his Nobel Prize—accepted a less rich professorship at Columbia and moved his family to New York.

Elliot found himself taking deep gulps of cold air into his lungs as if they were oxygen-starved. He wondered what the crushing, closed-in sensation was. He wondered if what he felt was what a son was supposed to feel upon learning of his father's death. He wondered whether he should cry—or why he was not crying—although he felt so physically wrenched apart. He wondered whether he loved his father. He felt helpless even to define the components of such a love.

This he knew: he wanted desperately to tell his father that he appreciated what he had been to him.

They were just passing the bricked-up entrance to the perpetually unfinished Central Park Shuttle, a subway that was to have linked eastside and westside IRT lines as Sixty-ninth Street, when Denise tugged at Elliot's arm, stopping him. Behind them, unnoticed among years' worth of graffiti and handbills, was a recently put-up poster announcing Dr. Vreeland's appearance at a Citizens for a Free Society rally the next morning.

"Elliot, I'm sorry but I *had* to," said Denise.

"Well, you didn't have to pull off my arm. I would've—"

"That's not it," she interrupted. She paused, biting on her lower lip. "Daddy's not dead."

Elliot's expressions changed from confusion, through relief, to anger as cold as the wind whipping through his hair.

"Ell, it's not what you think. Mom told me to tell you that. She called me out of Juilliard."

Elliot regarded his sister as though she might still be lying. Her habitual truthfulness stilled this thought. "Then what the—"

"No time to explain now. We have to get home. Fast. Which is our first problem." Denise referred to a total transit strike in the city that encompassed not only all subways and busses but medallion taxis as well.

Elliot thought a moment, considering and rejecting an illegal walk across Central Park, then motioned Denise to follow.

It took only a few minutes to walk Sixty-ninth Street the two blocks over to Broadway. They crossed to the west side, stood at the curb and waited. They waited five minutes. Ten minutes. Fifteen minutes later they were still unable to find anything resembling a gypsy cab.

"Are you sure you know what a *tzigane* looks like?" asked Denise.

"No," Elliot admitted. "That's the problem. When you're cruising illegally, you try not to look like anything in particular. A dozen might have passed us already."

"Then how do we find one?"

"We don't. We wait for one to find us."

To prove his point, within a minute a black sedan stopped at the traffic light they were opposite. The *tzigane*—a heavyset black man—waved out the window. Elliot waved back to the driver, then told Denise in a low voice. "I'll parley the price."

Presently the light changed, the sedan pulling alongside. The *tzigane* reached back, opening the rear curbside door. "Climb in."

Elliot shook his head just enough for Denise to catch, then walked around to the driver's side. "First," he said, "how much?"

The *tzigane* twirled a plain gold band on his right hand—a nervous habit, Elliot supposed. "Where you headed?"

"Park Avenue between Seventy-fourth and Seventy-fifth."

"Two thousand blues—up front." Elliot winced. The price

was four times what a medallion taxi had charged for the same run several weeks earlier. The *tzigane* continued twirling his ring back and forth. Elliot walked around the car, gesturing Denise to get in, and a moment later followed her; the car remained motionless. The *tzigane* turned to him and said, "Blues first."

Elliot removed his wallet and handed bills forward. They were blue-colored notes, no engraving on one side, on the other side hasty engraving proclaiming them "legal tender of the United States of America for all debts, public and private." More than anything else, it resembled *Monopoly* money.

"This is a thousand," said the *tzigane*.

"That's right," Elliot replied. "You'll get the other thousand when we arrive." The *tzigane* shrugged, revved his turbine, and with a jolt the sedan started down Broadway.

Not a minute later, when the car passed Sixty-fifth Street, Elliot suddenly leaned forward. "Hey! You missed the turnoff to the park."

"Relax, there ain't no meter runnin'."

Elliot began contemplating ways for Denise and himself to jump from the car. "But why aren't you taking the shortcut?"

"Only medallions and busses allowed through—and this is a private car, right?"

"Sorry."

"That's okay, bro."

Elliot did not relax, however, until the sedan pulled up in front of his address, a luxury high-rise. A uniformed doorman, Jim, came out of the building to open the car door for them. After paying his balance—with an extra three hundred New Dollars as tip—Denise and he got out. "Thanks," Elliot said.

"Any time, my man." The *tzigane* smiled then added, "Next time maybe you won't be so tight. Laissez-faire."

Elliot began to greet Jim with his usual smile, but Denise nudged her brother, who remembered himself at a point appropriate to someone wishing to appear pleasant under trying circumstances. As Jim opened the building door, he nodded in the direction of a half-dozen reporters—some with videotape cameras, others cassette recorders, still others with only notebooks—sitting at the far end of the lobby. "Your mother said you shouldn't talk to them," Jim whispered to the couple.

It was too late, though. The reporters looked up as they entered then literally pounced. "Hey, you're the Vreeland kids, aren't you?" one man shouted, rushing forward with his camera.

Jim blocked him. "Mrs. Vreeland said *no interviews.*"

A newspaper woman managed to block Elliot. "*Please,*" she said, "just tell us the cause of death."

Elliot glanced at Denise helplessly. "A heart attack late this morning," Denise told the woman.

Immediately the others began throwing out more questions, but Jim held them back as Elliot and Denise fled the lobby to the elevators. Luckily, one was waiting for them. They rode it up to the fiftieth floor and walked to their apartment, a gray steel door at the corridor's far end with the number 50L and the Vreeland name.

It was a warm, luxurious apartment with oriental rugs, many fine antiques, body-sensing climate control, and numerous paintings—mostly acrylic gouache by their mother, Cathryn Vreeland, who had a moderate artistic following. In typical New York fashion, the windows—and a door to the apartment terrace—were covered with Venetian blinds, now lowered to darken the apartment from the afternoon sun.

As Elliot and Denise entered the apartment, they heard the muffled sound of voices coming from the master bedroom. "...political suicide, sheer madness," Elliot overheard a hushed whisper. They continued through an L-shaped hallway into the master bedroom, where Dr. and Mrs. Vreeland were bending over a large FerroFoam suitcase on the bed, trying with noticeable difficulty to close it.

Whatever doubts remained in Elliot's mind vanished in shocking relief.

The elder Vreelands did not immediately notice their off-springs' entrance, engaged as they were with their discussion emphasizing each attempt on the suitcase. Dr. Vreeland said, "You would think they would at least be bright enough to fol-low EUCOMTO's policy, rather than this regression to further insanity." His speech retained only a trace of his native Vienna.

"They're trapped by their own logic," said Mrs. Vreeland, pressing hard on the suitcase. "You predicted this and pre-pared for it, so stop berating yourself about something you couldn't control."

"I didn't take the possibility seriously enough, Cathryn. I had no business risking my family—" Dr. Vreeland looked up. "Thank God you're finally home. Did they give you any trouble at school?"

Denise shook her head. Elliot said with some difficulty, "No."

Dr. Vreeland looked at his son with sudden compassion. "I'm terribly sorry, Ell. We had to catch you off guard to make my cover story credible. You know I wouldn't have done this if it weren't necessary."

Elliot forced a smile. "Uh—that's okay, Dad."

His father smiled back. "Good. Now," he said briskly, "do you two think you can help us get his damned suitcase closed?"

Chapter 3

Perhaps the single most important element guiding Martin Vreeland was a meticulous study of history.

He had learned the lessons of politics well, therefore harboring few illusions regarding to what extent those with power would go to maintain it—and fewer illusions respecting by whom and for whose gain political power was always exercised.

Had he not believed the incorruptible were statistically insignificant, he would have been an anarchist.

His latest bestseller, *Not Worth a Continental*, stated his views on the current crisis clearly:

> The true cause of the general rise in prices that is usually called inflation is one of history's best-kept secrets: it is known to almost everybody but its victims. To listen to most political debates on the phenomenon, one would think that it was some malarious fever—still incurable—which is to be treated with the quinines of joint sacrifice, Maoist self-criticism, and liberal doses of governmental controls. Yet, even today, one can look up "inflation" in most dictionaries and find in its definition a proper diagnosis of the disease and by that diagnosis an implied cure.
>
> Inflation is the process whereby central bankers in collusion with politicians—to mutual benefit—have counterfeited warehouse receipts for a commodity the public have chosen as a medium of exchange, and traded those counterfeits to those they have defrauded and forced them into accepting them.
>
> By doing this they gain something for nothing.
>
> Those who accepted the counterfeits, on the other hand, have taken nothing for something, but not realizing this, they calculate their own future spending as if they had received more something.
>
> The primary effect of all this nothing being passed around is a discounting of the medium of exchange—seen by everybody as a rise in prices of everything else—as people lose the ability to distinguish between something and nothing.
>
> The most important secondary effect is mass-scale malinvestment caused by the general false sense of prosperity.
>
> By the point at which there is more nothing being traded than some-

thing—our current situation—a hedonistic inversion is so rampant
that even the bankers and politicians are losing.

But by then it is much too late for them to save themselves—and
they see little profit in saving us.

The cure for inflation is to stop inflating.

Elliot had known his father was under fire from high places
for incessant—and widely reported—attacks on government
economic policies, but Dr. Vreeland had told him that direct
reprisals were relatively unlikely. A Nobel prize afforded some
protection; the high public profile of a bestselling author, more;
popularity among the million members of the radical Citizens
for a Free Society, still more; and perhaps most important was
his wide repute among the fiscally conservative delegates—
and personal friendship with the current chancellor—of
EUCOMTO, the European Common Market Treaty Organization.

What Dr. Vreeland now told Elliot was that while he had
considered reprisals unlikely, he had not considered them out
of the question—especially as a prelude to a major political
upheaval of some sort—thus he had taken various precaution-
ary measures. Among these were preparing secret caches and
asylums for emergency retreat, with extensive contingency
plans for each. He had also found it advisable to cultivate,
through timely gifts to "underpaid officials," loyalties that might
be useful during uncomfortable periods.

Earlier that day this last had paid off: one of his friends in
the Federal Bureau of Investigation had transmitted him a
message that the Vreeland name had been found on a list of
persons to be secretly arrested that coming weekend. "We leave
tonight," said Dr. Vreeland. "All of us. And probably from a
country now a dictatorship."

This simple proclamation shook Elliot's sense of security
almost as much as the earlier one declaring his father dead.
While he had been aware of current political-economic devel-

opments—been steeped in them—he had never accepted emotionally that they might have personal consequences. Mr. Harper's classroom warning was driven home as Elliot's father explained what his sudden "death" was all about.

"We have little time and a lot to accomplish," said Dr. Vreeland to Elliot and Denise. The three were at the dining table while Cathryn Vreeland prepared a long overdue lunch for herself and her husband. "Each of us has necessary tasks to perform with no room for error. One slip—even one you might think insignificant—may prove our downfall."

"Any choice about what we have to do?"

Dr. Vreeland looked at Elliot seriously. "Certainly," he replied, then paused several extended moments. "Listen, you two. You're both old enough to make any crucial decisions about your lives. It's much too late for me to impart values to you; but if you don't have them, then I'm not much of a father. Ell, there are only two choices my situation allows me to offer you: either you leave now before you hear my plans—in which case you're completely on your own as of now—or you accept my authority with out reservations until we're safely out of the country."

Ten seconds passed. No one spoke. Finally, Denise broke the silence: "Where are we going, Daddy?"

"Everything in due time, honey. Just let me proceed at my own pace." Dr. Vreeland faced Elliot again. "You didn't answer me." Elliot answered slowly, deliberately. "You know what my answer is, Dad."

Dr. Vreeland nodded. "Denise?"

"I'm in," she said cheerfully. "Give my regards to Broadway."

"Good. For the official record, then ..."

Martin Vreeland, Ph.D (so the story would go), had died of a heart attack brought on by overwork and the tensions of his public position. The official death certificate would confirm this, and his personal physician's records would document a nonexistent previous attack. Preceded by an immediate-family-only funeral service the next afternoon, the body was to be "immediately cremated." The neighbors had been told that Cathryn Vreeland and her children would be staying that night with her sister-in-law; since she did not have a sister-in-law, this could not be swiftly followed up.

"If you find yourselves unable to avoid the press," said Dr. Vreeland, "then say nothing factual. Make only generalized, emotional statements about me"—he smiled—"preferably laudatory. I will be leaving the apartment in disguise as soon after five as possible."

Denise asked, "Won't Jim think it unusual that a stranger he didn't let in is leaving the building?"

"No. First, Dominic will be on by the time I leave, and if he sees me, will simply assume that this 'stranger' came in before his shift. Second, I don't intend leaving through the lobby. I'll use the fire exit out to Seventy-fourth Street."

Cathryn Vreeland brought a plate of sandwiches from the kitchen, joining her family at the table. "Spam," she said. "It was all the Shopwell had left yesterday that I had ration tickets for."

Dr. Vreeland picked up a sandwich, bit into it with a grimace, then continued to talk and to eat intermittently: "The three of you will leave this apartment at 7 p.m., and will rendezvous with me on the west side of Park at Seventieth Street, where I'll be waiting with a rental car—and to anticipate any questions, all arrangements have already been made. From the moment we get in that car, we will no longer be in the Vreeland family. We will all be carrying full identification, including passports, exit permits, and visas—each with our new names—and we'll continue using them until we legally identify ourselves in our country of final destination."

"You still haven't said where that is," said Denise.

"To be perfectly candid, I don't know yet. We will be driving to International Airport, taking, at 10:05 tonight, Air Quebec Flight 757 to Montreal—one of the cities in which I have emergency assets and a number of friends. We might be there just a few days, but if much longer, you'll have a chance to practice your French."

"*Et ensuite?*" asked Elliot.

"*Trop compliqué,*" replied Dr. Vreeland, referring both to variables involved in choosing their next destination and to his inability to say all that in French. Dr. Vreeland paused several seconds, then managed to regain his original train of thought. "In packing your belongings, anything with our real names on it—or any pictures of me—must be left behind, no matter how treasured, no matter how valuable."

"We're going to have to leave almost everything behind, aren't we?" Denise asked wistfully.

"I'm afraid so. There's very little here that can't be replaced, nor would I, in any case, consider personal possessions to be worth risking my family's imprisonment. Even if your mother considers me excessively paranoid."

"I'll say," Mrs. Vreeland confirmed.

Everyone turned to her. Cathryn Vreeland rarely ventured unsolicited opinions; when she did, they commanded full attention. She would have commanded it anyway: the flame-haired woman could easily have been a top commercial model, and though she was thirty-nine, bartenders still demanded her proof-of-age. "When Marty first told me his plan, I suggested that he leave alone, while we three stay behind long enough to close out affairs here normally. He wouldn't hear of it."

"And still won't," Dr. Vreeland said. "I am not about to flee the country, leaving my family behind to answer FBI questions. There will be too many discrepancies in my story within twenty-four hours. If we were leaving the country under normal circumstances, we'd be selling and giving away most of our belongings anyway."

"One set of items we *will* risk taking," continued Dr. Vreeland, "is twenty-five Mexican fifty-peso gold pieces—at today's European exchange worth about eleven-and-a-half million New Dollars." Elliot whistled. "Don't be too impressed. When I bought them back in 1979, I only paid nine thousand old dollars for them, and they'll buy about four times that in real goods today. But, Ell—this concerns you personally—I don't want its value to cloud your thinking. If by 'losing' it or paying it as a bribe I can improve our escape chances one iota, I won't hesitate to do so for one second."

"Are they here?" Elliot asked.

"No, that's just where you come in. You're going downtown for me to get them."

Elliot's eyes widened.

A few minutes later, Dr. Vreeland drew Elliot alone into the master bedroom. "You'll be going to an—uh—'exotic' book-store off Times Square," said Dr. Vreeland. He wrote the address on a piece of paper.

Elliot took the paper, studied it a moment, then crumpled it up. "Do I have to eat this?"

"Not necessary," said his father. "Your contact is a bald, bearded man—somewhat overweight—called 'Al.' As a sign you're to ask him for a copy of *Not Worth a Continental*—be sure to mention my name as author. His countersign is, 'I may sell dirty books but I don't carry trash like that.' Your counter-countersign is, 'What do you recommend instead?' He will in-vite you into a back room and give you a package. The coins will be inside. Got all that?"

Elliot nodded. "Should I take my phone?"

"Absolutely not," said Dr. Vreeland. "We have to assume that all our phones are being monitored, and no matter what we say or don't say, they can be used to track our movements. I also won't trust the Internet until we are out of the country.

I'm assuming all our eMail accounts have been compromised by now, even our anonymous remailers. The only devices I'm willing to trust are decidedly low-tech. Which brings up one important piece of low-tech hardware."

Dr. Vreeland went to his dresser, returning with a small box, which he opened. Inside was a .38 caliber Peking revolver that he and Elliot had practiced with in New Hampshire. "Can you use it?" Dr. Vreeland asked.

Elliot picked up the pistol, swung out the cylinder—noting all six chambers loaded—and swung the cylinder back. "I can use it."

"Good. Only, don't."

"What if I'm stopped by a cop?"

Dr. Vreeland took a deep breath. "Under our present situation, a police officer must be regarded in the same manner as any other potential attacker. You can't afford to be caught with either a firearm or gold bullion. If you can talk your way free, do so: New York police must pass periodic shooting exams. But if your only chance of making rendezvous is using this gun, so be it."

"Terrific chance I'd have."

"The Keynesian Cops are understaffed at the moment"—Elliot winced at the pun—"Consider themselves underpaid and overworked, and are on the verge of striking again. If they're seen making an arrest openly, they're as likely as not to start a riot. They are *not* looking for trouble. Anything else?"

Elliot made a wry face. "Do you have any more ammunition?"

Chapter 4

After ducking through the fire exit to avoid reporters still in the lobby, Elliot started briskly down Park Avenue, the boulevard busy even with out its usual flow of yellow taxicabs. He walked toward the thirty-block-distant Pan Am Building—though it was no longer owned by that airline—passing seedy hotel after seedy hotel, passing a derelict structure at Sixty-eighth Street, once Hunter College. He turned west on to Fifty-ninth Street—past Burger King, past Madison Avenue, past the plywood and soaped plate glass at General Motors Plaza—and continued down Fifth Avenue.

Tourists from EUCOMTO states were abundant on the avenue, buying up bargains to the bewilderment of proudly nationalistic Americans and to the delight of proprietors eager for the illegal, gold-backed eurofrancs. Where once exclusive stores had displayed apparel of quiet taste, the latest rage among the fashionable was the Genghis Khan: coats of metallic-silver leather trimmed with long, black monkey fur.

A sign was posted on a lamppost at the corner of Forty-ninth Street; Elliot passed by hardly noticing it.

Warning!
to LOOTERS, VANDALS, MUGGERS, SHOPLIFTERS, PICKPOCK-
ETS, and other assorted CRIMINALS. This area is heavily patrolled
by ARMED GUARDS with orders to protect our businesses and
customers from you BY ANY MEANS POSSIBLE.
BEWARE FOR YOUR LIVES!
—*Fifth Avenue Merchant Alliance*

About fifty minutes after he had left home, Elliot entered a small bookstore at 204 West Forty-second Street, just outside the Federal Renovation Zone. It was crossways to the edifice at One Times Square originally the New York Times building,

most famous as the Allied Chemical Tower, now a federal building called, somewhat tongue-in-cheek, the Oracle Tower. The
Rabelais bookstore was without customers when Elliot arrived;
a man was seated on a stool behind the counter, a sign in back
of him declaring in large black lettering, "BE 21 OR BE GONE."
On one wall were such classic titles as *A Pilgrim of Passion*,
Suburban Souls, *Professional Lovers*, and *Saucer Sluts*; the
other wall offered more pedestrian titles by Salinger,
Hemingway, and Joyce.

If the man seated behind the cash register was "Al," thought
Elliot, then his father had been polite as an ambassador. He
was not "somewhat overweight." He was grossly fat, perhaps
tipping the scale at three hundred pounds. His triple chin—
one had to presume—was well hidden beneath a thick, black
beard, contrasted by his bald pate. He was chewing what Elliot
first thought was gum but soon realized was tobacco and was
reading Jean-Paul Sartre's *Nausea*, which matched Elliot's first
reaction to the man.

Elliot approached him with caution. "I'd like a copy of *Not
Worth a Continental* by Martin Vreeland," he said, according
to plan.

The man lowered his book, spat tobacco—into a cuspidor,
Elliot was relieved to see—and inspected Elliot carefully. "You
his kid?" he asked finally. Not according to plan.

Elliot nodded hesitantly. "Are you Al?"

"Yeah," he said, lifting himself off the stool with considerable difficulty. "C'mon, it's in the back."

Elliot's face fell. "But don't you need my countersign?" he
blurted.

"Nah. You look just like your old man."

Al led Elliot through a draped door to a corner of his back
room and gestured toward a large carton on the floor filled
with books. "Gimme a hand with this." Elliot got a grip on one
of the corners, then the two of them lifted it aside, revealing a

hole in the linoleum. Al lifted out a package sealed into a black Pliofilm bag, handing it to him. "The coins are in here," he said. "Count 'em if you want. I gotta get out front. Need me, just call."

Elliot looked at Al curiously. "Uh—mind if I ask a personal question?"

"Don't know till you ask the question."

"Well ... if you knew what's in here, then why didn't you just take it and run? Gold ownership is illegal. We couldn't have reported you."

Al laughed heartily. "I thought you were gonna ask how much I eat or somethin'. I didn't steal the gold 'cause it don't belong to me." He turned and went out front.

After placing the plastic on a nearby table, Elliot broke the sealed plastic, opening it. Inside was a specially designed leather belt—forty-odd inches long, two inches high—with no tongue or eyelets but a slide-buckle instead. At the bottom was a zipper concealed between two layers of leather. Elliot slid the buckle out of the way, unzipped the belt, and peeled apart the leather.

Inside were the twenty-five Mexican fifty-peso gold pieces, built into matching cutouts in the leather that extended most of the belt's length. They were beautifully struck, in virtual mint condition, and even in the back room's dim light reflected considerable luster.

Each coin was about one and a half inches in diameter. The traditional eagle with a serpent in its mouth embellished the obverse of each coin; on the reverse was a winged Nike—goddess of victory—bearing a wreath, to her right the 50 PESOS mark, to her left the legend 37.5 grams ORO PURO. Elliot removed his own belt, replacing it with the new one, which he had to thread through several belt loops twice as it was too long for his thirty-four inch waist. Then he replaced his jacket and overcoat.

Al was busy with a customer when Elliot came front; he stood away a polite distance, awaiting an opportunity to take his leave. Repressing a desire—more out of embarrassment than anything else—to spend his time examining Al's erotica, he instead alternated between observing Al's conversation—impossible to eavesdrop on because of Al's radio playing loudly—and watching the OPI News Summary streaming across the Oracle Tower.

ARMY GUARD IS WITHDRAWN FROM FORT KNOX, KY. ONE YEAR AFTER ANNOUNCEMENT THAT U.S. GOLD RESERVES ARE DEPLETED...

Elliot was suddenly struck by the strangest feeling of déjà vu. He could see that Al was doing something with his hands, but could not have told exactly what.

PRESIDENT LAUNCHES PHASE 7 OF ECONOMIC POLICY EXPAND-ING WAGE-PRICE CONTROLS AND RATIONING...

Al's customer purchased a book but Elliot could not shake the feeling that he had noticed something significant that he had failed to comprehend.

FBI CHIEF POWERS ATTRIBUTES LAST NIGHT'S FIREBOMBINGS OF BUREAU OFFICES TO OUTLAW "REVOLUTIONARY AGORIST CADRE"...

It was almost dusk when a moment later Al's customer left; Elliot walked forward to the counter and thanked Al for his help. "Don't mention it," said Al. "The least I can do under the circumstances—your old man being dead and all."

"How did you—?"

"It was on the radio while you're in the back," Al interrupted.

Elliot felt somewhat awkward about keeping up the pre-tense with a man whom his father—by his actions—regarded as a confidant; nevertheless he interpreted his father's instructions to mean that no one outside the family should know the truth. "Well, I'd better get moving."

"Keep your eyes open," replied Al. "This is a lousy area to be alone at night. Laissez-faire."

Everything suddenly fell into place: Al was wearing a plain gold band on his right hand and during his parley with his customer had twirled it back and forth—the same manner as the *tzigane*.

Elliot briefly considered asking Al if the ring twirling meant anything but felt another question would be prying. Besides, it was silly—and he had better get home quickly if he wanted a decent amount of time to pack. "Laissez-faire," he replied.

Al just smiled.

At almost ten to six, Elliot once again entered his apartment building. The reporters were gone from the lobby. At the door this time was Dominic, a small Puerto Rican man, whom he greeted on his way to the elevators. He waited several minutes before an elevator arrived, then rode it up to the fiftieth floor and fumbled for his keys while walking down the corridor to his apartment. After inserting the correct keys in the correct order, he opened the door and shouted, "I'm home!" There was no answer. Elliot looked into his parents' bedroom, but no one was there, so he tried Denise's room. It was also unoccupied. Elliot then looked into his own bedroom, the guest room, the bathrooms, and even the storage closets; there was no sign of anybody, and all the suitcases were gone.

He started over again, thinking that there must have been a sudden change in plans, and there would be a note somewhere. He checked from the bathroom mirrors to the bulletin board in the kitchen. It was only then that Elliot Vreeland understood that he was alone.

There was no note.

Chapter 5

On his third time around the apartment—still wearing his coat—Elliot noticed signs of visitors who must have come before his family had left. Several ashtrays held cigarette butts, and no one in his family smoked. No one except Denise—Elliot amended—and she only when their parents could not see her. Whoever it was must have stayed more than a few minutes, too, otherwise there would not have been time for more than one or two smokes.

But who was it, and what could he—or she—or they—have said to make his family leave without even writing a note?

Elliot approached the problem systematically. He first went over to the video intercom and buzzed the lobby. The doorman appeared on the small screen, answering with a thick Puerto Rican accent, "Dominic here." Elliot Vreeland, 50L. Had he sent up any visitors in the past couple of hours? "No, sir. Nobody." What time had he come on duty? "Five o'clock." Had he been at the door all the time since five? Dominic looked as if he had been accused of desertion during wartime. "Yes, sir." Elliot thanked him, then cleared the screen.

Next, he checked across the hall with Mrs. Allen, his mother's closest friend. She was a rather plump, jolly widow in her seventies, but when she saw Elliot, she was not very jolly. "Oh, my dear boy. What a tragic day this is! I know how hard this must be on you. When I lost my poor Gustav—"

Before she could tell him about her poor Gustav, Elliot said, "Mrs. Allen, do you know where my mother and sister have gone?" He maintained the cover, just in case.

"Why, certainly, dear."

"Where?" he asked anxiously.

"They've gone to your mother's sister-in-law. My dear, didn't they tell you?"

"Uh—yes," Elliot replied as his stomach sank. "I guess in the confusion I forgot." "Oh, you poor thing. Perhaps you'd come in for a cup of hot cocoa to settle your nerves."

Elliot thanked her warmly but declined, saying that he had better go over there before they worried about him.

He returned to his apartment and, after looking up the listing for Air Quebec, went to the Picturephone in his parents' bedroom, calling to ask if there were any messages for him. He used the family code name his father had given him, saying they were supposed to leave for Montreal that evening on Flight 757 and were accidentally separated. An attractive Air Quebec reservation hostess told him with a Quebecois accent that company policy prevented accepting personal messages between passengers. However, she could have the airport page them. "Uh—no thanks." Then, a flash of inspiration. "Is the reservation still intact?"

She punched data into a computer console, then turned back to the video camera. "Yes, the reservation is still intact. Do you wish to change it?"

"No, thank you," Elliot answered, delighted. "Thank you very much."

The reservation was intact; it had not been changed or canceled. Whatever had necessitated leaving the apartment so early, his family had to be expecting him to rendezvous with them on Park Avenue as scheduled at seven o'clock. He checked his watch. It was only half past six. He had wasted thirty minutes but still had time to pack and meet them on time—if he hurried.

Elliot was just about to start back to his own room when he heard the apartment's front door open.

It could only have been his mother or Denise.

He was about to call out but stopped himself. He heard voices. Unfamiliar, male voices. His reactions now raised to full alert, Elliot backed again into his parents' bedroom in time to hear one voice say, "Better check the master bedroom."

Quickly, Elliot slipped into the bedroom's storage closet and shut the door. He waited in pitch blackness, listening to his heart race, as footsteps passed by the closet, checked in the bathroom, then left the bedroom again. When he was certain whoever it was had left the room again, Elliot slipped back out of the closet, shut the bedroom door until just two inches remained, then pressed his ear close enough to pick up conversation.

After a half-minute pause, another voice—a lighter voice belonging to a young-sounding man—asked, "How long d'ja think we have to wait?"

"Don't know," said the first—heavier, gruffer—voice. "He could come any time."

That narrowed it down somewhat. They were—most probably, at least—waiting either for himself or his father.

The younger voice spoke again, "Jesus, I've never seen the chief so pissed before."

"We'll be seeing a damn sight more if you let the kid slip through your fingers again."

"*My* fingers? How the hell was I supposed to know you hadn't—"

"Shut up."

Elliot sensed how the cards had been dealt. But what did "the chief" want with him?

The logical answers were discouraging. His father's cover story might have been broken, the authorities—most probably the FBI—wanting Elliot as bait to catch him. They might have wanted Elliot to answer questions about his father's political activities—especially if they did still think him dead. They even might have found out Elliot was carrying a fortune in gold.

This last preyed upon his mind. How might the authorities know? So far as he had been told, the only person outside his

family with knowledge of the gold was Al. But if Al had been
so inclined, he could have informed any previous time, or simply have invented some reason not to have turned over the
belt. Besides, Elliot had been careful not to let slip to Al that he
was heading home ...although if he were important enough to
go after in the first place, they might have sent men to his
apartment as a matter of course.

Nonetheless, the important question had been answered.
The men outside were enemies, and he had to escape.

Armed confrontation was just too risky. What other way out
of the apartment was there? The only door out to the apart-
ment-house hallway was in the living room. Wait a second.
There was also that window right over there. He could easily
fit through, but he was still on the fiftieth floor, and even jumping terrace to terrace, there was no way he could rappel himself down that far. But if he could find a rope, perhaps he could
lower himself down to the terrace below, break in, escape
through that living room. If the neighbors were away ...50L,
49L ...That would be the Herberts. Only the Herberts had
moved out last month when Mr. Herbert's realty company went
under. The apartment was still vacant.

Elliot returned to the bedroom's storage closet, flipped on
the light, and began scratching around. First he needed a strong
rope—at least twenty feet—and he began searching for the
nylon rope used to tie up the family's speedboat on Lake
Winnipesaukee. They always took it home for the winter after
having had two such ropes disappear from the boathouse. He
did not find it. Damn! His father must have forgotten, and by
now somebody else would have stolen it, too. Elliot smiled to
himself as he realized that it did not matter anymore.

A few additional minutes provided nothing more promising
than twenty-five feet of plastic clothesline that he found on
top of a carton filled with copies of *Not Worth a Continental*.
Elliot measured out the line to a bit over four arm spans, then

tested it. The line would stretch like all hell, but perhaps if he were to double it over, it might support his weight. If he swore off sex and hard liquor for the rest of his life ...and there were a full moon for good measure.

Wasting no time, Elliot went over to the terrace window. He had opened it only an inch when he heard a loud thud from behind. Elliot whirled around, but no one was there. Then he realized what had happened. The change in air pressure from opening a high-rise window had caused the slightly ajar bedroom door to slam.

Immediately Elliot drew his gun, then dropped automatically into a one-knee shooting stance, aiming directly at the door. He was breathing very heavily—nervous, sharp breaths.

No one entered.

He waited in that position but still no one entered. Then he quietly crept to the door, pressing his ear against it. He heard— just barely—the two men still talking in the living room. Either they had not heard anything, or they had discounted it.

Relaxing enough to reholster his gun, Elliot returned to the window, now opening it without difficulty.

It seemed somewhat colder than during daylight hours. As he climbed out, he could see his breath illuminated by the bedroom lights.

The moon was about as far from full as it could get.

The terrace faced Park Avenue, extending half the apartment's length; the bedroom window was at the far end away from the living room. Nothing short of a small explosion could be heard by anyone there. Closing the window to prevent invading cold air from eventually betraying him, he glanced across the street to the opposite highrise and suddenly realized what a foolish risk he had taken. If anyone had been watching his apartment, the watcher would have seen his figure silhouetted against the window. Nonetheless, this was no time for recriminations, and there were no observers Elliot could detect.

After doubling over the clothesline, Elliot looped it around the bottom of the railing; this was not only to maximize the usefulness of his now only twelve-odd feet of rope, but also to minimize leverage on the rail. Now he tested the hookup by pulling against the line. It held. He wished there were a way to secure the rope around his waist but there just wasn't enough for that. He satisfied himself with wrapping the line several times around his right wrist.

The terraces were stacked directly on top of one another so there would be nothing but air between himself and the ground, six hundred feet below, while he was lowering himself. He would also have to swing himself out several feet, once he was lowered, so he would have enough momentum to drop into the terrace underneath.

Swearing not to look down, Elliot climbed over the railing, supporting himself with his left hand, until he was standing with his back to the air and his toes wedged into the slim space between bottom rail and terrace concrete. He took a deep breath. Now came the tricky part—gradually transferring support to the line without dropping onto it like a hanged man. He did not think the plastic line would stand such a sudden jolt.

No point delaying.

Holding tight onto the line with his right hand and the railing itself with his left, Elliot began lowering himself to his knees until he was precariously balanced with his legs sticking out and his kneecaps tight against the bottom rail. Then, still holding the railing, he lowered his knees off the concrete and began transferring his weight to the clothesline.

The rail began pulling out of the concrete.

The next few moments blurred in Elliot's mind. All he knew was that he was suddenly hanging in midair with his legs flailing. There was a sharp pain in his right wrist as the rope bit into it. And there was no way he could lower himself any farther without letting go of the thin line that was between him and the ground.

Don't look down, he told himself again, then slowly—excruciatingly—he began pulling himself up.

The rail moved out another half an inch.

He succeeded in raising himself high enough to grab the rail directly again and, in an endless moment he was never able to recall clearly, managed to pull himself—one knee at a time—back onto the concrete. In another few moments he climbed back onto his toes again and from there over the railing onto the terrace. He lay there for several minutes, almost unconscious.

When he was able to, he examined his wrist where the line had burned it; aside from a deep red mark and a stinging, it seemed all right. He examined the line. It was also undamaged. He looked at the posts holding the railing and learned that only the first was loose. If he anchored the line farther down—and this time looped the line so it would slip along—he could try it again.

But he knew he wouldn't. It was not that he was a coward—though at the moment he could see the merits of being one—but climbing down a plastic clothesline on a rail with *at least* one loose post was not Elliot's notion of heroism. It was his notion of death. His luck had held out once, but he didn't feel like pressing it. He would have preferred to take his chances with a shoot-out any day. Moreover, he was willing at the moment to defy anyone in his position to try climbing that line again.

There had to be another option. There *had* to be.

Elliot belly-crawled across the terrace until he was in front of the door and could see into the living room from under the lowered Venetian blind. This gave him a first sighting on his adversaries. There were only two. Both men were plain-clothed. One looked in his thirties, the other was middle-aged. The older man had his jacket off, revealing a shoulder holster and pistol ...and this man was muscular enough that Elliot had no desire to tangle with him. In any case, both were still in the living room, which is what he had crawled over to confirm.

Sliding back to concealment, Elliot hooked the rope over the top of the railing, letting the ends hang directly down to the terrace below. He then reopened the window, climbing back in, but this time he left the window open. By no means was he certain his brainstorm would work. But it felt a good deal less uneasy than the alternatives.

Drawing his revolver, Elliot aimed out the window toward the empty sky and fired. Though expected, the reverberating explosion startled him. Elliot made a dash for the bedroom door, went through, then closed it from the other side, now pressed against the wall that cornered the living room.

Had they fallen for it? Elliot risked a look around the corner. Yes! Both men had rushed out to the terrace to learn what the explosion had been; the older man was just dashing onto the terrace when Elliot checked.

Waiting a split second more, Elliot darted through the living room and escaped to the hall.

It would be only a few seconds before they concluded that someone had just climbed the rope, rushing out to search the apartment below. Thinking quickly, Elliot ran into the laundry room, shutting the door.

A few seconds later he heard running in the hallway. The two voices seemed to pause just outside the laundry room. "He's armed," the older voice said. "Probably went off accidentally while he climbed down."

"Think he knows we have his family?"

Elliot was too stunned to notice whether there had been any response; perhaps the older man had shrugged or shaken his head. "But he knows we want him. I'll take the lower apartment. You phone the chief. Now *move*."

Elliot heard the fire door open and slam, then a softer slam seconds later as his apartment door was used again.

His ears were ringing as he tried to regain his composure. He had escaped with the intention of rendezvous with his family.

They would not be there.

He knew who the earlier visitors had been.

He knew why there had been no note—why the flight reservation had been undisturbed.

His father's plan had been brilliant. What could have gone wrong? Dr. Vreeland's words echoed back at him. *"One slip— even one you might think insignificant—may prove our downfall."*

Was it his fault? Had he caused his family's arrest by failing to secure a proper countersign from Al?

Elliot found himself shaking and got angry with himself. This was no time to lose control. He had to get out fast. The stairs? No, the older man would be down there.

He stuck his head out into the hall, followed it, then pressed for the elevator, withdrawing into the laundry room until it arrived. An endless minute later it showed up. Empty.

Elliot got on—riding it straight down—ran out through the Seventy-forth Street fire exit, and from there to the dead chill of the city.

Chapter 6

Elliot had not run more than a few blocks before shortness of breath forced him into an alleyway. There he just leaned against a concrete wall, allowing the day's events to bear down upon him. After a few minutes, though, when the shakes had stopped, when his fears for his family had tripped out from overload, when he realized how cold it was, the improbabilities of his situation began to take on melodramatic—even comic—overtones. Echoing the punch line of a classic television sitcom he had seen on videodisc, he silently exclaimed, *What a revoltin' development* this *is*!

He faced several problems, each of which seemed insurmountable. First, to survive. Second, to escape the combined forces of city, state, and federal government. Third, to devise some plan to rescue his family. Until today, his most pressing problem had been how to get a passing grade from a stupidly dogmatic teacher.

Elliot still had no idea what the authorities intended for his family or why they now wanted him. He considered that they might have known, when they first came to the apartment, that his father was still alive. Or that they had come on a totally unrelated mission and upon finding his father alive were now holding his family for conspiracy to evade arrest.

He wondered if his father's FBI informant had been mistaken or treacherous, and the Bureau wanted them for a totally different—perhaps harmless—reason. Maybe they simply wanted to place them in some kind of protective custody.

Perhaps he was taking all this in entirely the wrong way. Maybe the best thing he could do would be to retain a lawyer to find out what was going on. Conceivably—

He stopped short, realizing that shivering in an alley was

not the best condition in which to think things through. He had to go some place warm and quiet where he could take stock of what had happened.

Elliot decided that, for the moment at least, he could risk the streets. The chance of being recognized at night in mid-Manhattan was rather slim. Nonetheless, by morning the situation might be changed drastically. Who might be questioned on his whereabouts: Mrs. Allen? Dr. Fischer? Phillip Gross?

He moved out into the street. He was on Seventy-third, just off Lexington Avenue. Almost instinctively, he turned downtown, not having any specific destination in mind, but moving just to keep warm.

A question started gnawing at his mind: To whom could he turn? He was not foolish enough to believe for a moment that he could single-handedly bring about his family's release. He was going to need potent help—and quickly. All right, who?

Neighbors were out, for obvious reasons. Family? The only relative within half a continent was an uncle in Chicago, but Elliot doubted this uncle had either the resources or the inclination to be of any use. Martin Vreeland had given his brother the same investment advice he himself was following; Georg Vreeland had ignored his brother's insight, and by some unfathomable logic now blamed Martin for his own resulting financial collapse.

Friends or university associates of his parents? Elliot had never paid them any attention, thus he knew nothing useful about them. Ansonia? Elliot did not have anything in particular against Dr. Fischer or Mr. Harper—or any of his still employed teachers, for that matter—but he did not have anything favoring them, either. They might very easily help him, but they might turn him over to the police. Classmates or friends? Aside from Marilyn Danforth, whom he had occasionally slept with, Elliot's only real friend was Phillip. Marilyn was apt to be unreliable, and while he trusted Phillip completely, Elliot did not see how his friend could be of any real help in a rescue attempt.

The bookstore proprietor he knew as Al? His father had obviously trusted him, but Elliot was by no means certain that it had not been Al who had tipped off the police. That business with the rings made him uneasy. Could it have been some kind of signal? Had his own movements been monitored all that day?

Was the *tzigane* a police agent?

Elliot decided to contemplate a possible link between Al and the *tzigane* on the theory that it might illuminate any obvious treachery.

First, each man had been wearing a plain gold ring on his right hand. Well, nothing unusual here. Jewelry, being the only legal form in which the public could own gold since it had been renationalized, was presently quite popular as an inflation hedge. Elliot himself was wearing a plain gold band Denise had given him that past Christmas. Two particular men wearing undistinguished rings was no more of a coincidence than if they had been wearing the same style of shoes.

Second, both men had been twirling their rings back and forth, repeatedly. How many ways were there to play with a ring, anyway? Elliot managed to generate four categories: twirling, up and down the finger, a screwing action combining the first two motions, and a final category involving removal of the ring entirely from the finger. As an afterthought, he added two more categories: a null set of ring wearers who did not play with their rings, and a set comprising combinations within and permutations among the four primary categories—a likely possibility for any code requiring more than a minimal vocabulary.

Elliot turned west onto Fifty-ninth Street.

Then he thought of behavioral aspects. What percentage of ring players fell into each category? Come to think of it, how many ring wearers regularly played with their rings in the first place—and how frequently?

In despair, Elliot decided he had insufficient data even to start considering any other probability than that of Al and the *tzigane's* coincidence of ring twirling being just that.

So, logically, there was no reason to assume any conspiracy involving Al and the *tzigane*. For the moment—on the basis of his father's trust in the man—he could assume that Al was a free agent who might be useful in aiding his family.

Elliot was on Fifty-ninth Street nearing Fifth Avenue when a boy who looked about eleven, raggedly dressed and scarcely protected against the cold, approached him. "Mister, can I have a couple hundred blues to buy somethin' t'eat?" The boy said it mechanically. Elliot wondered how long he might have been surviving this way. He took out his wallet, removing a wad of blue money much more impressive than its purchasing power, and peeled off five $100 bills. The boy took it, then—instead of thanking Elliot—he backed off, making a rapid arm gesture.

Suddenly—out from behind parked cars, garbage cans, and alleyway—came five more boys ranging in age from fifteen to one about twenty whom Elliot tagged as the leader. They did not have the polish of the more professional gangs of Harlem or the Bronx: no club jackets, no racial identity, no firearms. But they had Elliot surrounded and were armed with knives, broken bottles, a chain, and a hooked tire wrench.

The leader—his hair dyed in blond and black stripes—stood back just a bit, looking Elliot up and down. Elliot suddenly felt extremely self-conscious about the quality of his clothing. "Hot shit," said the leader. "A brownie." He brandished a knife.

This was his first mistake. An experienced knife fighter would have held his weapon low—at his hip—blade forward, ready to strike; instead, the leader stood in a semi-crouch with his arms extended, the knife in his right hand. He grinned. Even so, Elliot was not in a good position to defend himself if he lunged.

Then the leader made his second mistake. In an attempt to show off, he began tossing the knife back and forth between his hands. Elliot edged back—feigning panic in an attempt to get the space he needed—then kicked the knife away while it was in flight between the leader's hands.

Elliot did not wait to see the expression on the leader's face before he went for his gun.

He had only managed to withdraw it from its holster—but not from his jacket—when one boy swung at him with the tire wrench. Elliot blocked the blow—painfully—with his left shoulder and found himself rolling with the force onto the ground. Nonetheless, he managed to free the gun and get a shot off in the direction of the leader. He missed. The leader shouted, "The motherfucker's got one!" and scurried down the street, followed in close order by his compatriots.

Elliot was still dazed when half a minute later a police car pulled up nearby. A blue-uniformed officer got out to see if Elliot needed medical assistance; another drove off in the direction of the gang. The officer helped Elliot up.

Somehow, without quite knowing how, Elliot found that the gun was no longer in his hand, but on the sidewalk next to him. The jumble of thoughts following added up to, Well, I've had it now.

"You all right, son?" Elliot just nodded. Then the officer noticed Elliot's revolver and picked it up. She examined it a moment, looked at Elliot, and handed it to him. "Better put this away before my partner sees it, or I'll have to take you in."

Elliot was still too dazed to be sure what was going on. Was this an attempt at entrapment? He coughed, managing enough air to get out "Thanks." Then he risked taking the gun from the officer, holstering it.

"Sure you're all right?"

"Uh—I think so."

"Then I'd better get my partner back before the blood-thirsty fool gets herself killed." She started running down Fifty-ninth Street in the direction the police car had driven.

"Thanks a million!" Elliot shouted to his samaritan. Upon reflection, he realized a million was not very much thanks these days.

Fifth Avenue at night was even busier than in daytime, though the bumper-to-bumper traffic of automobiles and motor scooters had been replaced with an equally dense population of bicycles and pedestrians. Each night, between Fifty-ninth and Forty-second streets, the avenue was closed off to all motorized traffic except the electric patrol carts of Fifth Avenue Merchant Alliance Security—and FAMAS had justified the privilege. By totally ignoring any nonviolent, noninvasive behavior—no matter how outrageous or vulgar—and concentrating exclusively on protecting its clients and their customers from attacks and robbery, FAMAS made Fifth Avenue a safe haven from the city's pervasive street violence. Anything else went, from sexual displays of every sort to the street merchandising of neo-opiates or—for several hours, at least—your own personal slave.

Within his first five minutes Elliot was approached by two beggars (one of whom looked as if he had taken a graduate degree in mendicancy from the University of Calcutta), had been invited to a gay dance hall, watched a man in a dress and high heels chase a midget, and been approached by a black-market currency dealer. Elliot might have made a deal with this last if his rates had been better.

Nor was this discouraged by the avenue's property owners. They knew it was precisely this atmosphere that attracted their customers. Neither did the city government interfere; its own OTB gambling casinos on the avenue were one of the city's few remaining reliable sources of revenue—and more than one city council member had secret business interests in the enclave.

As a result, Fifth Avenue had evolved into the center of the city's nightlife, maintaining a carnival atmosphere—dazzling, noisy, and sensual—in which its patrons were as often as not more interesting than its own diversions, which were plentiful.

Elliot checked his watch; it was only a little after eight thirty. He found it astonishing, but his entire life had been pulled apart in just over six hours. More immediate, though was the thought that the Rabelais Bookstore might still be open.

After locating a pay phone, Elliot searched his pockets for a vendy. Officially named Federal Vending Machine Tokens, vendies were the same size and weight as the old dimes, nickels, and quarters, but had completely replaced coins in common exchange. By official definition vendies were not money: NOT LEGAL TENDER was conspicuously stamped on the obverse. They circulated as change anyway. Though vendies were sold legally only by banks and post offices at a price set daily by the Treasury Department, the official price tended toward the black-market one to prevent the hoarding that had greshamed all fixed-value coins out of exchange. In turn, the black-market price was a fixed ratio to the stable eurofrancs.

Depositing a dime vendy—today worth about fifty New Dollars or €.04—Elliot obtained the Rabelais Bookstore's telephone number and called it. There was no answer.

It was still early. Surely it was prudent that he should avoid the streets as much as possible, but he was not sure where else was completely safe, either. Perhaps Phillip could be useful after all. Elliot redeposited his vendy, punching in Phillip's number from memory. Ten rings later he gave up, deciding to try again later.

Casually Elliot started down Fifth Avenue again, observing the gaudy spectacle around him. Two male transvestites passed by arm-in-arm. New Orleans jazz mixed in the street with infrasonic rock. Pushcart odors—sweet, then garlicky—wafted by his face. Brief clouds of warm, moist smoke vented out of cinema cabarets into the street, slowly there to dissipate. He was smiled at several times by streetwalkers, managing to ignore them until a more assertive one—his own age, quite pretty, and wearing an expensive evening gown with stole—started walking alongside him. "Hi," she said.

Elliot continued walking and nodded curtly. "Hello."

"Would you like to have a date with me?"

Elliot could not resist looking her over but answered politely, "Thank you, but no." He speeded up a bit.

She matched his pace. "I'm different from the others." Elliot glanced over as if to say, *Oh?* "For five thousand blues I'll do it in my pants."

Elliot reflected that all the weirdoes were certainly out, than gave her another glance. He couldn't resist. "Run that by me again?"

She smiled, continuing to match his pace. "I said that for five thousand blues, I'll go to the bathroom in my panties. I've been holding it in all day. You can watch me—even feel it if you want to. I wet myself, too. How about it?"

Elliot studied her with a fascinated horror mounting within him. He was almost jogging now. "You can't be serious."

"But I am. You'll like it. It's really—"

Her voice cut off as she stopped short, her face losing all expression. Almost automatically Elliot also stopped, thinking that she was about to faint. But several seconds later when she did not, Elliot knew with certainty what had caused her to stop. He backed slowly away.

"Oh, damn," she said in a baby-soft voice. "Now you've made me do it."

Five minutes later, he escaped into the lobby of the New

York Hilton from Sixth Avenue entrance. After hurrying into a telephone booth, he tried both the Rabelais Bookstore and Phillip again. There were still no answers.

Elliot then sat in the booth, taking account of his assets. He found that he had twenty-six thousand and some-odd blues in his wallet—a fair-sized sum. This surprised him. His allowance was generous, but not that generous. Then he remembered closing out his savings account just several days before to prevent the final erosion of his few remaining New Dollars.

For the first time in hours, he remembered the gold he was carrying. The idea started percolating through his mind that perhaps this might be the means of financing his family's release, whether through bribery, lawyer's fees, or even hiring criminals for a prison break. He knew that the gold was not his but his father's; nevertheless, his father had said that if by "'losing it' or paying it as a bribe" he could improve their escape chances one iota, he wouldn't have hesitated "for one second."

In the meantime, though, the gold was illegal and unconverted—of no immediate use.

He was hungry and still not sure whether he wanted to take a room. After first visiting the lobby magazine shop, where he bought a paperback copy of *Between Planets* by Robert A. Heinlein, he rode the escalator down to the Taverne Coffee Shop on the lower level. There he ate a Monte Cristo sandwich with several cups of quite good coffee (but then eating out always seemed a luxury; hotels and restaurants were not rationed at consumer level) and he read about half the novel.

Elliot was a science-fiction fan, Heinlein by far his favorite author. This particular novel was an old friend that he had read many times before. Its seventeen-year-old protagonist was in a similar predicament. Unfortunately, the specific problems he encountered had their solution on Venus, not Earth. At half past ten, Elliot paid his check and called Phillip again.

No answer.

Ten minutes later, Elliot had taken a single room for $11,500, registering as Donald J. Harvey, the hero of the Heinlein novel. An exorbitant bribe to the room clerk, added to advance cash payment, forestalled any questions about identification or travel permits.

The room was clean, comfortable, warm, and well lit. Though as functionally nondescript as a thousand other hotel rooms, its very anonymity made it more beautiful to Elliot than almost any other place he had seen. He punched a do-not-disturb notice into the hotel computer, locked and chained the door, then undressed for a leisurely whirlpool bath, hanging his precious belt on the towel rack so he could keep an eye on it.

He took the opportunity to examine his shoulder. On it was a purple-and-red bruise. He thought it strange that such an ugly wound did not hurt very much, but restrained from questioning his luck. The injury did not seem to require any immediate attention, though, nor would he have known what to do if it had.

After bathing, Elliot got into bed—with belt under his pillow and gun on the night table—and finished reading the Heinlein. Finally, he called the desk, leaving a wake-up Picturephone call for eight o'clock.

Momentarily overcome by an attack of lonely fright, he soon managed to guide his mind to other matters. Thinking about the poor streetwalker made him feel a bit less sorry for himself.

What a revoltin' *development that was*!

Chapter 7

Elliot was back in the classroom. Mrs. Tobias stood at the front of the room wearing a police uniform. Marilyn Danforth walked up to Elliot and said, "Pardon me, but do you mind awfully if I defecate here? I have to go *so* badly." This embarrassed him greatly because his parents and Denise were at the back of the room watching him. Mrs. Tobias started talking: "And now I'd like to introduce the boys in the band. First, we have Mason Langley on chains." Langley stood up, rattled his chains a bit while bowing, then sat down again. "Next is Bernard Rothman. What are you playing, Mr. Rothman?" "I have no idea, Mrs. Tobias." "Well it doesn't really matter," she said. "And last, but not least, we have Cal Ackerman on the tire wrench. For our first selection ..." At this cue, Mason Langley started rattling his chains again while Cal Ackerman walked calmly over to Elliot and rammed the tire wrench into his left shoulder.

As the blow hit, Elliot awoke. The rattling of the chains transmuted into the ringing of a Picturephone. The pain from Ackerman's blow to his shoulder was intensely real, though, which he realized reaching over to answer the phone. Elliot punched the switch allowing him to see without being seen, then answered. It was his 8 a.m. wake-up call. Elliot thanked the operator and switched off.

As his mind cleared, Elliot quickly realized that the pain was not from Ackerman's phantasmal blow, but from the real one in his encounter with the gang. Tenderly, he tried moving his shoulder. He found he had full mobility—nothing seemed to be broken or sprained—but it did hurt like the devil. He resolved to ignore it as best he could.

Elliot decided to breakfast in his room rather than risk half an hour in a public restaurant again; he had no wish to be a sitting duck. Calling room service, he ordered papaya-mango juice, oatmeal, a cheese omelet, hash browns, muffins with jam, and a pot of coffee. Elliot had heard often—and believed— that breakfast was the most important meal of the day. Oh, yes. Could they provide a toothbrush with paste?

They could.

While awaiting delivery, Elliot used the toilet, washed, dressed—again donning his belt and shoulder holster—and had just reloaded his revolver with two bullets from a ciga- rette-case-sized holder when there was a knock at his door. Elliot looked up. "Yes?"

"Room service," said a male voice behind the door. "Your breakfast, sir."

Elliot swung his revolver's cylinder shut, holstered the pis- tol, then started to the door; halfway there, he stopped short, realizing his holster was in the open. He swore under his breath, told the door he would be right there, and headed back to the bed where he picked up his jacket and put it on. As an afterthought, Elliot picked up the ammunition case, hiding it in his jacket pocket.

A moment later, he opened the door; it was indeed room service. The waiter—a Slavic-looking man in hotel uniform— rolled in a wheeled breakfast cart. "G'morning, sir."

"Morning," Elliot replied. "Over by the screen will be fine."

The waiter set up the breakfast cart in front of the room's television wallscreen, then handed Elliot the chit to sign. He signed it—the waiter looking on closely—and when Elliot be- gan writing his tip onto the bill, the waiter interrupted imme- diately: "That won't be necessary, sir."

Elliot stopped writing. "Eh?" Then he understood. "Oh, of course." He reached into his pocket, removed his wallet, and counted out blue cash—almost endlessly. "Don't spend them all in one place."

The waiter smiled, taking the cash. "I don't spend them at all. My wife meets me at my lunch break, takes all my tips, and goes shopping while the blues are still worth something." He pocketed the money. "Thank you very much, sir. Enjoy your breakfast."

A few minutes later Elliot ate breakfast while watching a television newscast. On the wallscreen was a news announcer sitting in a studio: blown up behind him was a handsome, military-looking man in his fifties, wearing a stylish business suit. The caption under the blowup identified the man as Lawrence Powers, director of the FBI.

The news announcer was saying, "...the FBI director's address to the National Association of Law Enforcement Officers at their convention last night."

Film of Lawrence Powers addressing a police banquet was inserted onscreen. "These firebombings of our FBI offices," Powers said in his distinctive, deep-Southern voice, "are only the latest example. The Revolutionary Agorist Cadre can be viewed as no less a threat than as an unholy alliance between the Mafia and anarchist-terrorists."

The news announcer returned to the screen, continuing: "The FBI chief's appearance at the convention last night was a surprise to many. It was not expected that Mr. Powers would wish to appear in public so soon after the suicide of his wife."

The blowup of Powers was replaced by one of an equally handsome man in his late forties, blond, blue-eyed, and clean-shaven. The news announcer flipped to his next story, during which Elliot stopped eating and gave the screen his full attention.

"Private memorial services will be held today," said the newsman, "for Nobel Prize-winning economist Dr. Martin Vreeland, who died yesterday morning of a heart attack at forty-eight. Dr. Vreeland, often called the father of EUCOMTO's New Economic Miracle of fifteen years ago, became well known as

an intransigent advocate of a limited-government, laissez-faire
enterprise system. He was to have addressed the New York
rally of Citizens for a Free Society this morning. Dr. Vreeland
is survived by a wife and two children."

Elliot now knew that the police had decided to let the world
believe—for the time being—that his father was dead.

On second thought, he hoped it was only for the time being.

Nonetheless, by the time he had brushed his teeth, the world
did not seem as frightening as it had the night before. If things
went well, he might even have his family free by that evening.
He had a firm conviction that Al would know exactly to whom
he should go. Elliot decided shortly that it was time he got a
move on.

Not long after nine, Elliot settled his tab, starting to walk to
Times Square. It was one of those bitterly cold, windy—though
cheerfully bright—mornings to which even lifelong New York-
ers seldom grow accustomed. He pulled sunglasses and a scarf
(he had no hat) from his overcoat pocket, then turned up his
collar. Elliot had gloves, also, but resisted putting them on to
keep his hands free for possible shooting. Within minutes,
though, his fingers were numb enough that he could hardly
pull a trigger anyway, and he donned the gloves as well. His
ears became numb, too, and his shoulder ached, but there was
nothing he could do for them.

When Elliot arrived at the Rabelais Bookstore, there was a
sign inside the door, which he read through an iron grill, that
said, "CLOSED." He panicked a moment, then read further to
find a listing of hours: on weekdays the store was open from
ten to ten. It was only nine-thirty, so Elliot walked back to
Hotalings and perused foreign magazines for half an hour, finally buying a *Paris Match* to avoid being murdered by the
manager. He read French well enough to understand a cover
story entitled *"La Mort des Etats-Unis?"* A cover photograph—
a still taken from the film *Planet of the Apes*—showed the Statue

of Liberty half-buried in mud.

For reasons he could not fully identify, Elliot greatly resented the story, finding it strikingly presumptuous. Surely the country was in trouble, but it had been far worse during the Civil War, and the United States had survived that. Where did these foreigners get off already writing an obituary?

Elliot rolled up the magazine, shoving it into a coat pocket, and again walked to the bookstore. This time it was open. On the stool behind the counter was a man Elliot did not recognize, as thin as Al had been obese, with a pencil mustache and greasy black hair. He looked up from a tabloid headline "TEEN VAGINA!" and stared at Elliot. He pointed to the notice back of the counter saying, "BE 21 OR BE GONE."

"Uh—I'm not trying to buy anything," Elliot said quickly. "I just want to talk to Al."

"Ain't nobody here by that name."

"But he was here yesterday—I talked to him. A bald man with a beard. Overweight."

"Oh, *him*," the skinny clerk said. "Goddam brownie. He quit last night. Said he was sick of this goddam New York winter and was headin' south."

"Did he leave a forwarding address?"

"Nope. Now beat it before a cop catches you in here."

Elliot beat it.

Soon he stood at Times Square, cursing himself methodically. *You fuckhead, you prick, you numbskull! ...What are you a* brownie? *...If you'd walked back here last night instead of phoning, you might have caught him in time ...You were carrying a fucking* revolver *and still you were afraid.... What chance would there've been of two attacks in the same night? ...Now you've missed the one person you know to be on Dad's team .... You've probably blown the entire game....*

Elliot vowed never again to allow fear to control his mind. Then he took a deep breath and walked on.

He had only walked a few steps, though, when he realized he was not walking to any place in particular. He was lost. He knew the names of the streets, all right, and where they went, but he did not know where they would lead him. *Where to, kid*? he asked himself silently, *where to*? There was no answer.

He stood, gazing up at the Oracle's news marching across the top of One Times Square:

TEAMSTER PRESIDENT WARNS POSSIBILITY OF ARMED FORCES WILDCAT STRIKES IF PENTAGON DOES NOT MEET DEMANDS ...

Are you just going to stand here forever?

NEW DOLLAR AGAIN DROPS SHARPLY AGAINST EUROFRANC IN HEAVY TRADING ...

C'mon, c'mon, Elliot told himself, we haven't got all day.

SENATE DEBATE ON WAGE-PRICE CONTROLS STALLED PENDING CFS PROTEST MARCHES IN SIX CITIES TODAY ...

A helluva lot of good you are! Elliot told himself. An echo in his mind agreed.

In despair, he decided to choose a direction—any direction—and start walking. He hesitated another moment, then began marching up Broadway.

He had hardly started when a wiry, short man with curly black hair rushed up to him and said intensely, "If Thou art God, I offer myself and, in exchange, ask proof!"

Elliot kept walking. Not another Gloaminger.

"I said, 'If Thou art God—'"

"I heard you the first time," Elliot told him.

"Oh, hell," said the Gloaminger. "You're not Him, either."

"Don't you people ever give up looking?" Elliot asked.

"No time to talk," the Gloaminger said. He handed Elliot a

tract and walked up to a little girl nearby. "If Thou art God, I offer—"

Elliot looked the pamphlet over. It was called *God Here and Now?—An Introduction to Gloamingerism*, and was published by the Church of the Human God. The Septagram—symbol of the Gloaminger's "Seven Paths to One God"—embellished the front of the tract.

The Gloamingers believed that God was a human, on earth "at this very moment," but that He did not know Who He was. The question was supposed to trigger His memory in time for the Apocalypse. "Ask the question of the next person you meet!" the pamphlet said. "GOD WALKS THE EARTH TODAY. Now! He may reveal Himself to you!"

Elliot tossed the pamphlet into the nearest trash container. He was not about to start looking for God. He had enough trouble just finding his family.

Ten blocks farther up Broadway Elliot noticed wooden NYPD barricades along each sidewalk, and began to see an unusually large number of city police distributed around him—some sitting in police cars, some mounted on horseback, some on foot directing traffic or talking into headset transceivers. Elliot wondered what they were all there for, then remembered. The march and rally, of course! Broadway would be the parade route.

The first impulse he had was to put as much distance between himself and all those police as possible, but they did not seem to be interested in anything other than assuring an orderly demonstration, paying him no attention. His caution gave way for a moment to an even greater curiosity to see the demonstration his father was to have addressed, Elliot deciding that in the anonymous throng of bystanders he would be as unnoticed as the musicians in a striptease club.

Elliot first spotted the marchers as he approached Columbus Circle. He had no idea how many there were, but it seemed to be thousands, stretching uptown as far as he could see. He could hear from the distance that they seemed to be chanting repeatedly, but he could not yet make out the words. They were still too far off for him to read picket signs or banners. Finding himself a relatively uncrowded spot near the barricades at Columbus Circle, he waited.

Soon the march was upon him, led by a huge linen banner stretched across the first rank that read, "NO MORE CONTROLS!" with "Citizens for a Free Society" written in smaller letters underneath. Behind the banner were hundreds of smaller, handmade signs mounted on rolled cardboard (wooden picket signs were illegal), with slogans such as "CONTROL POLITICIANS, NOT PRICES! ...SMASH RATIONING! ...IN GOLD WE TRUST! ...NO MORE BLUES!" and dozens that read "WAS VREELAND MURDERED?" This last shook Elliot.

Other signs had a distinct left-wing tinge. "THE FED IS SAPPING OUR SURPLUS LABOR VALUE!" and "MISES OVER MARX!"

A number of demonstrators carried black flags.

Now he concentrated on listening to the chanting, difficult to understand immediately but clearer with each repetition. A voice on a bullhorn asked, "WHAT DO WE WANT?" The marchers answered, "FREEDOM!" The bullhorn asked, "WHEN DO WE WANT IT?" The marchers responded, "Now!" Elliot noticed as many middle-aged demonstrators as he did students, though the latter distinguished themselves by wearing black scarves wrapped around their foreheads.

The bullhorn stopped, the chanting quieted, but soon there started a new voice. It began chanting softly, and soon the marchers joined in, raggedly at first, then unifying and building up to a crescendo, "LAISSEZ-FAIRE! ...LAISSEZ-FAIRE! ...LAISSEZ-FAIRE!"

"Hey, Vreeland! Elliot Vreeland!" a voice cut through the chanting.

Elliot froze, trying to be as inconspicuous as possible in the hope that whoever had called him would believe he had experienced a case of mistaken identity. It was not to be.

"Hey, Vreeland! Elliot!"

Elliot saw that the voice belonged to his classmate, Mason Langley. Asshole, Elliot thought. He doesn't even understand what this march is about. Elliot started praying that no one else would pay any attention in the midst of all the chanting, but it was already too late. He saw a New York policeman start looking around at mention of the name "Vreeland." His only hope would be if Langley would just continue marching...

No such luck. Langley started pushing his way through the marchers trying to get to him. Elliot saw the policeman speaking into his helmet transceiver and knew he only had seconds; he slid under the barricades, and nonchalantly slipped into step with Langley and the marchers.

"I *thought* it was you," Langley said. "Why didn't you—"

"Shut up," Elliot whispered savagely, "or you might get us both killed. Quick—give me your picket sign."

Langley did so, somewhat confused, but it was already too late. The policeman shouted, "There! It's the Vreeland boy!" and started running toward him. Elliot thought quickly, knew his one remaining chance, and kept marching.

As the policeman caught up to Elliot and grabbed him, Elliot looked up innocently, shouting, "Hey, what the hell d'ja think you're doing?"

The reaction was as expected. The policeman realized his mistake too late to prevent several marchers from clobbering him with their picket signs. The cardboard did not do him very much damage, but it did cause him to release Elliot, who took the opportunity to push through the marchers in the confusion and emerge on the east side of Columbus Circle. Then, picket sign and all, Elliot bolted into a full run up Central Park West.

When he felt he had run as far as he could without bursting his lungs, he slipped into the outside front basement of a brownstone building and sat on the steps, catching his breath.

Then he examined the picket sign he had been carrying.

It read, "FREE THE AGORA!"

Chapter 8

"I can't serve you without proof-of-age," the bartender said, not without kindness. "Sorry."

Elliot placed a thousand blues on the counter. "Just coffee. In the back, please." The bartender took the bills, nodding.

Rick's Café Américain was now on Columbus Avenue near Seventy-first Street.

The proliferation of videodiscs and wallscreens—combined with an ever-increasing nostalgia mania—had caused a revolution in nightlife. Gone were most stand-up comics, mimes, dance bands, and dinner theatres; they had been replaced by cinema cabarets. On weekends the cafe was the domain of Ansonia students, who came to watch continuously run Humphrey Bogart films. Elliot had been there with Marilyn and Phillip on several occasions; a few minutes ago he had remembered it as an intimate place with secluded rear booths where a person could be undisturbed a long while.

Not very much after Elliot had settled himself in, the bartender brought Elliot his cup. Elliot took a sip, suppressing a choke. "There's whiskey in here," he said hoarsely.

The barkeep looked surprised. "Irish coffee. Isn't that what you ordered?"

Elliot was about to tell him that when he said coffee he just meant *coffee*, but cut himself off. "Not exactly, but this will do fine. Thanks." The bartender left, shaking his head slowly, leaving Elliot with the thought that this might just give the man incentive to divert any nosy police.

Soon Elliot felt more collected than he had been in a day. Even his shoulder did not hurt quite as much. He got down to some serious thinking.

One. Each time he was now seen in public would be at the

risk of impromptu arrest. As inefficient as the police were, the long-term odds were stacked in their favor.

Two. It seemed to Elliot that the possibility of proceeding through legal channels was, if not closed entirely, at least sharply restricted. Especially since he did not even know what charge he was being sought on. What if it were for his father's murder? In any event, he knew no lawyer he was willing to trust at the moment.

Three. Unless he could make trustworthy countereconomic contacts, the gold would remain of no use to him. And he was running out of blues frightfully fast.

Finally, four. Even if his resources were unlimited, he still had no idea of how to proceed with getting his family free. He did not even know of anyone who did.

Conclusions. He had to hide out with someone who could be trusted—someone who could act as a business agent for him. Hobson's choice: the only person whom he was at all inclined to trust was Phillip Gross. Elliot checked his watch; it was coming up on noon. Phillip and he were both scheduled for first lunch; he decided to walk over to Ansonia and catch him before Contemporary Civilization.

He never made it to Ansonia's second floor. Elliot had just climbed the stairs past the first floor when he ran into Dr. Fischer on her way down. They both stopped, staring at each other for several heartbeats. Then Dr. Fischer said softly, "Come into my office, please."

He thought about running. He knew that if he ran, nobody could catch him. But there was something about the way Dr. Fischer seemed to be looking right through him that made him decide not to run. He followed her past the reception area into her office.

Dr. Fischer closed the inner door. "There were police here this morning asking about you," she said, "asking if anyone knew where you were. They said they were making inquiries for your mother, that you had gone on a rampage when you learned your father was dead." She paused a moment. "They mentioned that you had taken one of your father's guns."

Elliot nodded. "I was wondering what story they'd come up with."

"It's true? The Administration has murdered your father?"

Elliot turned white. "How much have you heard? What's your source?"

"Only rumors," Dr. Fischer said quickly, calming him. "It is being said in many places that your father did not die of natural causes."

Elliot took a deep breath. "As far as I know, ma'am, my father is still alive. At least he was yesterday afternoon when—"

"Afternoon?" she interrupted. "But your sister said—"

He waved it away. "My sister was acting. My mother's orders."

"But she was so convincing," Dr. Fischer said.

"She's a drama student at Juilliard."

Dr. Fischer went to her desk, pulled out a cigarette which she inserted into a holder, and lighted it. After taking a deep drag, she said, "It's dangerous for you here, Elliot. The police will return—next time, I fear, with a search warrant."

"I was planning to see if maybe Phillip Gross could put me up."

She looked as if the idea surprised her, then smiled slightly. "Yes. Very good. But you should not be seen together, even here. You may stay here until shortly before Phillip's class is out, then walk to his apartment. I'll tell him that you'll be waiting for him nearby." Elliot nodded. Dr. Fischer relaxed slightly, took another drag on her cigarette, and smiled again. "Have you eaten lunch?"

After two cheeseburgers, apple brown Betty, and milk, which Dr. Fischer brought down to him from the cafeteria, Elliot resigned himself to a wait while Dr. Fischer sat at her desk doing paperwork. He got out his *Paris Match* and began struggling through an article questioning whether EUCOMTO should sell its new hypersonic transports to the People's Republic of Taiwan.

At two thirty, Dr. Fischer told Elliot that the coast was clear, and he left Ansonia. It was set up that he would meet Phillip on the approach to his Lincoln Towers apartment. Elliot walked west on Seventieth Street to the junction of Broadway and Amsterdam Avenue, then, after checking for police, he crossed over to Amsterdam. He walked down a block to the Lincoln Towers driveway, leaned against he wall of the now-empty public library—out of sight of the Lincoln Towers guardhouse—and covered his face with the *Paris Match*. Periodically, he glanced over the top.

At a quarter past three, Phillip showed up. Elliot lowered the magazine, allowing Phillip to spot him, then waited for the traffic light to change. Several moments later Phillip crossed Amsterdam and joined him. "Fancy meeting you here," Elliot said dryly from behind the magazine.

Phillip assumed an habitual sardonic expression. "Come on," he said tapping Elliot on the shoulder. "We're exposed out here."

They started into the complex, Phillip nodding to the security guard as they passed, and to the German doorman at 180 West End Avenue when they entered the building. A few minutes later they entered his seventh-floor apartment, furnished in the eternal New-York-Jewish-Upper-West-Side mode. Phillip told Elliot to wait, then disappeared a few moments into one of the bedrooms. "I had to reset the burglar alarm," he explained when he returned.

They took off their outer coats, Phillip hanging them up, then he suggested Elliot make himself more comfortable by removing his jacket as well. Elliot hesitated a moment, then took it off, revealing his holstered revolver. Philip looked at Elliot queerly. "You know how to use that thing?" he asked.

"It saved my life yesterday. Twice."

"Did you shoot anybody?"

"No. I missed."

"Accidentally or on purpose?"

Phillip never received an answer to the question for at that moment his uncle walked into the apartment.

Morris Gross was a thin, Semitic-looking man in his early seventies with sparse white hair and wire-rimmed spectacles. Still standing in the entrance alcove, he removed an overcoat, scarf, and a Russian fur hat. Elliot started wondering how he could explain his gun when Phillip, noticing his friend's expression, leaned over, whispering, "Easy, you're among friends."

"Hello, hello," said Mr. Gross as he entered the living room. He spoke with a Yiddish accent.

Elliot stood up along with Phillip. "Uncle Morris," Phillip said, "you remember Elliot Vreeland."

"Yes, of course." Mr. Gross approached Elliot, and they shook hands. "I'm deeply sorry to hear of your father's passing. He was a man of rare courage."

Elliot felt mixed emotions—embarrassment about the cover story, worried hope that his father's death was only a cover story. "Uh, thank you, Mr. Gross." Elliot glanced over to Phillip for guidance; his friend nodded reassurance. "I'd like to explain about the gun."

"No need," said Mr. Gross. "I've had to carry them on occasion myself. I manufacture jewelry, you know."

"You're home early," Phillip said. "Your stomach acting up again?"

Mr. Gross nodded. "Gold went up another 31 percent today. I can't stockpile it fast enough. I left Nikki to close the office." He turned to Elliot. "Will you join us for dinner tonight? Or do you have family responsibilities?"

"Of course you will," said Phillip, taking Elliot off the spot. "We won't take no for an answer, Ell."

"Thank you," said Elliot. "But do you have someplace where I can hang my holster, first?"

A few minutes later, the boys were alone in Phillip's bedroom, Elliot settled into a leather recliner, Phillip prone on his bed. Over the next hour Elliot gave a chronological and fairly complete account of the events leading up to his current dilemma. Phillip listened attentively, without interrupting. When finished, Elliot asked his friend whether he would help. "Of course," Phillip said simply. "What do you want me to do?"

"To be honest, I don't know. I suppose I should get a lawyer, eh?"

"I'm not a legal expert, Ell. I don't know, either."

"Well, the two of us can't go up against the entire U.S. government single-handedly, can we?"

Phillip barely cracked a smile. "I don't think so."

"Then what do you think I should do?"

"You're asking my advice?"

Elliot cocked a brow. "You're getting at something."

Phillip remained silent.

"Yes, I'm asking your advice."

"Then," said Phillip, "I think you should repeat your story for my uncle and ask *his* advice."

Elliot considered this for a long moment. "Phil, I don't know your uncle. Do you really think he'd help me?"

"He might. You can ask."

"But how will he take this? There are a lot of legal and political overtones he might not like."

"I guarantee you a safe conduct out of here whether he likes them or not."

"But does he know anything about this sort of business?"

Phillip smiled again. "I think so. When he was fourteen, he fought for the Irgun in the founding of Israel."

Elliot shut up.

Phillip glanced over at the wall clock, then got up. "I'd better start on dinner."

"You're cooking?"

"Why not? I'm quite a chef."

Elliot grinned widely. "Can I watch?"

"Absolutely not." Phillip switched his television wallscreen from disc playback to live reception and touched it on. "Rot your mind a bit," he said, then left.

Elliot caught most of a drama called *Presidential Healer*, a series about a United States President who cured his subjects by laying on of hands, then *Dr. Witch*, a comedy about an African witch doctor who had attended medical school and was now practicing in Long Beach, California. After being chased out of the kitchen by Phillip, he turned to *Hello, Joe—Whadd'ya Know?* It concerned the adventures of an intellectual gorilla named Joe—the product of primate educational research—who was a philosophy professor and resident sage at Gazpacho College. This episode concerned the problems that arose when Joe found himself scheduled for both a cello recital and the finals of an international chess competition on the same night.

There were no commercials. There were, however, a number of public-service announcements, leading into the six o'clock news.

A man and a woman—two well-known TV-series actors— were sitting in a shooting set on canvas chairs. "Remember," said the male actor, talking sincerely to the cameras, "that just one little ounce of gold bullion can put you away in a federal penitentiary for up to twenty years."

This made Elliot's day.

"And the FBI," said the actress, "now has a twenty-four-hour free hotline to report anyone engaging in black-market speculation. Black-marketeers steal from *all* of us, and prolong this economic crisis. Don't help a brownie. If you know of any, remember your patriotic duty and call now."

An 800 series inward-WATS telephone number was su-

perimposed on the screen; in disgust, Elliot changed channels in time to hear the promo for another station's evening
news: "—tape of a mass demonstration on Broadway that
ended with violence. This story and others in one minute!"

"Dinner is on!" Phillip called from the dining room. At that
moment, however, Elliot would not have budged if the gods
had personally offered him ambrosia and nectar.

A teletype machine soloed in an overture, then: "Good
evening," said a sandy-haired newsman. "I'm Monahan Scott
with the news.

"This morning's anti-wage/price control march down Broadway by an estimated sixty thousand members of Citizens for a
Free Society ended in violence soon after it began when a New
York City policeman—apparently without provocation—at-
tacked one of the marchers. Neither the identity of the officer
nor that of the demonstrator is known. Frieda Sandwell was
there and spoke to one of the demonstrators."

The picture zoomed in to Columbus Circle with clouds of
tear gas chasing demonstrators, one of them retching on the
street. Another marcher was seen being clubbed by two po-
licemen. There was a shot of a policeman being kicked in the
groin by a woman marcher. The screen then cut to a teen-age
boy with a bloody gash over his black head-kerchief, being
interviewed by the flawlessly groomed Frieda Sandwell. "Well,
we was just goin' along peacefully," the boy said, "when this
crazy pig yells somethin', charges into the march, and grabs
one of our people."

"Did you hear what the officer shouted?" asked Frieda
Sandwell, shoving a microphone in his mouth.

"It sounded like, 'Let's tear the freedom boys!'"

"Hey," said Phillip, entering the bedroom. "Your dinner's
getting cold."

Elliot switched off the television and without saying a word
followed his friend to supper.

Chapter 9

Phillip was every bit as good a chef as he declared.

Elliot was treated royally to a dinner that started with grapefruit halves and tossed green salad, proceeded through fillets of coconut-orange chicken, green beans with almonds, and candied yams, then was topped off by Southern pecan pie served with chickoried *café au lait*. Elliot complimented Phillip, among other things, on his abilities in matching up ration points.

After dinner, over cognac and cigars (Elliot accepted the former only), Elliot repeated his story for Mr. Gross: how his father's name had been on a secret arrest list, the plan to leave the country, his trip to find the gold and what he had learned upon his arrival home—even his theory about the possible link between Al and the *tzigane* cabdriver. He retold the events after his escape from the apartment, finishing up this time by including what he had learned about his part in precipitating a riot. Several times Mr. Gross asked for clarification of a point or for additional information.

Mr. Gross puffed on his cigar one last time, then snuffed it into his ashtray. Elliot noticed himself holding his breath and consciously took in air. Finally, Mr. Gross said, "Have you considered the possibility that your family may already be dead? I don't ask this to be cruel. When I was your age, I lost my entire family except for one brother—Phillip's father, whom we lost later—to the Nazis."

Elliot swallowed, about to answer in the affirmative, then suddenly changed his mind. "I've thought about it, Mr. Gross, but I find it inconceivable that the authorities would just kill three private citizens in cold blood."

"It was inconceivable in 1943, too. But it happened." Mr.

Gross allowed Elliot to digest the thought for several seconds, then added, "But, to be honest, I think it is likely that all three are still alive at the moment. This is not wishful thinking; there are a number of sound reasons why this should be true. Even so, while we must proceed on the assumption that your family can still be helped, I want you to face the possibility that it may be too late."

"I understand."

"All right."

"Maybe," said Elliot, "it would be best to try forcing the authorities into the open. Possibly hire a lawyer to get a writ of habeas corpus. Or maybe I should just march into the offices of *The New York Times* and tell them the entire story."

"I can see your point, and if that's what you decide to do, I'll be happy to help in any way I can. But I advise against it."

"Why?"

"Call it intuition if you like," said Mr. Gross, "but it is my belief that, if your family is still alive, you'd be running the risk that exposing their kidnaping—and I use the term advisedly—might make certain you would never see them alive again."

"Then what are you saying? That I should sit tight and not do anything?"

"No, action must be taken—quietly."

"Are you telling me to hire a detective?"

"This would be beyond any normal investigators. They would have their licenses revoked if they stepped on any political toes."

"Then what are you suggesting?"

Mr. Gross took a sip of cognac and paused a moment. "In the jewelry business one meets many people. Some of them tell me that almost anything can be obtained—for a price. You told me that you have the means. The question remains how much you are willing to spend."

"All of it," said Elliot firmly. "All the gold I've got. I figured that out yesterday."

"Then, if you like," Mr. Gross continued, "I'll ask some of my associates what is possible. I can't do anything until tomorrow, so you'll spend the night here. Phillip will make up the couch."

"Mr. Gross, you're a real lifesaver."

"I hope to be."

At that instant, the grandfather clock in the dining room began striking eight o'clock. Mr. Gross rose. "Five minutes slow, Phillip. Your turn to wind."

Mr. Gross retired to his bedroom to read, and Phillip, having finished his kitchen duties, asked Elliot if he were up to a game of chess. Elliot was, and Phillip set up on the dining table.

After picking the white pawn out of Phillip's clenched fists, Elliot opened with pawn to king's fourth. Phillip responded king's pawn to fourth rank also. Elliot played king's bishop to queen's bishop fourth, then said, "By the way, how *did* you know that Mrs. Tobias was being fired?"

Phillip grinned. "Let's leave it that the ventilation shaft between the second floor men's room and the headmaster's office directly below is a useful source of information. And she wasn't fired." He moved his king's bishop likewise.

White queen moved to king's bishop third. "Why did she quit?"

"A power play," said Phillip. Black queen's knight's pawn to fourth, threatening white bishop. "Mrs. Tobias wanted to teach her political views, Dr. Fischer said she was hired to teach, not to propagandize."

Elliot's queen took the pawn at king's bishop seventh. "Don't you think that's a rather nasty violation of her academic freedom? She was a bitch—granted—but fair is fair."

"Nonsense," said Phillip, taking Elliot's bishop with the knight's pawn. "It's no more a violation of her freedom than refusing to charter a plane to Los Angeles when you want to go to Miami. What she did on her own time was her own business."

"You can't take that bishop, Phil."

"Huh? Why the hell not?"

"Because I mated you last move."

Phillip stared at the board, then said softly, "Shit."

Elliot grinned fiendishly.

Bright sunlight awakened him. After a few minutes trying to keep it out, he gave up, pulling himself into a sitting-up position. A few moments rubbing his eyes, several seconds to remember where he was. He rubbed his calves, removing the kinks—the couch had been too short for him—then came wide awake, hearing that the apartment was absolutely silent except for the ticking from the grandfather clock. It was about nine thirty.

In line of sight with the grandfather clock was a note on the dining table impaled on the white king, the night's battlefield still displaying his victory. He padded over.

Ell,
We didn't want to wake you because you seemed to need the sleep. There's hot coffee in the percolator and you can feel free to rustle up anything you want to eat. Suggest you stay put. My uncle and I will return by mid-afternoon.
Keep your powder dry,

Phil

It seemed to Elliot, after he had performed the usual morning rituals, that no day had ever passed so slowly. He felt that there was an immense pressure compelling him to action ...but he could not move. He felt as if some great achievement was demanded of him ...but that he did not have the strength to perform it.

He tried reading a novel chosen from Phillip's shelves: he was unable to read more than a few pages before his mind began to wander. He turned on the television. The games seemed impossibly insipid, and he turned the set off angrily.

Finally, he selected a holosonic cassette and put it on Phillip's music system; it was the Reiner-Chicago Symphony recording of Brahms' Third Symphony. Finding it soothing, he was able to sit for the first time in hours. Elliot sank into Phillip's recliner, and when the second movement began, he closed his eyes.

The Grosses returned home together at about four o'clock. "It's all set," Phillip's uncle said as soon as the door closed. "The chairman doesn't like to take this sort of case, but—knowing your father was at stake—decided to help."

"The chairman?" Elliot asked anxiously.

"Merce Rampart," said Mr. Gross. "Chairman of the Revolutionary Agorist Cadre."

Elliot stood stunned, as if again hit by the tire wrench. His mind was a jumble of conflicting imagery. All in the same instant he felt betrayed, vulnerable. "These are your 'associates'?"

"Yes," Mr. Gross said.

"You approve of what they do?"

"Wholeheartedly."

"Phil? How do you feel about all this?"

"I don't know much more than you do, Ell."

Elliot stood there a moment, weighing the lives of his family against political considerations he was not yet fully competent to weigh. At present the government was on one side, and he—along with his family and an "unholy alliance between the Mafia and anarchist-terrorists"—was on the other. But what if loyalty to his family required him to choose the wrong side?

His father's words came back to him: *"It's much too late for me to impart values to you; but if you don't have them, then I'm not much of a father."*

"All right," said Elliot. "I'll see this Rampart. What do I have to do?"

Part Two

A sleeper met in his dreams the Prince of Darkness, finding him to be erect of figure and fair in countenance. He addressed him, "O handsome Prince! Men know nothing of your beauty, but always depict you as fearful-looking and hideous!"

Lucifer smiled, replying, "Those figures have been drawn by my enemies, who blame me for their eviction from Paradise. It is in malice that they portray me so."

—SHEIKH MUSHARIFF-UD-DIN SA'DI, 1184-1291, best known as Sa'di of Shiraz, translated from *Bustan* ("Garden")

Chapter 10

"Sign here."

Mr. Gross gestured to the document he had just placed on the coffee table, extending Elliot a pen. Phillip was in the kitchen preparing dinner.

"I knew there was a catch somewhere," Elliot said. "What is it?"

"A skeptic, eh?" replied Mr. Gross. "Well, I can't say I blame you. Read it for yourself, then, if you have any more questions, I'll answer them if I can."

Elliot picked up the paper and began reading it aloud:

"GENERAL SUBMISSION TO ARBITRATION

"*Agreement*, among the undersigned Submittor, the Independent Arbitration Group [there was an address], hereafter IAG, and all other persons who have made or may make General Submissions to Arbitration ...

"In consideration of the mutual promises herein ...and other good and valuable consideration, the Submittor agrees that any disputes arising, or which have arisen, between Submittor and any other person(s) who has made or makes a General Submission to Arbitration shall be arbitrated by IAG under its Rules then in effect. Submittor acknowledges receipt of a copy of the Rules."

"Which I just happen to have a spare copy of," said Mr. Gross, handing Elliot a booklet.

"Mmmmm," Elliot acknowledged. He then skimmed over a technical passage about filings, notices, and such, then concluded:

"Arbitration shall enforce the law of the contract to effectuate its purposes, and shall decide the issues by the application of reason to the facts under the guidance of the Law of Equal Liberty (each has the right to do with his/her own what he/she wishes so long as he/she does not forcibly interfere with the equal right of another)."

"Okay I get the point," said Elliot. "But what does this have to do with me?"

"Everything," Mr. Gross said. "Every single person who works with—or does business with—the Revolutionary Agorist Cadre has signed just such an agreement as this, either with this group or another with which they have swapped reciprocal jurisdiction. The Cadre will not do business with—will not even talk to—anyone who has not signed a Submission to Arbitrate."

"Why?"

"A number of reasons," Mr. Gross said. "Being an underground organization, the Cadre cannot sue in a government court if someone breaks a contract or otherwise damages them. Also, the Cadre do not care to use gangster tactics to enforce their contracts. Broken arms, setting fires, murder—this is all that's left when one is deprived of a peaceful method of settling disputes. And such methods are—in any case—against agoric principles. The Cadre cannot set up their own court— dragging people into it the way the government does—because such a court would be—and would be called—a kangaroo court. It would not have the mystique of having a State behind it, and nobody would respect its decisions."

"Wait a second, wait a second," Elliot interrupted. "You're telling me that this Independent Arbitration Group, that they're not part of the Cadre?"

"Of course not. How could they be? It's a perfectly legitimate arbitration organization. Check with the Better Business Bureau, if you don't believe me."

"Then how can a 'perfectly legitimate' organization have an illegal organization as a client?"

"It would be easy enough for the Cadre to get around this by simply having board members file Submissions in their own names—leaving the Cadre as an organization out of such matters—but, as it happens, the government wants the Cadre to have a Submission on file."

"What?"

"Muhammad hasn't come to the Mountain," continued Mr. Gross, "so occasionally the Mountain goes to Muhammad— meaning that the government has been notably unsuccessful in dragging the Cadre into statist courts and prefers having channels available for claims the government itself wants to file against them. I would be surprised if the federal government hasn't already demanded arbitration over the firebombing of its FBI offices."

"You're kidding."

"Oh, I'm quite serious."

"But that's crazy," Elliot said. "First off, if the Cadre people are anarchists, why would they ever agree to meet peacefully with their enemies in the government?"

"The Cadre have no choice in the matter. The Submission clearly reads that the Submittor agrees to arbitrate *any* dispute with *any*one else who has filed one. If they did not, their Submission would likely be revoked."

"But why don't their prosecutors involved simply arrange to have their police arrest any Cadre people who show up for the trial?"

"'Hearing,'" corrected Mr. Gross. "There are no formal charges; only litigation of damages. But to answer, the Cadre take no chances; all such hearings are conducted in countries that don't have extradition treaties with the United States."

"Wait a second, wait a second," Elliot interrupted. "If the government can sue the Cadre this way, why can't the Cadre sue the government? They're revolutionaries; they must have complaints against it."

"They have sued, but there are practical limits. For one thing, the Cadre cannot sue the government as a corporate entity, only certain individuals in the government. More importantly, an arbitral decree is only as binding as the parties to it can be

compelled to make it. On the countereconomy, an arbitral decree is the basis for a boycott and ostracism against anyone
who doesn't comply with it—a 'casting out' that is virtually
equivalent to being turned naked over to one's enemies. In
this case, all the Cadre can ever win—practically speaking—is
the small fee the arbiter requires both parties to put up as a
compliance bond—and if the Cadre force the ante higher, the
government will refuse to play. The federal State is not about
to stand for any private arbitral decree that would do real damage to any of its employees; they would be protected by invok-
ing 'sovereign immunity.' And the Cadre have no way of forcing the government to pay up: in all-out war the Cadre would
lose hands down."

"Then how does the Cadre expect to win?"

"They hope to starve the government to death."

"Nobody's going to starve here," said Phillip, entering the
living room. "Dinner is served." He disappeared back into the
kitchen.

Elliot picked up the pen and signed the General Submission to Arbitration.

"You must leave for Aurora. Tonight."

The Grosses and Elliot were at the dining table, finishing
off Swedish meatballs with rice and a good German
Liebfraumilch.

"Aurora?"

"A code name, of course," Mr. Gross continued. "I can tell
you that it's somewhere on the Eastern seaboard. Anything
more than that is on a need-to-know basis restricted to the
Cadre."

"But what is it? Does it have to do with the northern lights?"

"It's symbolic, mostly," Phillip said. "Aurora was the goddess of dawn in Roman mythology and represents hope; the
Cadre also used the name because the first two letters—*Au*—

are the chemical symbol for gold."

"More literally," said Phillip's uncle, "*AU* is also the abbreviation for 'Agorist Underground'—which is precisely what Aurora is. It's the seat of a chain of secret agora—marketplaces—where countereconomic traders meet to do business."

"How do you get there if you don't know where it is?"

"The Cadre handle that. In your case, you'll be sealed into a baggage trunk with an air tank as companion, and will be shipped there. And if you want to enjoy the trip, I suggest you pass up a second helping of Phillip's meatballs."

Elliot pushed his plate away, but his concern was not with motion sickness. "You're not coming?"

"No. Neither Phillip nor I is under suspicion right now, and my taking you to Aurora this weekend would have its risks, if for no other reason than my being missed by friends. But don't worry, you're welcome back here at any time, for as long as you think necessary."

"Thank you, sir."

"Our pleasure."

After Elliot had helped Phillip clear away the dishes, they set up the chessboard again, this time Phillip—undistracted—gaining the advantage. By seven thirty, down by a bishop and a pawn, Elliot resigned. Mr. Gross suggested at this point that Elliot take a Dramamine. Elliot took it.

At eight, halfway through the play-off game, the doorman announced a delivery on its way up; Mr. Gross ruled a draw by fiat, ordering the boys into Phillip's bedroom. They chatted aimlessly there until Mr. Gross called them to the living room ten minutes later. "They're waiting in my bedroom," Mr. Gross explained, anticipating Elliot's question.

In the middle of the living room, next to the couch, was a trunk with its lid open; it was large enough to hold a man—and had to. There was a thick layer of foam padding on bottom and side interiors, a safety harness, and four FerroFoam air tanks built into the lid.

Elliot regarded the trunk dubiously. "Small, isn't it?"

"Nonsense," said Mr. Gross. "It's one of the largest on the market; they use them over at the Met Opera. You'd better get right in." Elliot looked hesitantly at the trunk another moment. "What's the matter? Claustrophobic?"

"No, agoraphobic."

Mr. Gross smiled. "You'll get over it."

After Elliot was properly bundled, he said warm goodbyes, then was strapped into the harness. His arms and legs were immobilized, a mouthpiece adapted from SCUBA equipment was inserted, and the lid was closed. It became pitch dark, and Elliot heard a lock click.

Someone knocked on the trunk and seemed to whisper (shout?), "Take it easy. You won't be in there long." Elliot declined answering for fear of losing his mouthpiece.

The trunk was pushed upright, Elliot being suspended by the harness—sitting on it—as if he had been attached to a parachute. As the trunk leaned forward, then tilted back, Elliot deduced that a hand truck had been slid under. A forward lurch, a bump—he was moving.

Soon after the journey began, the trunk stopped for what seemed a substantial pause, Elliot overhearing discussion that he could not understand. He thought he caught the words "wrong apartment," then the voices ceased, and the trunk started moving again.

He was on his back again shortly thereafter, feeling and hearing vibrations, endless changes in momentum, ups and downs, sideways movements ...

Elliot awakened with a jolt. The trunk was at rest. *Must have fallen asleep*, he thought. *No doubt the Dramamine.* He heard the lock click again, and the top opened; still groggy, he was blinded by a flood of light. A hearty male voice boomed, "Playing hooky, my boy? Well, your essay was due today, and you're not getting out of it that easily!" The man bent over the trunk, smiling widely. Elliot squinted, nearly choking on his mouthpiece.

It was Mr. Harper.

Chapter 11

"Wait a second, wait a second," Elliot said as soon as his mouth was unplugged. "Not you, too?"

"Eh?" said Mr. Harper.

There was a somewhat elderly man with him—heavy-set, wearing a rumpled gray suit—but he did not say anything.

"Isn't there anyone I know who isn't mixed up in this conspiracy?"

"The boy seems to be fine," the elder man said. "I'll see you later, Ben. Laissez-faire."

"One moment, Doctor. I'm not certain he did not receive a concussion. He seems confused." Mr. Harper turned back to Elliot. "Now, what's this about a conspiracy?"

"The Cadre, I mean," answered Elliot. "It just seems that everyone I know or meet is mixed up with it in some way." He paused. "Now that I think about it, Al and the *tzigane* are probably members, too."

"Slow down," said Mr. Harper, releasing Elliot from the harness. "I don't know who you're talking about, but if they're Cadre allies, I don't want to know."

The two men helped Elliot out of the trunk. He stood dizzily for a moment, then examined his surroundings. He was not sure what he had expected—perhaps a rat-invested warehouse or a dimly lit cellar—but this was certainly not it. Instead, he found himself in a larger-than-living-room-sized hall that looked like a cross between an airport VIP lounge and a hospital emergency room.

On the wall behind the trunk hung a white first-aid cabinet with a red cross painted on, near it a green oxygen tank with face mask, an examining table, a stand with an empty hook—used to hold blood—and emergency heart resuscitation equipment. Against the opposite wall were a liquor bar, tables and comfortable chairs, and facing the bar a video wallscreen. Though the room was carpeted, a Plexiglas runway was overlaid between the trunk and the room's only door. There were no windows.

The room's only decoration was a modified Gadsden flag draped on the wall adjoining the bar and medical areas (opposite the door), a golden field with "LAISSEZ-FAIRE!" in an upper left corner, a coiled rattlesnake facing left with its tongue out, and in the lower right, "DONT TREAD ON ME!"

Elliot decided this hall was quite used to receiving visitors.

The doctor told Elliot to get onto the examining table and there examined him for concussion—testing his pupillary responses, checking his reflexes, asking Elliot if he had a stiff neck; Elliot answered that his neck was fine.

Then he told Elliot, "Open your coat, jacket, and shirt." Elliot did, pushing his holstered gun over to the side, and the doctor listened to his heart, removing the stethoscope to tell him, "You'll live to be much older than me." He turned back to Harper. "And now, Ben, I'll leave this youngster in your capable hands."

With a "Good night, all," he left.

"Seems in a hurry," Elliot said as soon as the door closed.

"Dr. Taylor is probably anxious to return to his poker game," Harper replied.

Elliot buttoned up his shirt. "Sorry to take him away from it."

"You did him a favor. He was losing."

After jumping off the table, Elliot asked, "Mr. Harper, what are you *doing* here?"

Harper guided Elliot over to the bar. "Forget that name. Around here I'm Ben Goldman. Call me Ben."

"All right ...Ben. But what—"

"And it would be a good idea," Harper interrupted, "for you

to use another name around here. Vreeland is far too sensitive at the moment." Harper went behind the bar. "I'm drinking Jack Daniels on ice. What will you have?"

"You're offering a student a drink?"

"Why not? Are you an alcoholic? Or a teetotaler?"

Elliot shook his head, sitting at the bar. "I just can't imagine what Dr. Fischer would say. Jack Daniels will be fine—water, please."

"You're giving Dr. Fischer less credit than she deserves. She's highly intelligent." Harper handed Elliot his drink. "*Skoal.*"

For the next forty-five minutes, "Ben Goldman" gave Elliot a basic rundown of what was expected of him if he were to receive aid from the Revolutionary Agorist Cadre. "This room is Aurora Terminal," Harper explained, "and is the only part of Aurora that anyone but an ally pledged to keep our secrets is permitted to see. The Cadre's goal—a laissez-faire society—precludes our use of what would be traditional revolutionary tactics; we are forced to rely mainly on stealth. And, as such, the main precondition for anyone to deal with us is a good deal of discretion. You must refrain from learning more about Cadre business than the part that directly concerns you, and *never* discuss Cadre business with anyone but another ally. The rest will follow easily enough if you keep just one rule: *mind your own business.*"

"I get you."

"Fine. Now finish your drink and you'll get the Grand Tour."

Past the Terminal door was a long corridor, fluorescently lit, with a large sliding portal opposite the Terminal and a single door at the corridor's far end; Mr. Harper led Elliot to the latter. The door was constructed of steel—without any visible doorknobs, hinges, or buzzer—however, Elliot noticed a small mirror above the door, correctly deducing that it concealed a video camera.

When the door slid open, Elliot found himself facing a burly-looking man pointing a weapon he recognized as a Taser, a nonlethal electrical-dart paralyzer. The guard wore black turtleneck sweater and black slacks, a photo-identification badge with his picture on it but no name or other markings, and a red "SECURITY" brassard on his arm. Nonregulation hair and beard.

"Identity," said the guard, pointing the Taser directly at Harper.

"'A is A,'" Mr. Harper replied, obviously bored with the procedure.

The guard lowered the weapon. "Go on through."

They turned a 45-degree right bend in the corridor, ending up at an alcove with a security commandant behind a desk that housed another Taser. Both men were uniformed like the first guard—though the commandant's arm brassard identified him as such—with photo badges clipped to their turtlenecks. The alcove also housed folding chairs, a row of lockers, and several machines Elliot recognized from preflight security checks; he spotted a metal detector and a fluoroscope.

"Still clean," the commandant said. The guard with the Taser nodded.

Mr. Harper and Elliot passed through the metal detector, then were fluoroscoped. Harper was passed without comment, but Elliot was asked to surrender his pistol and ammunition case. The guard placed them in a locker, handing Elliot the key. The nature of Elliot's belt was also discovered; the commandant asked what was inside. Elliot hesitated momentarily, then answered honestly, "Gold coins."

"Will you give us permission to inspect?"

"Do you have to?"

"I'm afraid so."

"Commandant Welch can't pass you otherwise," Harper explained.

Elliot agreed reluctantly, opening the belt, then watching

the inspection closely. Inasmuch as the belt turned out not to be concealing any weapons, cameras, recorders, transmitters, or radioactive materials, it was immediately returned intact.

"You're cleared," the commandant said. "Proceed to registration."

Elliot picked up his jacket and overcoat, then followed Harper farther down the corridor. "Do you have to go through this every time you come in?" he asked.

Harper nodded. "Even if it's only walking down to Aurora Terminal."

"Poor Dr. Taylor."

"Registration" turned out to be a small office not far from the security alcove, empty but for five cubicles that looked like voting booths except for a chair inside; curtains on each booth could be drawn across to assure privacy. Inside each cubicle was a computer station. There were no computers present, of course; Elliot knew enough not even to wonder where they might be.

Each station had a video display, a modified typing keyboard, an instant-photo camera aimed at the chair, a facsimile print-out unit, an optical scanner, and a light pen; the cubicle also housed a dispenser for the photo badges.

While Elliot watched, Harper went into a cubicle and without sitting down or drawing the curtain immediately typed in a bypass program. After placing his palm on the optical scanner, he was automatically reissued his photo badge.

Harper told Elliot that he would meet him when he was finished, then left, clipping the badge to his jacket.

Elliot sat in the cubicle, the video display activating as he sat down.

LAISSEZ-FAIRE, NEW ALLY. WELCOME TO AURORA. WE HOPE YOUR STAY WITH US IS PLEASANT AND PROFITABLE.

THE ELECTRONIC DOCUMENT RESULTING FROM THIS INTERVIEW WILL
CONSTITUTE YOUR BASIC CONTRACT WITH THE REVOLUTIONARY
AGORIST CADRE AND WILL BE FULLY ENFORCEABLE AFTER ARBI-
TRATION AS PER MUTUAL SUBMISSION AGREEMENTS.

PLEASE ANSWER ALL QUESTIONS FULLY AND HONESTLY, IN THE
UNDERSTANDING AND BONDED ASSURANCE THAT ALL INFORMATION
YOU GIVE WILL REMAIN FULLY CONFIDENTIAL AND IS PROTECTED
AGAINST ACCESS FROM ANY NONAUTHORIZED SOURCE.

The computer display proceeded to give Elliot instructions
on how to use the keyboard, scanner, and light pen to supply
answers, to correct errors, and to ask questions relating to the
contract or further instructions.

About an hour later, Elliot was certain that the computer
now knew more about him than he did, and using the light
pen on the optical scanner, he had signed a contract with it.
The computer asked Elliot if he wanted a hard copy of his
contract, to be issued to him at his own risk; Elliot decided
that he did want one and in a few seconds one slid out of the
facsimile printer.

Elliot's contract did not discuss what services Elliot was to
receive from the Cadre; it was concerned with procedural
matters, Cadre security requirements, and limits on liabilities
relating to damages Elliot might do the Cadre and vice versa.
In essence, Elliot had agreed to "rules of the establishment"
and granted them the right to lock him up for certain specified
periods (never over six months) to give them time to reroute
should he endanger any Cadre secrets. In return, the Cadre
were betting him that he had a fat chance of ever getting his
hands on such information in the first place; if he had learned
the information unintentionally, they agreed to pay him for
the time.

After the contract signing, Elliot's palm print was recorded,
his picture taken, and both were duplicated onto the photo-

identification badge he was issued, the palm print as significant data on a magnetic strip embedded inside the card. Then certain signals were recorded by which Elliot could identify himself to the Cadre and other allies from remote locations; he chose **QUEEN TAKES PAWN, MATE** and **DO YOU HAVE ANYTHING FOR CLOGGED SINUSES?**

Finally, he clipped the badge to his jacket and emerged from registration. Mr. Harper was chatting with the two security men in the security alcove when Elliot came out; since Elliot had last seen him, Harper had changed into more casual attire, and his hair was damp. "Ah, there you are."

"Have I kept you waiting?"

"Not a bit. I was just up to the sauna awhile. Cleansed out the poisons of modern living.

"There's a sauna here?"

"On the fourth floor," said Harper. "Also a steam bath— though I find them uncomfortable—a sun room, swimming pool, a Jacuzzi, and gymnasium."

"Well. A regular YMCA."

Harper smiled as if Elliot's remark had sparked a hilarious memory. "You look tired," he said. "Come on, I'll show you to your room."

They walked past more offices, soon reaching an elevator; the control panel showed ten floors. Harper told Elliot to observe as he unclipped his photo badge, inserting it into a slot on the control panel; Harper then pressed three.

After the doors closed, Elliot asked him, "When will I be meeting Merce Rampart?"

Harper looked at Elliot quizzically. "You won't."

Elliot started to protest, then changed his mind.

"Any other hoops I have to jump through?" he asked.

"Just enjoy your self and keep out of mischief. You'll find this complex well designed to both ends."

After the elevator doors opened, Harper reclaimed his badge, leading Elliot down a hall to a door marked "316." He explained that his door had been preset for Elliot's photo badge only.

The room looked like any commercial lodging: double bed, dresser, desk, Picturephone, video wallscreen, and full bath. Its only unusual features, so far as Elliot could see, were its lack of windows and the addition of a stripped-down computer station otherwise identical to the ones in registration. Mr. Harper explained that the station could provide everything from a commodities report to Aurora's commissary menu, and would be activated by the insertion of a badge.

"You mentioned something about a Grand Tour?" Elliot asked.

Harper smiled. "Oh, that was just my little joke. In any proper utopia you're always given the Grand Tour. You know: 'Here is the food-production facility. It produces three times the food of the old, reactionary system, with just one third the effort!'"

"I take it this isn't a proper utopia?"

"I'm afraid not. You'll have to muddle along on your own. But it's close to midnight. Aren't you tired?"

Elliot shook his head. "I've been pretty keyed up lately."

"Well, I am," said Harper. "Suppose we get together for breakfast. Say nine thirty?"

Elliot nodded.

"Good. If you need me, the commandant will know where to find Ben Goldman." He paused a moment. "By the way, what alias have you chosen?"

"Joseph Rabinowitz," Elliot answered puckishly.

Harper was amused. "In that case," he said, leaving, "*shalom.*"

After Harper had gone, Elliot waited a few moments, then tried his door from the inside. It opened. Well, he thought, for the time being I'm a guest, not a prisoner. He decided to find out how far that went, punching *Operator* on his Picturephone and asking for an outside line.

The commandant informed him that he was not cleared for outside communication.

Well, mostly a guest.

Elliot decided to take the Grand Tour on his own, starting at the bottom and working his way up.

As Grand Tours went, this one began slowly ...

The second floor had the elevator at one end, the commissary at the other, and a number of function rooms in between on each side.

The commissary was a combination cafeteria-bar with about a dozen middle-aged men and women eating, drinking, and socializing, with empty tables for another hundred or so. At one end of the commissary was a selection of food and a bursar (not a cashier; payment was by photo-badge credit), with pricing in terms he did not recognize. This caused Elliot to wonder how much of a bill his visit to Aurora was already running up; the place had the look of an expensive private club, and the high security no doubt shot up costs even further. He also speculated that the main reason Mr. Gross had not accompanied him was that Aurora was too expensive to visit except on major business.

The recreation rooms were slightly more lively, though Elliot's first impression was that the inhabitants of Aurora looked more like a Chamber of Commerce convention—well, maybe Jaycees—than a revolutionary cabal.

In Recreation Room One were several table-tennis matches in progress, a number of bystanders watching and waiting to play off the winners. Also in use here were pool and billiard tables, a dart game, and several electronic playmates.

Elliot spotted Dr. Taylor and his poker game in Two, a room devoted to gambling—betting also on the roulette wheel, blackjack, one-arm bandits, and even contract bridge.

Recreation Room Four was simulation gaming, everything from simple games such as *Diplomacy* and *Stratego*, to full-scale interstellar war-gaming and *Dungeons and Dragons*. In one corner, a couple had the audacity to play checkers.

Several rows of slightly younger Aurorans were watching a videodisc on a communal wallscreen; the film they were watching was *Fahrenheit 451*, a scene showing the old librarian and her books being consumed by flames ...

Aurora's library had a fair collection of books, videodiscs, and holosonic music cassettes. Book titles included *Human Action* by Ludwig von Mises, *Atlas Shrugged* by Ayn Rand, *Counter-Economics* by Samuel Edward Konkin III, *The Probability Broach* by L. Neil Smith, *Power and Market* by Murray N. Rothbard, *The Moon is a Harsh Mistress* by Robert A. Heinlein, *Anarquía* by Brad Linaweaver and J. Kent Hastings, *Kings of the High Frontier* by Victor Koman, and *Wiemar, 1923* by Martin Vreeland. Videodiscs ran the gamut from *Horsefeathers*, *Bananas*, and *The Great Dictator*, to *The Fifth Element*, *The X-Files*, and *NaZion*.

Musical recordings followed no detectable pattern.

A poetry reading was in session in Recreation Room Three, a lounge. A man in his late forties—brown-haired, mustached, with a golden "Sons of Liberty" medallion around his neck—was sitting on the carpet with half a dozen lovely young women in a circle around him. "It was twenty-five years ago," the poet said, "when this was a fantasy. Nobody really believed it would happen. But I knew."

He closed his eyes and recited from memory:

> "Alongside night
> Parallel day
> By fearful flight
> In garish gray
> Will dawn alight
> And not decay
> Alongside night?"

The fourth floor seemed deserted. Elliot found no one in the gymnasium, sun room, or Jacuzzi whirlpool, and was about to leave when he stepped for a second into the swimming pool area and saw a woman swimming underwater.

She was slender and lithe, long black hair flowing behind her, and was nude.

Elliot decided that this called for some of the discretion Mr. Harper had mentioned, but he could not take his eyes from her, then it was too late. She broke water and spotted him.

Looking at her as she stood still—arms akimbo, bare breasts above water level—Elliot could see that she was much closer to his own age then he at first had thought, though her development could have indicated elsewise a woman in her twenties. She was the only person of his age he had seen in the complex. They stared at each other for several heartbeats, then she spoke.

"You're staring at me," she said. She spoke with a mildly Southern accent.

Elliot blushed. "Uh—sorry. I didn't know I wasn't supposed to be up here."

She did not make any attempt to move or otherwise to conceal herself. "Nobody's stopping you from swimming," she said. "It's just that it's rude to stare."

"You caught me by surprise. But I'd better leave if I'm making you uncomfortable." Elliot turned to go.

"No, don't—"

Elliot turned back, his pulse skipping a beat.

"I was finished anyway. The pool's all yours."

She climbed out of the water, grabbed a towel from a deck chair, and without draping it over herself calmly walked through a door into what Elliot presumed was a locker room.

Elliot considered stripping down for a swim himself, wargamed the idea of waiting for her to try apologizing again, then decided against both. Instead, taking the elevator back down to the second floor, he picked a book almost entirely at random out of the library's science-fiction section and returned to his room. After washing out his clothes, hanging them in the bathroom to dry, he began reading in bed.

Somehow, he had trouble keeping his mind on the book.

Chapter 12

The Picturephone was ringing.

Elliot reached over to answer it, knocking over *Illuminatus!*, the book he had been reading the night before. About the fourth or fifth ring, he managed to find the *answer* button; Mr. Harper appeared on the screen. "Good morning, Joseph," he said.

"Huh? Oh, right. G'morning." Elliot picked his watch up from the night table. It was just after eight. "I thought our breakfast appointment wasn't until nine thirty?"

"Change of plans," Harper said seriously. "I'm sorry, but I won't be able to make our breakfast date. Something important's come up."

"Bad news?"

"I don't know yet. But I'm afraid I'll have to abandon you here awhile. I apologize but it can't be helped."

Elliot stifled a yawn. "Anything in particular I ought to know?"

"Check with the security desk sometime this afternoon. The commandant will tell you if I've left any messages for you."

"Okay. And thanks a lot."

Elliot successfully remained awake by swinging his legs off the bed as soon as the screen cleared. He sat motionless for a full minute, then found enough energy to walk into the bathroom. Somewhat more awake after splashing water on his face, Elliot got back into his still slightly damp clothes. It was then he realized that he had forgotten to ask Harper whether he could afford to buy breakfast.

Though crowded, the commissary did not present any particular problems. Elliot selected grapefruit juice, pancakes, eggs, bacon, and coffee, handing his photo badge to the bursar, who said, "That comes to seventeen cents four mils," and charged the breakfast without further comment.

After carrying his tray to a small table on the far side, Elliot took his juice and resumed reading the library book.

Two eggs, a pancake, and a chapter later, a pleasant voice interrupted him: "Can I join you?"

Elliot looked up to find his mermaid of the pool, now clothed in a summery dress he found even more enticing than nudity. The same glance noted peripherally that his table was not the only one still partly unoccupied. "Go right ahead," he said, then, summoning every last watt of willpower, he turned back to the book.

His intentions were shattered about a minute later when he risked peering over the book and caught both her eyes again. "Any good?" she asked.

"I haven't gotten very far yet. I seem to be having trouble concentrating lately."

"Eye trouble?"

"Not from this side.

Elliot tucked the jacket in as a place mark and closed the book.

"Honestly," he said. "I didn't intend spying on you last night."

"Forget it," she replied. "An acute case of culture shock. We're both victims of it, you know."

"I couldn't agree more," said Elliot. "What are you talking about?"

"Each of us thought the other was representative of the culture here, when actually both of us arrived yesterday for the first time."

Elliot went on guard. "How do you know that?"

"Because both of us reacted defensively to a situation that anyone who'd been here even one extra day would've accepted as normal."

Elliot bit into a strip of bacon, then, chewing, said, "If you got here yesterday, how do you know what's normal?"

"Because after I left you at the pool I walked back to the sauna and found an orgy in progress ...What's the matter?"

Elliot reached for his coffee, a few sips managing to stop the chokes caused by remembering what Mr. Harper had told him about the sauna last night. "A piece of bacon went down the wrong pipe," he lied.

"So anyway," she continued, "if that sort of thing goes on, no one who's been here any time at all is going to get upset over a little midnight skinny-dipping. Are you just going to leave that other bacon strip?"

The price of a lie, he thought. "Help yourself." She took it. "By the way, I'm Joseph Rabinowitz."

She looked Elliot over carefully. "Highly unlikely."

"All right, I'm *not* Joseph Rabinowitz. Who aren't you?"

She lit a cigarette, nervously. "I'm not Lorimer."

"How do you do," said Elliot. "Is that not your Christian name, or not your surname?"

"Neither. Or both."

Elliot wiped his mouth. "Lor, have you done any exploring around this place?"

"Nothing above the fourth floor, the health spa—Joe."

"Same here. How about us seeing what we can stick our noses into before somebody tells us to stop?"

As soon as Elliot had finished breakfast, he dropped his book back at the library, and the two strolled to the elevator, encountering buttons for half a dozen upper floors they had not seen. "Your badge or mine?" Elliot asked.

"Try yours first. If it doesn't work, try mine."

Elliot inserted his photo badge into the control panel, pushing five. The elevator doors closed, then, without its having moved, they immediately opened again. He repeated the procedure with the sixth through tenth floors, getting the same result. He was about to try the entire sequence again with Lorimer's badge, when the elevator doors closed of their own accord, the elevator descending.

"I think somebody is about to tell us to stop," he said. Lorimer nodded.

A few moments later the doors opened to reveal a muscular security guard, Cadre uniformed, pointing a Taser at them. Elliot smiled weakly. "Uh—hello, there," he said. Lorimer smiled, too.

The guard did not smile. "Just what are you two up to?" he asked sternly, motioning them out of the elevator.

"Just exploring," said Elliot.

Lorimer started fluttering her lashes, doing an adequate impression of Scarlett O'Hara. "Honestly," she said. Her accent had moved south.

The guard was not seduced; he must have been made of stone. "I think I just caught a couple of statist spies."

"Do we look like spies?" Lorimer asked. Her accent moved still farther south—any farther and she would have been speaking Spanish.

The guard gave her a look suggesting that she, in any event, would pass the physical.

"What makes you think we're spies?" Elliot asked.

"Why were you trying to get up to the maximum security floors? If you wanted to explore, why didn't you look through the trading floor?"

"Maximum security floors?" said Elliot. "Trading floor?"

The guard looked them over, and saw they were genuinely confused. He motioned with the Taser. "Come on."

He led Elliot and Lorimer to the security alcove, and told the commandant—a different one from the previous night, "Two for Aurora Proper."

The commandant then asked them, "Anything you want from the lockers?"

"I have a pistol," said Elliot. "Do you think I need it?"

"I couldn't say," he replied. "Cadre are not allowed on the

trading floor."

"Why not?" Lorimer asked.

"Privacy," the commandant explained. "The allied businesses in Aurora have delegated to the Cadre the right to monitor incoming and outgoing goods and communications, to ensure that the location is kept secret. To make sure that the Cadre can't try to use this authority against them, they forbid us to enter into their domain and maintain their own security force to keep us out. Their guards are armed; except during emergencies we are not allowed to be."

"Well," said Elliot, "if I'm allowed to, I guess I will take my revolver."

"Right. Surrender your badges, please."

Taking their badges and feeding them into a collection slot, the commandant then got Elliot his revolver. After Elliot had put on his holster, the guard led the couple down the same corridor through which they had entered the Cadre complex initially, retracing the 45-degree bend around which was the steel door defended by still another guard. The door was opened for them, and they were instructed to walk to the Terminal corridor's end and wait at the large portal opposite the Terminal. They did—Elliot meanwhile noting the Terminal door locked—and a few minutes later the portal slid open.

They were facing a freight elevator.

After they had got on, the door automatically slid shut, the elevator creeping down. When the door opened again, they were looking down the main promenade of what looked to be a small village.

Elliot and Lorimer faced a carpeted mall—daylight simulated by sunlight fluorescent panels in a low acoustic ceiling—twenty-feet wide and stretching ahead over twice the length of a football field. On each side of the promenade was an array of storefronts and offices the likes of which Elliot had never seen, and shopping in the mall were over a hundred persons obviously of widely varying nationality, creed, and custom.

"This is clearly impossible," said Elliot. Lorimer did not disagree.

They began down the promenade, on the left passing the Black Supermarket (it looked like a supermarket); next to it, offices of the First Anarchist Bank and Trust Company— AnarchoBank for short; farther down, NoState Insurance; and beyond that, a post office: The American Letter Mail Company, Lysander Spooner, founder.

On the opposite side of the promenade were The Contraband Exchange (jewelry, novelties, duty-free merchandise), Identities by Charles (makeup and disguises), and a restaurant, The TANSTAAFL Café. There were several dozen more shops and offices that looked even more intriguing.

"Well, what do you think?"

Lorimer paused a moment before answering. "I think it might be easier to hide the Lincoln Memorial."

"We might be under it."

They walked farther, passing The Gun Nut and an office for Guerdon Construction, coming to a door marked "The G. Gerald Rhoames Border Guard and Ketchup Company." Elliot and Lorimer took one look at it—then at each other—and decided to go in.

A bell on the door tinkled as they entered; the shop was old-fashioned, almost Dickensian in style, with a small, well-dressed man seated behind a glass counter. He stood as they came in. "Yes?"

"Mr. Rhoames?"

He bowed slightly.

"We were wondering what you sell here," Lorimer asked.

"My sign does not convince you?" He spoke with a British accent contaminated by overexposure to Americans.

"Should it?"

"Surely not. Gentlemen should deal neither in frontier

guards nor ketchup. I am a cannabist."

"You eat human flesh?"

"Good heavens, no, dear lady. I am a cannabist, not a canni-bal. A cannabist deals in *Cannabis sativa*, the most select parts from the female hemp plant. I am a seller of the finest hybrids from Colombia, Acapulco, Bangladesh."

"Wholesale or retail?" Elliot asked.

"Both," said Mr. Rhoames, "though naturally my store here is quite limited. Over three kilograms entails outside deliv-ery."

"What would an ounce of Acapulco go for?"

"Thirty-nine cents."

"What?"

"Very well, then. Thirty-three."

Elliot pulled out his wallet, extending a blue. "Do you have change of a hundred?"

Mr. Rhoames looked at it with disdain. "Surely you do not think I was pricing in fiat? The price is thirty-three cents *au-rum*."

"Well, how much is that in dollars?"

Mr. Rhoames shrugged. "I suggest you utilize a bank here and exchange them."

"Thanks," said Elliot. "Come on, Lor." They started to the door.

"I say—on the subject of dollars ..."

They turned back to him.

He reached behind the counter, his hand returning with a small box. Inside were five manufactured cigarettes with gold dollar signs engraved on the paper. "A house blend, grown hydroponically in my own tanks."

"I'm sure they're excellent, but I can't do anything until I get my currency exchanged."

"No, no, no," said Mr. Rhoames. "On the house."

"Why, thank you," said Lorimer. "That's very kind."

"Nothing at all. Come back anytime."

When they were fully out the door, Lorimer turned to Elliot and just said, "Well."

"I'll reserve my opinion until I see how these others are," Elliot replied.

A two-minute walk returned them to the AnarchoBank, inside three tellers' windows with a half-dozen customers in line, and a sign on the wall: "Offices in AURORA, AUTONOMY, AUCTION, AURIGA, AUDACITY, AUBERGE, AUSTRIAN SCHOOL, AUNTIE, and AUM."

Elliot and Lorimer bypassed the line, instead walking over to a good-looking black woman behind a desk marked "New Accounts." "Excuse me, but who do I see to exchange New Dollars?"

"Do you have an account with us?" she asked pleasantly; Elliot shook his head. "Then I'll take care of it. Won't you sit down?" After Elliot and Lorimer had been seated, she asked, "How much would you like exchanged?" Elliot took out his remaining currency, counting out twenty-seven hundred in blues. "You'd like gold or eurofrancs?"

"Uh—gold, I guess."

She made use of a desktop computer console, then said, "We'll have to buy your New Dollars at what we estimate is Monday's rate." She explained, "That's the earliest we can sell it. And at 28.165 New Dollars per milligram gold, we can offer you ninety-six mils."

"How much will that buy around here?"

"Not very much. A carton of cigarettes at Black Supermarket or a light lunch at TANSTAAFL Café. As a reference point, a dime vendy trades at par with four mils, a quarter vendy at ten mils—that is, one cent."

Elliot thought a moment, then said, "My money will buy me two dozen phone calls?"

"If there were pay phones in Aurora—which there aren't—

yes."

"In that case," said Elliot, "I'm interested in another transaction."

Concealing his motions from both the woman and Lorimer, he unzipped his belt slightly and pulled out a 50-peso piece. He placed it on the desk.

"For eurofrancs," said Elliot.

Ten minutes later, Elliot had exchanged his blues for a handful of vendies and had been given €405 for his gold piece—ten eurofrancs per gram gold and an 8 percent premium for the coin. The New Accounts officer also showed them AnarchoBank gold coins of various weights, including a one-gram wafer so thin it was sealed into plastic.

"Listen," said Elliot, after he had been given a thorough sales pitch for minimum-balance checking accounts, interest-bearing time deposits, and a small pamphlet called "The Wonderful World of 100% Gold Reserve Banking." "I don't mean this to sound nasty—honestly—but how can I be sure this isn't a fly-by-night outfit?"

"That's a fair question," she replied, though I'm afraid the best way we can prove ourselves to you requires that you simply do business with us long enough to be assured of our honesty. Short of that, you can receive a copy of the auditor's report from the Independent Arbitration Group, or check with any of our overseas correspondent banks. AnarchoBank is a wholly owned subsidiary of the Union Commerce Bank in Zurich, and does business through it with aboveground banks throughout the world."

Elliot and Lorimer got up. "Well, thank you," said Elliot.

The New Accounts officer extended another pamphlet to him. "Your application for a Bank AnarchoCard," she said.

For the next hour, Elliot and Lorimer window-shopped, looking at duty-free Swiss watches in the Contraband Exchange, picking up a prospectus for Project Harriman, a countereconomic lunar mining venture, and scrutinizing the wide range of illegal chemicals on sale in Jameson Pharmaceuticals, displayed as in the patent-medicine counters of a discount drugstore. A sign on the wall announced: "NO PRESCRIPTIONS REQUIRED ON ANY PURCHASE—Consult Your Physician for Indications." And past rows of morphine, paregoric, methadone, and heroin was another smaller sign on the wall, but reproduced on each package: "WARNING: Narcotics Use is Habit-Forming."

Another counter displayed LSD 25 ...THC ...Mescaline ...cocaine ...Sweet & Low...

In Nalevo Personnel Lorimer was told by a placement manager that they could guarantee her employment at twenty grams gold a week in one of the finer bordellos.

The Black Supermarket impressed them not for what it had—aside from tax-free liquor and cigarettes its merchandise was the kind any supermarket would sell—but for what it did not have: no shortages, no rationing, no listings of "lawful" ceiling prices. Elliot felt a momentary twinge when he saw a shelf stocked with Spam; he had pushed his family to the back of his mind and felt guilty for enjoying himself.

It became evident that the trading floor was primarily a convenience for wholesale countereconomic traders, who shook hands on huge deals here, and made their deliveries outside. It was only slightly unusual to see a person walking around with face masked, though Elliot suspected that most of the people shopping on this floor were "expendable" agents of the actual buyers, whose faces would never risk being seen.

After a five-minute wait for a table, Elliot and Lorimer were seated in the TANSTAAFL Café, a sign on the wall translating the word as *There Ain't No Such Thing As A Free Lunch*, and rightly crediting the acronym to E. "Doc" Pournelle. The special luncheon for Saturday offered split-pea soup, sandwich, french fries, and beverage, all for seven cents. After brief discussion, Elliot ordered it for both of them.

While waiting for the food, they paid a visit to the restaurant's old Wurlitzer jukebox, finding it stocked only with classical music. Elliot inserted a quarter vendy and pushed I-23; the machine responded by playing the Heifetz recording of the Tchaikovsky Violin Concerto.

Elliot and Lorimer spent another ninety minutes drifting around the floor—talking with document forgers, electronics technicians, and arbitration agents—and visiting, at Elliot's urging, The Gun Nut. On display was a weapon fancier's dream, everything from pistols, bazookas, and M-21 automatic machine pistols, to grenade launchers, subsonic generators, and lasers. Its real attraction for Elliot was a fifty-foot-deep shooting range behind a soundproof glass panel. After donning ear protectors, Elliot fast-drew into a Weaver stance at a paper target in the shape of an armed assailant. Afterward, he brought his target up to the front counter.

"The proprietor said, "That'll be ten cents. How'd you do?"

Elliot showed the man his target. He had shot a number of bull's-eyes, fewer holes farther out, none out of killing range.

The proprietor nodded respectfully.

"Lor," said Elliot as they exited to the promenade, "after this place I'd believe you if you told me someone was here hawking nukes."

Someone was.

The display mock-up had a sign underneath labeling it: "100 KILOTON ATOMIC FISSION DEVICE."

The salesman in Lowell-Pierre Engineering was telling them, "…but of course much smaller than the megaton capabilities of the hydrogen fusion devices."

"You provide the plutonium?" Elliot asked him.

"No, of course not," said the salesman. "You'd have to find your own source. But even if you did, you'd have to accept one of our supervisors to ensure that the device would be used only for excavation or drilling, before we would sell you one. We don't hand over nuclear weapons to fools who want to blow up the world."

"But you've sold these things?" asked Lorimer. "Really?"

"Of course," said the salesman. "Do you think we're in business for our health."

The freight elevator arrived for them without being summoned; Lorimer conjectured that they were being monitored from a remote security location. After returning to the Terminal floor, they again approached the steel door protecting the Cadre complex; it also opened, the same guard who had let them out pointing a Taser at them. "Password," he said.

"'A is A,'" Elliot replied.

"That's yesterday's password."

"But I wasn't given a new one."

"Give me the password, or you don't get in."

Elliot looked helplessly to Lorimer, who paused for a moment, then replied, "'Swordfish'?"

"Go on through," the guard said.

Elliot glanced at her suspiciously. "The commandant gave it to you while I was getting my gun, right?"

"Horsefeathers," she declared.

After each had registered, Elliot checked with the security desk as Harper had told him. There was no message, and Elliot began wondering why he had been brought to Aurora, whether the Cadre were doing anything to help him, and where the hell Mr. Harper was anyway. As they walked to the elevator, Elliot told Lorimer that he was still free. "What about you?"

"I don't have anything until an appointment on Monday."

"Any suggestions?"

"Well, how about a swim?"

"I don't have a suit," said Elliot.

"Neither do I," said Lorimer unblushingly.

Elliot did blush.

"Or," she continued, "we can try out some of that grass."

"Uh—I'd better keep my head clear for a while."

"Oh. Okay. Why don't we go back to your room and fuck?"

They entered the elevator, Elliot unclipping his badge and inserting it into the control panel. He studied Lorimer's expression, then punched for the third floor. "Am I really that dense?" he asked.

They were resting naked in each other's arms when the alarm was sounded.

Chapter 13

"G-raid alert! G-raid alert! This is not a drill."

The room television had been centrally activated, an authoritative gray-haired man in Cadre uniform appearing on the wallscreen. Elliot slid Lorimer's hand off his behind, then his leg out from between hers, abruptly sitting up.

"Commence evacuation sequence," said the gray-haired man. "Cadre are to implement Procedure Five immediately. All allies will please identify themselves to the nearest computer station for further instructions."

Elliot and Lorimer were out of bed quickly, pulling on their clothes.

"Remain calm," the man continued. "There is no danger if you follow our procedures. Repeat: G-raid alert. This is not a ..."

The message repeated itself in the background as Elliot and Lorimer dressed. Elliot struggled with a shoe. "Any idea what a G-raid is?" he asked Lorimer.

She shook her head. "Gas attack? Ground assault?"

"Maybe the government. G-men. Yeah, that's probably it."

"Too corny." Lorimer tossed her hair forward. "Zip me."

After fastening the dress, Elliot slipped an arm around Lorimer's waist, spinning her around. "Listen, whoever-the-hell-you-are, what say we shack up somewhere for the next few catastrophes?"

Lorimer tickled the back of Elliot's neck. "When do we leave, stranger?"

"Get your stuff, meet me back here in three minutes. I'll see what the computer says."

Lorimer gave him a grace kiss on the mouth. "Be right back." Elliot propelled her out the door with a pat on the rump.

As the door shut, Elliot unclipped his photo badge from his jacket, inserting the card into his computer station. The video display lit up at once:

OPERATOR: ELLIOT VREELAND ALIAS JOSEPH RABINOWITZ CONTRACT 23-NY-890

PRELIMINARY INVESTIGATION MADE VREELAND FAMILY WHEREABOUTS: TWO WOMEN TENTATIVELY IDENTIFIED AS CATHRYN AND DENISE VREELAND CONFINED INCOMMUNICADO, 23 FEBRUARY, FBI MAXIMUM SECURITY PRISON CODE NAME "UTOPIA," CHESHIRE, MASSACHUSETTS. REMOVAL NOW NOT POSSIBLE.

ALL INVESTIGATIONS TO DATE DR. MARTIN VREELAND REPORT NEGATIVE. SEARCH TO PROCEED. WILL NOTIFY YOU RESULTS WHEN AVAILABLE.

They've killed him, thought Elliot.

ACCOUNT TO DATE:

TRANSPORTATION	AU 2.500 GRAMS
REGISTRATION	AU 1.000
ROOM (ONE NIGHTS)	AU 2.000
COMMISSARY	AU 0.174
INQUIRY	AU 20.000
TOTAL CHARGES	AU 25.674 GRAMS

PAYMENT ON ACCOUNT DEFERRED.
PLEASE REPORT AT ONCE TO SECURITY DESK, TERMINAL FLOOR, FOR EVACUATION TO NEW YORK

All but the last sentence winked off. Elliot pulled out his photo badge, and the display went blank.

For a long moment, Elliot sat in front of the lifeless console, arching forward over it to brace himself. That his father was not confined with his mother and sister meant almost surely that he had been murdered. Images of words he had just seen lingered: CONFINED INCOMMUNICADO ...UTOPIA ...RE-MOVAL NOT NOW POSSIBLE ...

The unspeakable emptiness felt when Denise had told him their father was dead returned, thricefold, multiplied also by the suffocating frustration of feeling impotent to do anything about it.

There was a knock at the door; Elliot got up and let Lorimer in. One arm held a Genghis Khan coat and a small travel bag; her other held a cigarette. "All set ...Hey, what's wrong?"

Elliot made an effort to control his voice, after a moment replying evenly, "My problem. I'll have to handle it."

Lorimer nodded solemnly. "I checked with the station in my room. I'm supposed to go to the security desk."

"Same here." Elliot violently yanked his overcoat from its hanger. "C'mon, we'd better get the hell moving."

As they rode the elevator down, stopping at the second floor for more passengers, Elliot was surprised at the tranquility pervading the complex. Were the agorists all on barbiturates? No one pushed frantically to get onto the elevator; those for whom there was no room seemed willing to wait in line for its next trip. Nobody ran panic-stricken down the halls. There were no sirens. It just did not seem as if a major emergency was taking place.

Upon disembarking on the Terminal floor, Elliot and Lorimer found themselves at the tail end of a long line to the security alcove; there were perhaps seventy persons stretched ahead of them, carrying a wide variety of luggage and apparel. Still, the atmosphere was cheery and matter-of-fact—not at all what he had expected. Elliot gained some small understand-ing by eavesdropping on two men in front of him—one of the

few public dialogues he had overheard, in fact, among the
necessarily taciturn countereconomic traders. "It's a goddam
nuisance," grumbled the younger of the two. "At these prices
you would think they could avoid this sort of problem."

"Two hours' warning of a raid is not what I would call unreasonable," his friend said.

"It might as well have been two minutes, for all the good it
does me. I have a half-quintal commodities account downstairs. Now what am I supposed to do?"

"Stop acting like an ass, Red."

That ended the discussion.

In forty-five minutes they were at the security desk, the line
now stretching behind. Commandant Welch was again on duty,
saying to Lorimer, "Badge, please." She handed it over, the
commandant inserting it into the console built onto his desk.
"You're in Group Eight. Claim any property checked here, then
wait for your number to be called." A guard led Lorimer over
to the lockers, where she retrieved a small leather pouch, while
the commandant took Elliot's badge. "Group Five," the commandant told him, "leaving Terminal in eleven minutes."

"But we're together," Elliot protested.

"Sorry," the commandant replied. "The computer makes the
assignments, not me."

Lorimer walked over to the commandant. "I'm going with
him."

"Nothing I can do about it. The next thing Elliot knew, a
voice from behind said sharply, "Don't try it, girl. I'm using an
M-21, not a Taser." Elliot heard the metallic click of a machine pistol being switched from semi- to automatic.

Elliot saw Lorimer's hand, halfway into her pouch, freeze,
and he glanced slowly over his shoulder. The man leveling
the weapon at her back was the guard they had experienced
the run-in with that morning in the elevator. Commandant
Welch stood, taking Lorimer's pouch and removing a .32 au-

tomatic pistol-with-silencer. "Your group leader will return this to you before he lets you off."

Elliot said, "I thought we were guests here, not prisoners."

"Your choice," the commandant replied. "We're authorized to protect this property, and we do it."

"Whose authority?" Elliot inquired.

"Why, yours," Welch answered. "You signed a contract agreeing to abide by our requirements, remember?"

"I never agreed to be pushed around like this."

"I'm afraid that's a matter of discretion. Mine at the moment. You're free to file any suits you want with the arbiters—after you leave."

The commandant nodded to the guard with the M-21, who lowered it from his shoulder, motioning Lorimer aside. "Statist swine!" she snapped.

It may have been at this moment that Elliot decided he was in love with this crazy female.

There was a rumbling murmur along the line behind her. Commandant Welch turned purple. "Wait!" he ordered Lorimer's guard. He turned to Lorimer again, speaking loudly enough for half the line to hear also: "Young lady, if you were my daughter I'd put you over my knee right now and strap the daylights out of you. Unfortunately, you're not, and I'm more concerned with making sure this evacuation proceeds with no further delay." He turned to the guard. "Put them both in Five. I'll reprogram when I get the chance."

"I have property in the locker," Elliot said.

"Get it and get out."

Elliot retrieved his pistol, holster, and ammunition, again putting on his holster, then the guard with the M-21 personally escorted the couple down the corridor to the Terminal.

Inside, about thirty people were standing around, waiting. Luggage and apparel lay throughout the room, with the video wallscreen adding meaningless noise to the already high decibel level. Bar was being tended; many had drinks in their hands.

The guard brought Elliot and Lorimer over to a young Chinese man standing near the bar. "She's an extra," the guard told him. "Transfer from Eight. Troublemakers, both of them." The guard handed the Chinese man Lorimer's automatic. "Hold on to this until the last possible minute."

The Oriental nodded, and the guard left.

"My name's Chin," the man said in accentless English. "I'm your group conductor. What was the trouble, back there?"

"The commandant tried to split us up," said Elliot. "The computer—"

"Enough," Chin said with a sigh. He extended the pistol; Lorimer took it back. "I sometimes wonder how some of the Cadre ever became anarchists. They would make splendid bureaucrats."

"Pardon me," said Lorimer, "but am I going to be stuffed back into a trunk?"

"No, you'll be traveling First Class this time," Chin replied. "Have a drink and relax. We'll be leaving in just a few minutes." The group leader turned to the bartender—king size, black, mid-fiftyish—saying, "Jack would you set up my two friends here?" The bartender nodded. Chin excused himself, disappearing out to the corridor.

Elliot and Lorimer both decided on soft drinks and upon receiving them moved over to one side of the bar. "You know," Elliot told Lorimer, almost shouting, "I can't figure this out. These people act like they were at a cocktail party."

She looked around and then nodded. "Spooky."

"Not really," a basso profundo voice answered, "once you understand the economics involved."

The voice belonged to the bartender, who was meanwhile pouring vodka and orange juice into a plastic cup. Elliot looked at the man closely, noting that his left eye was glass. "Uh—economics is sort of a hobby of mine," Elliot told him. "How's that again?"

The bartender poured the remaining juice into the cup, holding up the used carton. "You wouldn't get upset if you lost an empty container, would you? Same with this place. Within an hour there won't be anything here worth capturing." He crushed the carton, discarding it. "Squeezed dry."

"But it's not equivalent, is it?" asked Elliot. "This place must be worth a fortune."

The bartender shook his head. "Built for under a quintal and was paid for within a year of completion. Rental space on the trading floor went for twelve grams per centare year—you savvy 'centare'?"

"One square meter. But what's a quintal?"

"Defined metrically as one hundred kilograms. As I was saying, Aurora Proper had eighty-five hundred rentable centares. Fully subscribed before a gram was spent. Operated thirty-three months after earning back her investment. Cleared about two-and-a-half times her original capital expenditure." The bartender took a sip of his screwdriver and added, "The Cadre hotel operation was even more profitable."

Lorimer asked, "What about all the stuff on sale downstairs?"

He shrugged. "Anything crucial is being evacuated. The rest—risk of loss calculated into operating overhead."

"You seem to know a lot about all this," said Elliot.

"I should. I built Aurora, and several of her sister undergrounds." He wiped his right hand on a towel, extending the former. "Jack Guerdon, Guerdon Construction."

Elliot took the hand, wide-eyed. "Pleased to meet you, sir."

Lorimer also shook hands, then asked, "Mr. Guerdon, how could so huge a complex—with hundreds of people coming and going—be kept secret for four years? Longer, if you count construction time."

Guerdon grinned. "Well, I'm not about to reveal any trade secrets, but I can answer abstractly; countereconomic theory is freely available. To keep any secret, you divide it into data segments—perhaps 'modules' would be closer—and spread these modules among a few trusted persons—the fewer the better. An underground agora is a machine—a social structure—based on that principle. Access to the machine is freely available to many; knowledge of its location is its most closely guarded secret, in this operation known to almost no one except those directly involved in transporting goods and people—a few Cadre."

"But what about your construction workers?" Elliot asked.

"They were recruited from construction sites all over the world, were transported here secretly, worked only inside, and never knew where they were. If you think security is tight now, you should have been here during construction; a mosquito couldn't have gotten in or out."

"But spies must get inside, no?"

"Probably dozens—maybe hundreds," said Guerdon, "but what difference does it make? The Cadre make sure that anyone coming in isn't being traced from the outside—and you can be certain that they are technologically quite sophisticated in their methods—then once inside, you play by the Cadre's rules, which are set up to make sure nobody finds out anything they shouldn't or interferes with operations. But it's not a major problem; even the security guards don't know all the gimmicks built into this place—much less visitors—and this puts any potential spy at a tremendous disadvantage. If he causes any trouble, where can he go? The Cadre are controlling access, and nobody leaves until they say it's okay."

"Pretty totalitarian," Lorimer said.

"That's precisely why nobody gets in here until they've signed a contract agreeing to security procedures; nobody is forced to come here, but if they do, it's according to the Cadre's rules. However, the Cadre are not free agents, either; they are even more restricted by contract than are the visitors: a visitor here can do anything except disrupt operations or violate security; the Cadre are not permitted to do anything except maintain those freedoms. It's not just in theory, either; social structures created on paper are translated into balances of power in practice. The original agreements by which the agoras were set up dictated the forms used to enforce them."

"But still," said Elliot, "all this sounds tremendously expensive."

"Expense is a relative term. The initial capitalization and overhead were high-priced—and so are they with any office building, for that matter—but it was cost-effective to the Cadre's clients compared to the costs of doing business in the State-controlled economy."

"Won't the loss of Aurora hamper their business seriously?"

"For a little while. But things will be looking up in a few days."

Chin reentered the Terminal at that moment, saying loudly, "Attention, please."

There was no response.

Chin walked over to the wallscreen, switching it off, then vaulted on top of the bar. "Quiet!"

The assorted conversations died out.

"Group Five departure time," said Chin. "Show your boarding passes to the stewardess, please."

One of the walls began to move.

Chapter 14

The wall opposite the corridor—the wall with the "laissez-faire" modified Gadsden flag—slid several feet to the left, revealing a portable staircase five steps high, enclosed by an awning that concealed what lay beyond. The somewhat muted whine of turbines filled the Terminal.

Chin jumped off the bar, walking over to the staircase. "Okay, folks, let's get going. Pick any seats and strap yourselves in."

With the sole exception of Jack Guerdon, who was fixing another drink, everyone began lifting belongings and lining up near the staircase. "You're coming, Mr. Guerdon?" Lorimer asked.

"Isn't it customary for captains to go down with their ships? Why not shipbuilders, too?" Guerdon noticed that the two youngsters did not know whether to take him seriously, so he added, "Just some last-minute business. I'll be out of here in time enough."

"Well, glad to have met you, sir," said Elliot. They all shook hands and with a "Take care, now" Elliot and Lorimer joined the departing passengers.

The steps led into what appeared from the inside to be the cabin of an executive jetliner—eight rows of seats, four across with a center aisle—allowing for a somewhat cramped ceiling and no windows. Chin had been joking—there was no stewardess taking passes—so Elliot and Lorimer found two seats, the last two together, and strapped themselves in. Lorimer immediately lit a cigarette.

Chin shut the cabin door, saying, "No smoking, friends"; then, a few moments later, the turbine whine increased in volume and pitch, and Elliot felt the craft moving.

Chin came over and glared at Lorimer. She snuffed out the

cigarette and muttered to Elliot, "Damned prohibitionists."

Elliot clasped Lorimer's hand and smiled. She smiled back. Elliot was thinking that she had the most radiant smile he had ever seen when she was no longer there and, like the Cheshire Cat, only her smile remained. For some time after that, there was nothing at all.

Someone was shaking him, only he wanted to sleep some more. He tried saying, "Leave me alone—it's Saturday," but he found it hard to move his mouth.

"C'mon, now, up we come."

His mouth was now free, and he tried focusing. There was a long haired girl a little in front of him. "Denise?" he asked.

"Are you okay?" she replied.

Elliot realized he was standing, braced against a seat in front of him. He took a deep breath and felt his mind clearing, then looked up. Chin was packing up a portable oxygen kit, with Lorimer a few feet behind him. "You know, you gave us quite a scare, just now," Chin said.

"What happened?" Elliot asked.

"They gassed us," said Lorimer.

"Who? The FBI?"

"No, the Cadre."

Elliot looked over to Chin.

"There was a spy on board," Chin began explaining. "A real Mata Hari. Transmitter in a cigarette lighter. There was no real danger—we're shielded, of course—but the pilot knocked out everyone in the passenger cabin, including me, to avoid possible gunplay."

Elliot took another deep breath, then exhaled. "I'd find that much easier to swallow if I hadn't fallen asleep in the trunk to Aurora."

"It happens," said Chin. "Drink anything before the trip? Anti-nausea pills?"

"Both," Elliot admitted. "But they were given to me by a

loyal Cadre ally." He turned to Lorimer. "When you came in, did you fall asleep?"

She shook her head. "At least I don't think so. In sensory deprivation, how can you be sure?"

Elliot scowled. "Tell your friends I didn't like it," he told Chin. "Next time I'll go to the arbiters."

Chin shrugged. "What would you sue for? This gas leaves no permanent aftereffects. No damages to demand."

"I'll sue for arbitrary recompense for violation of my civil liberties."

Chin grinned widely. "Good for you. I'd be interested in the outcome myself."

Grabbing an attaché case stashed under his seat, Chin led the two into a waiting room with the other passengers already inside; it was empty except for a table and some folding chairs. There were no windows, of course. Some of the passengers were expressing, loudly, indignation equal to Elliot's. One man with Beacon Hill written all over him was wondering "whether this ghastly gassing is usual or not."

"I'm getting hungry again," said Lorimer. "What time do you have?"

"Eh?" Elliot checked his watch. "Ten to six," he replied absentmindedly—then a thought took hold, and he felt as if he should hit himself. "Lor, what time did we leave Aurora?"

"Don't know," she answered, tapping her bare wrist.

Elliot began calculating time lapses. "We returned to the Cadre complex just before two—I checked—and ... how long would you say we made love?"

"I wasn't watching the clock," she said drolly.

"Be serious. Forty-five minutes? An hour?"

"If you must measure," Lorimer said, "then closer to an hour and a half.

"That brings us somewhere close to three thirty. How long was I out, just now?"

"No more than five minutes after everyone else."

"Right. Then maximum possible travel time was about forty-five minutes—assuming my watch wasn't tampered with, which I can check as soon as we hit the streets."

"Fine," said Lorimer. "What does all this have to do with the price of congressmen?"

"It puts Aurora within four hundred miles of New York, assuming we were knocked out to prevent us from feeling the unmistakable accelerations of a jet. Far closer if we were in a hydroplane, a submarine, or the intermodal containers they switch from trucks to trains to freighters."

"Thank you, 'Joe.' Care for a banana?"

Elliot groaned, regretting his alias: *Hello, Joe—Whadd'ya Know?* "Television," he muttered.

A few minutes later, Elliot and Lorimer were seated facing Chin, whose attaché case was open on the table in front of him with a computer inside. "You're returning to Manhattan?" Chin asked Elliot.

Elliot looked to Lorimer. "It doesn't matter where I am," she said, "as long as I'm not caught."

"Manhattan," Elliot agreed.

"Got a safe house?"

"A what?"

"A place to hide out," Lorimer explained.

"Oh," said Elliot. "I have a standing invitation with allies but I doubt if it extends to two. I figured we'd take a room somewhere—probably in the Village."

Chin took out a pad of paper and began to scribble. "Check this place out first. Not fancy, but comfortable. Weekly rates. The owners aren't formal allies, but they're countereconomic. They won't ask nosy questions."

"Will they take gold or eurofrancs?"

"If you approach it right. You don't look like goldfingers."

"I'll be needing to make some other countereconomic

contacts."

"I was coming to that." Chin wrote on a second piece of paper. "Here's a phone number to call the Cadre—good for another week. Call only from a nonvideo pay phone. A recorder will answer. Give your identification code, the pay phone's number, then hang up. If you don't get a callback within two minutes, get lost—fast. If the callback comes but the person at the other end doesn't address you by name, then it's a trap, and there'll be a police wagon along as soon as they've located your phone."

"Why the restriction to calling from a pay phone?"

"If police capture our relay station, they can hold on to the connection from the other end whether you hang up or not—then trace it. Cell and PCS phones are even worse for us. Got all that?"

Elliot repeated it back with one minor error, and was corrected. "What if I have to contact the Cadre after the week is up?"

"Use this number at least once before it *is* up," replied Chin. "Once you're identified, you'll be cleared for monthly phone numbers, eMail aliases and public keys, contact points, mail drops, bannering codes—"

"Hold up," Elliot interrupted. "Bannering codes?"

"You don't know?" Chin asked.

Elliot shook his head, mystified.

"I thought you already knew because you're wearing the ring."

Tumblers clicked. The engine turned over. *Queen takes pawn, Mate.* "A Christmas present."

"Oh," said Chin. "A banner is an inconspicuous signal that allies use to flag one another during face-to-face contact. It's useful only at street level where the sheer number of transactions makes heavy police infiltration improbable. If you want further confirmation, the two of you can head off to a pay phone

for a conference call to the Cadre, call in each of your identification codes, and have the Cadre return your confirmed
names."

"I take it the current banner is a ring-twirling code?"

"That's right, based on Morse Code. But I thought you
didn't—"

Elliot interrupted: "I saw it used twice in the same day. Once
by a *tzigane* driver and once by ...someone else."

After pulling a hologram data cartridge out of his computer,
sticking it into a pocket for safekeeping, Chin led Elliot,
Lorimer, and two other couples out to a windowless garage in
which were parked half a dozen panel trucks painted like commercial delivery vans. The van to which they were taken read
"Hot Bialys" on the side. "A gambling joint or a nightclub?"
Lorimer asked Elliot.

"You aren't a New Yorker, are you?"

She shrugged. "Sounds like someone in a Damon Runyon
story."

Inside the van were two side couches facing across, seatbelts
for three on each side. There was a steel partition between
the rear and the driver's compartment—in the back, again, no
windows.

After a last "laissez-faire" to Chin, the six climbed into the
truck and fastened their belts. Elliot found himself with
Lorimer on his left and a plump, fiftyish woman with frosted
hair on his right. With his coat on—for it was chilly—he felt
like a slice of turkey sandwiched between two slices of bread—
one wheat, the other rye.

It did not help that after Chin had slammed the doors—a
heavy, metallic *whoomph* making ears pop—it now sounded
as if they were in a recording studio. Elliot tried knocking on
the sides to produce an echo; all he got for his troubles was
sore knuckles: the space was absolutely dead. The situation
did not improve when the van started moving; he felt changes

in momentum but little vibration and no road noise—not even the comforting whine of turbines.

The bleached-blonde woman across from Elliot—middle twenties—tried starting a conversation with her male companion, an emaciated chain smoker whom Eliot thought tubercular, but the acoustics inhibited not only sound but conversation as well. Lorimer also lit up immediately. The hour in transit was spent in smoky, but silent, meditation—transcendental or otherwise.

When the van came to a halt, a gravely voice came back through an intercom: "Last stop. Get ready to leave when I give you the word." Everyone unstrapped, lifting luggage onto their knees; Lorimer slung her travel bag over her shoulder. Elliot noticed a wire—running from the door forward to the driver compartment—suddenly tighten. "Ready ... ready ... go!"

With a muffled *crack*, the van's double doors swung open into the frosty night air. They were behind the Pan Am Building and Grand Central Station; Forty-fifth Street was deserted. Lorimer jumped out, followed immediately by Elliot and the Smokers Anonymous advertisement, the two young men helping the remaining three passengers out while Lorimer kept watch.

As soon as the Grande Dame's feet were on solid ground, the van sped off around the corner, its double doors swinging shut as it turned. None of the passengers had even glimpsed the driver.

Leaving Elliot and Lorimer with only another "laissez-faire," the two other couples started post-haste to the front of Grand Central Station; Chin had mentioned that *tzigane* cabs were lining up during the strike without police interference. "Think we ought to phone the rooming house?" Elliot asked Lorimer.

"Probably a good idea, but I wouldn't mind eating first. Anyplace good around here?"

"Best choices are over on Fifth Avenue or down in the Village. Which way?"

"Fifth Avenue," Lorimer said. "I've never been there on Saturday night. I hear it's a real witches' Sabbath."

Elliot pondered this a moment.

"That's almost adequate," he said.

Chapter 15

The headline on *The New York Times* Sunday edition—just then hitting the street—read: "PRESIDENT URGES DIPLOMATIC RECOGNITION OF TEXAN REPUBLIC."

Elliot handed the Forty-fifth Street newsdealer two quarter vendies, checking the *Times* to ensure all sections present. "Well, it's Saturday night, all right," he told Lorimer, then checking his watch against the newsdealer's, determined that it was seven fifteen by all accounts.

"You're really gonna lug that entire paper around?" Lorimer asked him.

"This, my dear, is for research."

"You're carrying it," said Lorimer. "Okay, where to?"

Elliot thought a moment, then smiled devilishly. "I know just the place," he said, tucking the paper under his left arm, taking Lorimer's hand with his right.

Fifth Avenue on a Saturday night was like Fifth Avenue any night—only more so. As they were just entering the enclave, they were brushed aside by a pickpocket being chased by two FAMAS guards. As he ran, the pickpocket scattered a wad of blues into the wind. He kept the wallet, though.

A four-block walk uptown brought the couple to a small club several doors from the Swissair office; the sign on the door said, "Ye Ole Rich Place," and below it, "Welcome Darwin and Huxley Students."

The maitre d' met them at the door, wearing a huge set of eyebrows, wire-rimmed glasses, false nose with mustache, and carrying a banana-sized cigar. "What's the password?" he asked.

Lorimer gave Elliot a dirty look. "You fink."

"You better give him the password, or we won't get in," said

Elliot.

"I'll give you a clue," said the maitre d'. "It's—"

"Swordfish, swordfish!"

"True Marxists," the maitre d' said. "Table for two?" Elliot nodded; the man grabbed two menus. "Walk this way," he said, imitating the Groucho stride all the way to their table. Elliot and Lorimer both did their best, but it was no contest.

While the maitre d' was leading them to their table, the real Groucho, as Rufus T. Firefly in *Duck Soup*, was on the wallscreen singing:

> "These are the laws of my administration.
> No one's allowed to smoke
> Or tell a dirty joke
> And whistling is forbidden."

Lorimer handed the maitre d' a one-eurofranc note and whispered. "Do you take this credit card?" He looked at the bill, holding it up close in the dim light, then with sleight-of-hand made it disappear. He himself then disappeared with the menus. Before Elliot could say anything, Lorimer told him, "You bought me lunch, I'll buy you dinner."

> "If any form of pleasure is exhibited,
> Report to me and it will be prohibited."

The maitre d' returned with new menus; the prices were in eurofrancs. Elliot nodded to Lorimer admiringly.

> "I'll put my foot down,
> So shall it be.
> This is the land of the free!"

After studying the menu and deciding on the "Zeppo," Elliot

asked Lorimer to order for him, telling her he wanted to phone the rooming house and the friends he had mentioned.

He walked to the telephone in the rear next to the rest rooms, closing the booth and punching in the first of the numbers Chin had given him. On the fourth ring a female voice said hello. "Mrs. Ferrer?" Elliot asked.

"No, hold on a second." There was a muffled shout of "Mama, it's for you," and in a moment another voice took over—just the barest trace of an Italian accent:

"Yes, who is speaking?"

"Mrs. Ferrer, my name is Joseph Rabinowitz—you don't know me. I just came into New York and was told you might have rooms available."

"Who tells you to call me?"

Elliot hesitated the slightest moment. Chin had not said to use his name. But either she knew the name or she did not; it would not hurt Chin in either case. Any risk was his and Lorimer's. "Mr. Chin."

"I have rooms for friends of Mr. Chin. We go to bed here at ten thirty: I expect you before then. Good-bye."

She hung up.

Elliot inserted another vendy, punching in Phillip's number from memory. A strange male voice said hello on the second ring; Elliot considered the thought that voices change over the telephone. "Mr. Gross?"

"No, Morris stepped out for a moment. This is his brother Abe. Who's calling?"

Elliot hung up, then sat in the booth a moment, shaking.

Was it a Cadre recognition signal he had not been given? Was there the slightest possibility that one of Mr. Gross's brothers had somehow survived—to appear after locating his brother so many years later? Or was it what it sounded like: Mr. Gross and Phillip had been arrested—possibly killed—and their apartment turned into a trap?

Chin's words suddenly surfaced in his mind. Elliot held his breath, picking up the receiver again as silently as possible. He listened a moment.

The telephone had not disconnected.

Elliot noiselessly cradled the receiver and left the booth.

In a moment he was back to the table, whispering into Lorimer's ear, "We're leaving. Now."

"But I already ordered."

"Emergency. I walked into a trap."

She nodded. Elliot helped her with her Genghis Khan, then donned his own overcoat. "Don't forget the *Times*," she reminded him, lifting her travel bag. He slipped on his gloves and took it.

At the door Lorimer stopped to cancel their order. "Is anything wrong?" the maitre d' asked.

"We were never here, eh, comrade?" she said softly.

He nodded. "Good luck, *tovarishchi*."

Lorimer stuffed a bill into his hand. "For the workers ..."

Elliot and Lorimer pushed out onto the crowded street, starting downtown at a moderate clip. "How did you know he was red?" Elliot asked.

"I have a sixth sense about it," she said. "I get it from my father. Well, where to now?"

"If you don't mind, to the rooming house. I seem to have lost my appetite."

"The rooming house? Wasn't that the trap?"

Elliot shook his head. "My friends."

"Oh! I'm sorry."

"Let's not even think about it," he said.

After a few minutes' conversation, Lorimer convinced him that starving would not do either of them any good. Elliot was forced to agree with her logic. In ten minutes they were in front of Grand Central Station, where almost two dozen cars were lined up—some undistinguished, others carrying the insignia of telephone taxi services unlicensed for street pick-ups. Removing his gloves, Elliot handed Lorimer the *Times*, approaching the first driver seated at the wheel of a red Nissan electric compact. "How much to West Eleventh Street?" Elliot asked while giving him the ring banner, the Morse Code letter A.

Though he wore a gold wedding band, the driver did not touch it. "Seven thousand blues, buddy. Hop in."

"No thanks."

They bypassed the second car entirely; the driver was wearing gloves.

A full-sized Checker, black and unmarked, was in the third position; the driver was female and ringed. Elliot twirled his ring once forward and once back, repeating his question. The driver twirled twice toward Elliot and once back—the correct response, U—and said, "That depends on what you're payin' with."

Elliot and Lorimer climbed into the car, shutting the door. "Do you take euros?" Elliot asked.

"Sure do. One'll cover it. What's the street number?"

"I'm not certain," said Elliot. "A restaurant—Manrico and Pagliacci."

"Got it." She stuck her hand out the window, flooring the accelerator, then picked up the microphone to her transceiver and in code gave her coordinates and destination to a base station known as Egotripper.

While they held on for dear life, the Checker turned left onto Fifth Avenue, hit green lights all the way down, turned right on Eleventh Street, and within a scant five minutes deposited them in front of the restaurant.

Manrico and Pagliacci's specialized in Italian cuisine set to operatic videodiscs—though not exclusively Italian opera. After they had again ordered—once more from eurofranc menus—Elliot directed his attention to the screen, in a mo-

ment recognizing it as the Metropolitan Opera recording of
the modern masterpiece *Die Achselnzucken des Atlas.* It was
the final act of the seven-hour-long opera, in which Johann,
the unseen hero, was singing his fifty-eight-minute *Radiorede*
aria.

After two orders of antipasto, manicotti, cappuccino, and
pastry—the last two accompanied by the grande finale—the
couple started walking east to the rooming house.

Elliot's left arm held both the newspaper and Lorimer's arm,
his right was in his coat pocket holding his revolver. Though
they were passing through slum and semislum neighborhoods—their obviously affluent appearance drawing a hostile
stare or two—they were unmolested. Elliot wondered if perhaps the local predators had moved uptown or west in search
of choicer game.

The buildings on Eleventh Street east of First Avenue were
old but not dilapidated; most were sandblast-clean, the street
in front of them unlittered, garbage tightly in cans. They passed
several armed private guards patrolling the street and an open
storefront with a sign, repeated in four other languages, that
said, "TOMPKINS SQUARE PARK COMMUNITY ASSOCIA-
TION—Security Officer on Duty." If Elliot had not known better, he could have mistaken the block for one in the West Eighties off Riverside Drive.

Between Avenues B and C was a building numbered 635
East Eleventh Street, several steps up to a door with another
sign, reading, "ROOMS FOR RENT—No Dogs or Welfare Para-
sites." Elliot pressed the door buzzer; in a short while a man's
voice asked over an intercom who was there.

"Rabinowitz," Elliot said. "I called earlier about a room."

In a few moments, a man opened a peephole. "I'm
Emmanuel Ferrer. You spoke to my son?"

"No, sir. To Mrs. Ferrer."

He opened the door and let them in.

The building's interior was not luxurious but was well appointed with wood-paneled walls and carpeted floors. Ferrer, a thin-haired man with a small paunch, led them up a twisting staircase to his second-floor apartment; a delicious mixture of cooking odors floated out the door.

Inside his living room, in front of a video wallscreen, were a thin woman about forty, a boy about Elliot's age, and a girl whom Elliot guessed thirteen. Mrs. Ferrer turned to her son and said, "Turn off the record, Raphael. Company." Raphael got up and disengaged the videodisc.

"This is my wife, Francesca," said Ferrer, "my daughter Carla, and—as you heard—my son Raphael. Please sit down." Elliot and Lorimer took seats near the couch, where the family was sitting. "Did you have a nice dinner?"

"Very nice," said Lorimer.

"Good, good. Would you like some coffee?"

"No, thank you. I'm still pretty full." Elliot shook his head also.

"My wife tells me that you were sent to us by Mr. Chin?"

"That's correct, sir," Elliot answered.

"Please forgive me if I sound suspicious but these are terrible times. Could you describe what Mr. Chin looks like to me?"

Elliot considered it a moment, then replied, "Yes, sir, but I don't think it would be discreet for me to do so."

Ferrer nodded; Elliot had evaded his trap. "How long were you planning to stay with us?"

"Well, that's sort of up in the air. We'd be interested in a weekly rate—starting off with one week."

"You'd want to do your own cooking?"

Elliot looked over to Lorimer. She nodded.

"And I should mention before we get too far along," Elliot continued, "that all I have to pay with is gold or eurofrancs."

Mr. Ferrer's attitude shifted visibly from cautious to respectful. "Let me show you the apartment we have available. If you like it, we can discuss price. Raphael, the key to 3A."

Ferrer led Elliot and Lorimer up another flight, taking them into a front apartment. Elliot decided at first glance that he liked it. Light and airy—as much as any apartment could be at night—it was decorated with Spanish modern furnishings. A good-sized living room with a picture window facing the street, a dinette off a small kitchen, and a bedroom with queen-size bed—full bath adjoining—were all spotlessly clean and carpeted throughout. All appliances, with the exception of a ten-year-old Sony portable television, were fairly new; the kitchen was fully equipped with cooking gear, utensils, and dishes.

Elliot caught Lorimer's eyes, receiving nonverbal confirmation that she liked the apartment as much as he did, and he asked Ferrer how much he had in mind.

"The price on this apartment is three grams of gold a week, or thirty eurofrancs."

Elliot nodded.

"Come downstairs again while my daughter brings up towels and makes up the bed."

"She doesn't have to go to all that trouble. I can take it up."

"I wouldn't hear of it," said Ferrer. "It's how she earns her allowance."

After they had returned downstairs, Ferrer directed Carla to her preparations, Elliot then paying him thirty eurofrancs cash. Mrs. Ferrer wrote out a receipt for one week's rent, a fabricated price in New Dollars written in.

"Is there anyone around here who sells ration books?" Elliot asked. "Or a grocery store not too fussy about regulations?"

"We have a food cooperative here that doesn't bother with such nonsense," said Ferrer. "If you like, we can have groceries delivered while you're here. I'll give you the order form."

They chatted about nothing in particular until Carla returned, then Mrs. Ferrer mentioned to her husband that it was ten thirty. "Yes," said Mr. Ferrer, rising, "early Mass tomorrow."

"Maybe Mr. and Mrs. Rabinowitz would like to join us?" chimed in Raphael. His sister directed a dirty look at him.

Elliot was pondering Lorimer's religious orientation—his own was militant solipsism—when Lorimer saved him by cutting in, "Thank you, but we're Jewish."

"Would you eat breakfast with us?" Mrs. Ferrer asked. "There is nothing to eat in your refrigerator and there are no food deliveries until Monday."

"Unless your dietary laws—" began Mr. Ferrer.

"We don't observe them," said Lorimer. "We'd be delighted to join you."

"Good. We usually eat when we get back—ten o'clock."

After good nights were said, Elliot and Lorimer were given keys and returned upstairs, Elliot removing overcoat, jacket, and shoes, then collapsing on the living-room couch. Lorimer got her travel bag and took out a purse, presenting fifteen eurofrancs to Elliot. "What's this for?" he asked.

"My half of the rent."

"I didn't ask you to split it."

"I'd be paying one way or another. This limits my obligation." Elliot shrugged, a difficult motion while supine, and took the bills, returning several to Lorimer. "I don't understand," she said.

"You paid for dinner. The least I can do is pick up the bribes."

She shrugged and took the bills.

"You know," said Elliot, "you have a lot of chutzpah for a goy."

She grinned. "If you're going to play a role, you might as well play it to the hilt."

"Maybe you can. But 'to the hilt' is exactly how I can't play it."

"Why not? You speak the idiom better than I do."

Elliot paused for a moment. Interesting, he thought. "Uh—never mind. Let's just hope Mr. Ferrer doesn't invite me to a steam bath."

She shrugged again. "Coming to bed?"

"Soon," he said. "I just want to scan the paper for a few minutes."

"Okay."

Elliot remained on the couch for another moment then dragged himself over to the dining table, pulling off the first section of the *Times*. After reading the article on the Texas-secession issue up to the continuation notice, he flipped to the bottom half of the front page for the first time.

There was a story headlined:

VREELAND WIDOW ASSURES PUBLIC HUSBAND DIED
NATURALLY.

Chapter 16

Sunday it rained.

It began after five, drops of sleet pelting their bedroom window like distant shots ricocheting. Inside the darkened room, a boy and a girl lay next to one another under covers, their body heat irradiating each other against the outer cold.

She reached over, turning on the light. "You still haven't slept any, have you?"

He stared blankly up at the ceiling. No.

"You think talking about it would help any?"

"It might make me feel better. That's all."

"That's all?"

"I wouldn't be any closer to solving the problem."

She reached over to the bed table, got a cigarette, and lit it. "How do you know? You don't have a monopoly on brains."

"I don't have the right to lay it on you.

"It would break a confidence?"

"No, that's not it," he said.

"Then feel better. Tell me."

"It's not your problem."

"For Christ's sake, you're keeping me up, aren't you? It fucking well is my problem."

Elliot did not say anything.

"Look," she said, "I'll trade you problems.

He smiled slightly. "I have a feeling you'd be making a bum deal."

"How do you know?"

"I don't. As a matter of fact, we still don't know the first thing about each other."

She tickled behind his ear. "The first thing?"

"Well, yes, there's *that*. But you can't fuck all the time."

"Why not?"

He smiled slightly. "Okay, we'll trade. You start."

"Don't you trust me?"

"Sure I trust you. You start."

"Bastard." She took a puff. "All right, I guess you won't turn me in. I ran away from home."

"Definitely a firing-squad offense," Elliot said, only slightly sarcastically.

"Quite possible. I took some microfilm with me."

"Getting more interesting."

"The FBI file on the Cadre and other subversives. The only complete copy left in existence after the firebombings of Bureau offices."

Elliot was slightly awed. "And it was just laying around home?"

"Well, not exactly lying around," she corrected him. "It was in a safe I saw being opened once. By my father. I was hiding at the time."

"What was this file doing in your father's safe?"

"My father is Lawrence Powers, director of the FBI."

Elliot turned over onto his elbow and examined her face closely. "You're not bullshitting?"

She drew a cross between her breasts.

"Why'd you do it?"

She hesitated a moment. "Why does anyone defect? Ideological reasons."

"But your own father?"

"I didn't shoot the motherfucker. I just stole his film. He'll live."

Elliot shook his head. "All right, don't tell me, then. But don't give me any crap about 'ideological reasons.'"

Lorimer hesitated a long moment, took a drag on her cigarette, then answered flatly, unemotionally, as if what she was reporting had happened many years before. But Elliot could hear an undertone of great tension and much bitterness. "My father," she began. "My father committed my mother to a mental institution. My mother was a saint whose only insanity was telling members of the press that she thought my father was a monster—which he is. Last week, after a shock treatment, my mother killed herself. She had been saving up sleeping pills. She knew my father had the connections to keep her in there forever. I stole the film while my father was at her funeral. A political showcase—I wouldn't have let my face be seen with him there anyway."

Elliot had listened closely, worried that he had bullied her into relating too-painful events. Lorimer was silent for a moment, then looked up and said, "Your turn," then added softly, "Prick."

Elliot answered quietly, "My mother and sister are locked up at a nice little prison in Massachusetts. Code name Utopia."

"My father's personal dungeon," said Lorimer. "Why do they rate?"

"I think it's because they can prove that my father did not die of natural causes."

She looked puzzled.

"My father was Dr. Martin Vreeland."

It was her turn to be shocked.

"Might as well start calling me Romeo, Juliet. By the way, not-Lorimer, what *is* your name?"

"Deanne Powers." She pronounced her first name in one syllable.

"Pleased to meet you," he said. "I'm Elliot Vreeland."

"Charmed," she replied.

Elliot extended his hand formally. They shook.

"Listen, Deanne—No, on second thought we'd better not break the habit of using our code names." She nodded. "Okay, then. Lor, we're teaming up for a while, right?"

"Right, *Joe*."

Elliot winced. "Okay. My problem is this. All I have to do is spring my mother and sister from your father's personal dungeon. The Cadre says they can't do it, but on Monday I start checking out other possibilities. There's also the slightest chance that my father is still alive—although I don't believe it anymore—but if he is, then the Cadre will give me their best shot at finding him, and if my father is dead ...well, dead is dead." He paused. "I know that may sound pretty coldblooded but I can't afford the luxury of feeling for a while."

"Feeling is a luxury?"

"When the only thing stopping your ass from getting caught—or shot off—is your being able to think clearly, then feeling is a luxury, yes. It's been pretty marginal for me lately. And for you, too, judging by what I've seen."

"You mean that bastard commandant?"

"Lor, much as I hate to admit it, I don't think the commandant was being a bastard. Or at least not much of one. A real bastard would've tried getting us locked up for six months—and seeing as how I don't know the way these arbitration hearings turn out, he might've made a good case of it. As it was, all he was going to do was evacuate us separately, and now that we know how Cadre communications work, we probably could've gotten in touch on the outside."

"Maybe not. The computer station in my room said I was going to Montreal."

"If we'd tried paying for the trouble instead of your silly-ass stunt of pulling a gun, he might've been more cooperative."

"That's not very complimentary," said Lorimer. "Actually, I thought it was rather machisma."

"Great. I could have paid tribute in the morgue. By the way, as long as we're laying it on the line, why did you proposition me? I may be egotistical but I'm no Don Juan."

"You may not be Don Juan but you're not Quasimodo, either."

"You're evading again."

"Okay, I can be blunt, too! I wanted to lose my virginity."

Elliot remained silent for a half-moment, then said, "But there was no ..."

"I haven't had a cherry since I was thirteen. Gymnastics."

"Are you trying to tell me that you couldn't manage to get laid before you ran into *me*?Are the guys in Washington all eunuchs?"

"Not Washington. Alexandria, Virginia. And usually not. But could you get it up with the daughter of the chief pig in the country?"

Elliot smiled. "It seems I did."

"That doesn't count. You didn't have to put up with an FBI agent tailing you on dates."

"Uh—I'll take the point under consideration."

"We've gotten way off the point," said Lorimer. "You were telling me about your problem."

"No, I finished. Tell me yours."

"Nothing like yours. All I have to do is remain at large with my picture soon to be in every post office in the country."

"That's easy," said Elliot. "Just put stamps on the posters and mail them. They'll never be seen again."

"Mmm. Well, neither of us is going to be in any shape to solve anything if we don't get some sleep. We have to be up for breakfast in under five hours." Lorimer reached over, crushed her cigarette into its ashtray, and shut off the light.

They were ten minutes late to breakfast.

Mr. Ferrer met them at the door saying, "Come in, join us."

"Awfully sorry we're late," Elliot said sheepishly.

"We overslept," Lorimer lied.

Ferrer led them to the table. "Nonsense, you can't oversleep."

Elliot's heart skipped a beat.

"If you slept longer, you needed it. Besides, we're just sitting down."

Breakfast was unusually plentiful for a private table: oatmeal, bacon, eggs, orange juice, and coffee, the only exception to standard American cuisine being Mrs. Ferrer's homemade Spanish *churros*—rolled flat fritters sprinkled with sugar—which she said she had learned to make from Mr. Ferrer's mother. Elliot decided that if these were the imitations, the originals would have enslaved him for life. He consumed his fill, washing them down with plenty of dark-roast coffee.

Afterward, Carla left to meet a girl friend while her brother drew kitchen duty. The two senior Ferrers invited the "Rabinowitzes" into their living room.

Mr. Ferrer walked over to the window, pulling aside the drapes, and looked out to the street. "Is it still so dreary out?" Elliot asked him.

"It's still raining," Ferrer replied. He paused an instant, then added softly, "It washed the garbage off the street."

"I didn't see any garbage on the street," said Lorimer. "Unless you mean the cans—"

"No, no," he interrupted, letting go the curtain, "not anymore. This was, oh, six years ago. You must have seen the slums just a few blocks from here. Six years ago this block was also a slum."

"What happened?" Lorimer asked. "Urban renewal?"

Elliot almost choked.

Ferrer said to him, "I see you understand." He took a seat on the couch, taking a cigarette out of a silver box on the coffee table and lighting up. "No, not urban renewal as you mean it. That only traded flat slums for higher ones."

"Why?"

"The way the housing projects were rented. The only people who got in were the unworthy poor. Welfare mothers with children they had only to get a bigger check. Drug addicts who had been cured—now they only took methadone. Friends of the politicians."

"Emmanuel, is no good to think about this after so long."

"It will not hurt, Francesca, for me to tell it once more." Ferrer took another puff on his cigarette. "Mrs. Rabinowitz, six years ago I owned a small printing and copy store near New York University. I was not rich from it but it kept food on the table and paid the tuition for my children's parochial school. Then one day in March, without any warning or reason, the Internal Revenue Service seized my business, my bank accounts, and everything in my apartment."

"You don't have to explain any further," said Lorimer. "I know exactly how that works."

"Very well. You know then that no matter how I tried, I could not find out why they did this, and that it would have taken years before I got a day in court. In the meantime, I had no job, no belongings, no money. I applied for unemployment insurance and was turned down. I applied for an apartment in a city housing project and was put on a two-year waiting list. I applied for welfare; it was denied."

"What did you do?" Lorimer asked.

Ferrer snuffed out his cigarette. "I took a messenger job and moved my family into this building—the one we're now in. It was abandoned. Every building on this street for three blocks was abandoned. Between inflation, taxes, and rent controls, the landlords—slumlords?—all had gone broke. When we moved in, this building was without electricity, running water, heat—"

"But plenty of rats and roaches," said Raphael, entering from the kitchen. "Of course there was a balanced ecology between them."

"The rats ate the roaches?" asked Lorimer.

Raphael shook his head. "The other way around."

"Pay no attention to him," Mr; Ferrer said. "He's heard me tell this so many times that he wishes it was only a story."

"Is the crossword puzzle around here somewhere?" Raphael asked.

"The magazine section is in the bathroom," said Mrs. Ferrer.

"To continue," Mr. Ferrer said, "we were the last family living in this building when a man visited us asking who owned it. I told him as far as I knew nobody did and started pleading with him not to make us leave. I thought he was from the government."

"He wasn't?"

Ferrer shook his head. "He told me not to worry, that he was just checking up. He had been to the city hall and the last owner had stopped paying taxes and disappeared two years before. Then he asked us how long we were living here—it was seven months—and said that as far as he was concerned we owned this building by possession and was I interested in making a deal to fix it up?"

"And you took him up on it?"

"Of course," Ferrer said. "He told me he owned a construction company that would do all the renovation work, and he knew a man that would put up the money, splitting the ownership and profits with me fifty-fifty. All I had to do was remain here and manage the building for another six and a half years to maintain continuous possession."

"Excuse me," asked Elliot, "but was this man very tall and black? A glass eye?"

Ferrer nodded; Elliot and Lorimer exchanged pointed glances. Guerdon.

"There's not much more to tell," Ferrer continued. "He made the same offer to people left in buildings all along this block. We eventually got together, forming the Community Association to split the costs of garbage collection, police and fire protection, and the food cooperative to buy in bulk—later to buy on the countereconomy to avoid shortages and rationing. We do not receive—or want—any government services, and we pay no taxes."

"Haven't you had any problems with tax officials, building inspectors, and the like?"

"Our construction friend said he would handle this and he has. Only one city official—housing, I believe—came by with a court order to make us leave. I told our friend about it and never saw the official or his court order again. Police detectives were around this block asking about the man a few days later, but then they gave up and left. This was three years ago, and we have not been bothered since."

Before they left, Mr. Ferrer remembered to give Elliot and Lorimer the food cooperative's order form, telling them to return it by that evening if they wished to catch the Monday morning delivery. Lorimer and he thanked the Ferrers for their hospitality, then returned upstairs.

Shortly after their apartment door closed, Elliot asked Lorimer if she had anything to keep herself busy awhile.

"I suppose I could watch some TV."

"You said that to make me ill, didn't you?" Elliot's face then brightened; he found in his coat pocket the Heinlein paperback he had reread half a week before, tossing it to her. "Try this instead."

Lorimer stuck out her tongue at him. "Snob. I bet I've read more science fiction than you." She retired to the living room with the book.

For the next hour, Elliot brought himself up to date, the *Times* spread over the dining table, the kitchen radio tuned to WINS, an all-news station.

What he thought most significant was what was not mentioned. There was no news of an FBI raid on a Cadre base (which should have hit the air by now, though missing his paper's deadline), there was no news concerning the weekend arrest of any dissidents. Had the dragnet his father had been fleeing never materialized—perhaps aborted by Lorimer's microfilm theft—or had it proceeded silently to capture the Grosses?

Later, Elliot told Lorimer that he was going out to buy a few items. "Anything you want me to bring back?"

"Something to eat later. I don't much feel like going out in this weather."

"Okay. How's the book so far?"

"Not bad," she said. "Almost as good as *Hello, Joe—Whadd'ya Know?*"

Elliot shook his head sadly and started for the door.

A very wet ten-minute walk brought him to nonvideo pay phones at the corner of First Avenue and Fourteenth Street. Elliot inserted a vendy and punched in the number Chin had given him to telephone the Cadre. The phone answered on the second ring, a recorded female voice saying, "You have reached 500-367-7353. After the tone, please record your message."

After the tone Elliot said, " 'Queen takes pawn, Mate,'" and read off the pay phone's number, hanging up immediately. Then he followed the seconds on his watch.

Sixty-seven seconds later the telephone rang; Elliot picked up immediately. Another voice, now male, said, "Joseph Rabinowitz?"

"Yes," said Elliot. "I can talk freely?"

"We believe this line secure. How can we help you?"

"Would there be any difficulty in putting me through to Chin?"

"Please hold while I try to relay you."

Elliot turned up his collar uselessly; rain still ran down his neck.

In about another minute, a familiar voice came on and said, "Joseph?"

"Hello, Chin."

"When did you last see me?"

"Yesterday afternoon," said Elliot.

"Oh, yes. Our private chat."

"No, I was with Lorimer."

"How's your health?"

Elliot pondered this last query for a moment, then replied, "Not bad. But—do you have anything for clogged sinuses?"

"What can I do for you, Joseph?" Chin asked.

"Information. Are you sure we're secure?"

"Relax. What's on your mind?"

"First," said Elliot, "I need an identity check. Lorimer."

"I can't give you her name without her permission. The best I can do is confirm or deny a name you give me."

"Check this, then. Deanne Powers."

"It checks," Chin said.

"She's really the FBI chief's daughter?"

"Yes."

"And you're sure she's on your side?"

Elliot could hear Chin's dry chuckle. "My friend, she has a higher psychometric loyalty rating than you."

"I don't recall taking any tests," said Elliot.

"What do you think your entire visit to Aurora was?"

"Uh—never mind. Next point. I want to find out if the friends—the allies—who arranged my visit to Aurora are okay. I don't know their Cadre names. Should I give you their real names?"

"No," Chin said. "They're listed in your file as your sureties. Wait a moment." In a little while, Chin said, "Stay away from their apartment. It's been captured."

"But are they okay?"

"I'm sorry. I can't tell you anything over this line."

Elliot swallowed a lump that had been building since yesterday. The Grosses were dead—they had to be dead.

"All right," Elliot said slowly. "Okay. Has there been any progress about my—family?"

Chin's voice was even gentler. "There have been no new entries in your file since you left, Joseph."

"Okay."

"Are you staying at the place I recommended?" Chin asked.

"Yes. Very nice people."

"Fine. I'll record that in your file so if we lose relay prematurely we can get word to you there. Laissez-faire."

On the way back, Elliot stopped at a grocery store, picking up a supply of cold cuts, sandwich makings, fruit, soft drinks, and a tube of toothpaste. He paid for them with vendies and the few remaining ration tickets he had in his wallet. A little farther east on Fourteenth Street he stepped into another store for a few minutes, again paying with vendies, walking out with a smaller purchase.

When he got back to the apartment, drenched to the bone, Lorimer was still on the couch, reading. After hanging his overcoat on the showerhead to dry, Elliot brought the second bag into the living room. "Catch," he said, tossing Lorimer a strange-looking roll.

She caught it. "What's this?"

"A hot bialy," he said.

Chapter 17

He found the advertisement classified in *The New York Times* under "Services Available."

It read:

How good is your security system? If we can't crack it, no one can. Money-back guarantee. Confidential free consultations, no appointment necessary. MISSION IMPOSSIBLE, Empire State Building, New York, N.Y. 10001

Lorimer dropped the clipping onto the bed table. "That's where you're heading today?"

Elliot, still undressed, sat down on the bed next to her. "There and also to the *Times* building, where I'll drop off my reply to another ad. Come with me?"

"Just for company?"

Elliot shook his head. "Whoever is looking for us individually won't be thinking about a couple. I also get the feeling you're pretty up on cloak-and-dagger."

Lorimer shrugged. "Something rubs off, I guess." She hesitated. "That's what my appointment today was supposed to be about. I've been told Merce Rampart thinks I could make a good operative."

Elliot looked at her seriously. "Have you met him?"

She shook her head. "I would've today."

"I wonder," said Elliot. "I'm beginning to think that there isn't any Merce Rampart. That he's just a bogey invented to throw everyone off the track."

"You're a cynic."

"Not at all. I'm a rational empiricist. And an impatient one. Are you coming with me?"

Lorimer nodded. "I had some shopping to do anyway."

"Me, too. A change of clothes. And some brown hair dye."

"Not that easy sometimes. When I dyed my hair last week, I had to pick up colored contact lenses."

"That's not your real coloring?"

"My hair's as blond as yours."

"Well that explains—Oh, never mind." He studied her. "You know, blonde you'd look a little like my sister."

"Thanks. I think. Now come up close." Elliot slid over; Lorimer looked into his eyes. He could not resist kissing her. After a time she asked, "Is that how you treat your sister?"

"No." He kissed her again.

"You have a one-track mind."

"That's me, all right. The Man with the Monorail Mind. "

Lorimer flipped off the bed covers. "Later. I'm taking a shower."

Elliot flicked an invisible cigar ash onto the carpet. Imaginary thick eyebrows gyrated up and down behind imaginary glasses.

"Mind if I join you?"

At ten thirty Elliot answered a knock at the door, Lorimer still in the bathroom drying her hair. It was Mr. Ferrer with their delivery from the food cooperative.

Elliot took in the first carton; then, after accompanying Ferrer down to his apartment for two more, returned upstairs with him to pay the ten eurofrancs due. After thanking Ferrer, Elliot asked him if there were anything he could do in return. "Would you be going near a newspaper stand today?" Ferrer asked.

"Going uptown a little later."

"Would you pick up a newspaper for me? Our newsboy did not show up today. Again."

"No problem." Ferrer thanked Elliot and returned downstairs.

Elliot went to the kitchen, turning on the radio—easy-listening music was playing—then began storing the groceries. When half an hour later Lorimer finally emerged, dressed in a tight cashmere sweater and slacks, coffee was on the table, tarts in the toaster, and bacon draining. "So you cook too, huh?" she said.

"Nope. You're my first victim. How'd you like your eggs?"

"Uh—I'll cook my own eggs, thank you."

"Just kidding. I can make them any way you want."

"I'm crazy about eggs Benedict."

Elliot gave her a dirty look.

"In that case," Lorimer said, "once over easy."

While Elliot dropped food onto their plates, the radio announcer took the opportunity to intone a station break, then continued by cueing what he called "more beautiful music for a beautiful Monday morning, a Boston Pops rendition of 'Slaughter on Tenth Avenue.'"

The arrangement came on as Elliot carried the plates into the dinette, joining Lorimer at the table. "That's odd," he told her.

"What is?"

"The announcer just gave this station's call letters as WINS."

"So?"

"So WINS is an all-news station, twenty-four hours. Has been since before I was born."

Lorimer shrugged. "Probably a new CRC ruling. They've been talking about cracking down on balanced-programming rules for years."

Elliot scowled. "Why can't the CRC mind its own damn business?"

"When has any government agency ever had its own damn business to mind?"

"Uh—let's change the subject," said Elliot.

"Spoilsport."

Though still overcast, the sun was shining through in spots, and the sky did not again threaten rain. Just after noon, Elliot and Lorimer walked up to Fourteenth Street, deciding against searching for a *tzigane* and beginning to walk across town.

It was not as windy as the previous week, consequently the freezing temperature was not especially uncomfortable. Had he not had so much on his mind, Elliot could have found this walk with Lorimer as carefree an outing as ever could be hoped for on a February day. As it was, he felt like a student on a half-day field trip, the momentary freedom merely underscoring his sense of being trapped.

As they walked along, past First Avenue, past Second and Third, Elliot began noticing that many of the faces he encountered showed uneasiness as great as his own. Too many stores were closed, hastily drawn signs taped onto plate glass behind drawn steel grilles, saying "NO STOCK TODAY." Though the subway strike had been thickening street-traffic density, today seemed particularly crowded. A mob at Union Square was standing around a fight, cheering it on. Elliot told Lorimer, "There's something in the air," then added silently to himself: *And it has nothing to do with meteorology.*

At ten to one o'clock, the couple entered United States postal zone 10001, the Empire State Building's directory informing them that their destination was on its forty-third floor. Taking the elevator up, they found a small office with its door marked "Mission Impossible Security Consultants" and went right in, a buzzer sounding as they entered.

There was a receptionist's desk but no receptionist. After a moment, a bald man with glasses emerged from an office wiping his nose. "Heddo," he said. "Cad I he'p jew?"

Elliot suppressed an immediate desire to walk right out again, instead replying, "We're responding to your classified in Sunday's *Times*."

"Jew bus hab de wrog opus. I dode hab edy ebplobet opedigs."

"What?"

"Hode od a bobet."

He took a decongestant from a jacket pocket, tilted his head back, and sprayed both nostrils. "Ah, that's better. I said you must have the wrong office. I didn't advertise for any personnel."

"But you did advertise your firm's services.Testing security systems? Money-back guarantee if you can't break them?"

"That's our ad, all right. But we deal with commercial and industrial systems. Are you sure you're coming to the right place?"

"I'm not sure at all," said Elliot. "Do you usually do business in your reception area?"

A surprised expression appeared on the man's face. "Not at all." He motioned the two into his office, directing them into plush chairs facing his desk; photographs of security devices decorated the wall. "I'm Benton Durand," he continued, taking his chair. "I apologize but today's been impossible—just impossible. First, this cold. Second, my secretary didn't make it in today—I think she caught my cold. And third, my phones have been out all morning." He wiped his nose again. "Can I get you anything? Tea, coffee? The coffee will have to be instant; I don't know how the machine works."

Elliot hoped this was not an indication of the man's technical competence. Moreover, he was not about to risk drinking anything within a hundred yards of Durand. He and Lorimer both declined.

"Mr. Durand," began Elliot, "my problem is rather touchy—legally. You advertise confidentiality. Will it remain confidential if you deem what I ask illegal, or we do not do business?"

"It will remain confidential, Mr.... Mr...."

"Rabinowitz," said Elliot.

"...Mr. Rabinowitz, but if you want me to help you steal or destroy property—"

"Nothing like that," Elliot interrupted, waving it away.

"Then if I'm worried, I'll talk to my lawyer. Go on."

"You're sure this office isn't bugged?"

"I know my business. This is private."

Elliot nodded. "Two members of my family are confined incommunicado in a federal maximum-security prison in Massachusetts. They have been arrested without due process, charges, or trial. If you can bypass that prison's security, I am willing to pay handsomely—in gold."

Durand blew his nose, shaking his head. "Impossible."

"Moral objections?" asked Lorimer. "Or is it the risk?"

"Neither one. Mr. Rabinowitz, I fully sympathize with you. But I can't help. I don't know anyone in the business who could."

"Would five hundred grams of gold change your mind any?" Elliot asked. "Five thousand eurofrancs, if you prefer. "

"Ten times that wouldn't change my mind. Maybe a hundred times would. Something this size requires a budget of—oh, half a million eurofrancs. At least we'd be in the same league as with the federal intelligence forces."

Elliot stood, Lorimer following. "I'm afraid I can't afford government prices."

Durand extended his hand. "I really do sympathize."

"Thanks, anyway," said Elliot, taking it. He and Lorimer started for the door.

Durand cleared his throat loudly, calling them back. "Er—there is one outfit—now that I think of it—that could possibly help you."

Elliot turned anxiously. "There is?"

"I don't know how to put you in touch, though. The Revolutionary Agorist Cadre."

"Uh—I'll keep that in mind," said Elliot, he and Lorimer both suppressing shocked smiles.

Durand sneezed. "This damn cold is driving me right up

the wall. Do you know of anything for clogged sinuses?"

Elliot got out as fast as possible.

A brisk fifteen-minute walk over to Broadway and eight blocks up through the garment district—business as usual—brought them to Times Square; the *New York Times* offices were a block farther up on Forty-third Street. Elliot sensed something incongruous but could not quite put his finger on it. Then he knew.

The news on the Oracle was gone.

Chapter 18

Police barricades on both the Seventh and Eighth Avenue sides of Forty-third Street blocked all access to *The New York Times* Building. After a brief discussion, in which she assured Elliot it was unlikely she could be recognized, Lorimer volunteered to ask the police what was happening while Elliot waited across the street.

Upon her return a little later, she told him, "They say there's been a bomb threat."

"Brilliant. Absolutely brilliant."

"You think it's a news blackout."

Elliot nodded, starting to walk briskly back to Forty-second Street; Lorimer struggled to keep up. "Where are we going?"

"Phones."

They found one at the comer of Forty-second. Elliot inserted a vendy, punching in the number he had used to call the Cadre. He received a busy signal. "Everybody's probably calling in," Lorimer said.

"I wonder." Elliot redeposited his vendy, punching "O" for the operator. Busy. He called 411. Also busy. He called the telephone in his family's abandoned apartment. Harsh, repeating squawks. "Tomorrow," he told Lorimer, "they'll probably announce the central switching office was captured by terrorists."

They crossed over to a newsstand not far from the Rabelais Bookstore; the newsdealer—a grizzled old man—had magazines out but no newspapers; his radio played music loudly from the booth. The old man shook his head. "Sold outa last night's papers, and that was it. Nothin' delivered today."

"Have you heard any news on your radio?" Lorimer asked.

"Not even a hockey score. Been switchin' stations all day.

WOR is all music, WCBS is off the air. Can't even find no call-in shows."

"The phones are out," said Elliot.

"That wouldn't stop none a *them* ratchetjaws. They can talk ta themselves fer hours. If ya ask me, I tink it's a war, and they ain't figured out how ta tell us yet."

"They've always figured out before."

He answered softly, drawing them close for a revelation. "Yeah, but this time it's gonna be nukuler, ya know? This time it's gonna be *nukuler*. Ya just tell me if I'm right."

"I'll be the first one," said Elliot. He turned to Lorimer. "We'd better figure this out."

They went into McDonald's next door, Elliot buying two hot cocoas at the counter, then carting them over to a table at the window. "Okay," he practically whispered to Lorimer. "Newspapers are stopped. Radio is under tight censorship—I think we can assume the same for TV. Phones are dead, wire services are out—"

"Wire services?"

"If OPI—the Oracle—is out, then the rest are out."

"Oh," said Lorimer. "You forgot public transit."

"That's been out for weeks."

"It's still a datum."

"Possibly. This might have been planned weeks—maybe months—ago. But what does it add up to? First off, do you have any ideas who's behind this?"

"Well, not the New York police alone. They're probably cooperating with federal and state authorities. Possibly Civil Defense."

"You're assuming it's the government?" She nodded. "Why not our—uh—friends?"

"You can rule *them* out, as far as I'm concerned."

"Not capable of it?" Elliot asked.

"Oh, certainly they are—or at least my father thinks so. But it would require a massive amount of property violations—coercion. Our friends are opposed to that sort of thing on principle."

"Isn't that a little naive?"

"You can think so if you want. I don't."

"Okay, I'll put that idea on the back burner for the time being. What about a foreign power?" he asked.

"Can you see the New York cops taking orders from Russia?"

"Uh—point granted. If it's a coup, it's being run from the top down. Which brings up another point. Military junta?"

"What difference would it make? The effect is the same whether it's coming from the Joint Chiefs or the Kremlin or the White House. Believe me, they're all playing the same game; the rules simply change to match the terrain."

"Okay. Then what you're saying is that we have a domestic dictatorship on our hands."

Lorimer considered this for a moment. "Umm—let's go back to basic theory."

"I knew I couldn't avoid the lecture," said Elliot.

She smiled. "Battleground training," she said. "We're told we have a government by popular consent. At least in one sense that's true. Every government always exercises the maximum amount of power its rulers feel the people will stand for without revolting. If *this* government—or an element within it—is drastically increasing its use of power, then the leaders either feel they have the popular support—or apathy—to get away with it, or they're taking desperate chances because they're being pressed to the wall."

"According to my father," said Elliot, "the government has been increasingly 'pressed to the wall' for the past quarter century by fiscal realities. And if you can judge by last week's demonstrations, there's little popular support. "

"Then you've just answered your own question."

"I see. You're telling me that the government at the moment is like a wounded rhino starting to charge anything in its path. Maybe we'd better get out of it."

"How much more out of it do you want to get?"

"That, my dear, is the sixty-four-million-dollar question. What's Montreal like this time of year?"

"Cold," Lorimer said.

"Then maybe we'd better think about buying long underwear."

"I thought you had business here?"

"All the advantages of working out of New York have been neutralized. Montreal could work just as well for what I have to do. Besides, I'm beginning to think Durand was right. There's probably only one outfit that can handle this—when they decide they're ready—and we can hang out damn near anywhere as far as they're concerned."

"But how would we get there? Even if we had all the papers—which we don't—we can't assume there'll be any means out. If they've seized communications, they're almost certainly controlling commercial transport, too."

"We can make arrangements through our friends," Elliot said.

"How? No phones."

"I can think of several ways even if phones aren't restored—which they probably will be in a day or two."

"Yes, but why run away?" Lorimer asked. "What are we, brownies? The minute trouble comes, you head for the hills with your rifle and survival foods?"

"Consider that if the government cut off food to Manhattan it would begin starving in three days. Bread riots on the sixth."

"One. I don't believe they could do it; half the food on this island comes in countereconomically as it is. Two, I don't believe it's politically tenable. And three, I can't imagine what the higher circles—the ruling elite—could see themselves gaining by such a plan."

"All right, let's keep it on a more personal basis, then. Have you thought about what they'll do to us if we get picked up even for jaywalking?"

She nodded. "But if anything, the odds just got a lot better for us. Unfortunately, though, worse for some others."

"What?"

"Think it through. Yesterday the two of us were singled out by the government as public enemies. Today there are thousands more people on their enemies list. The statists' resources are just as limited as ever, but they're spreading them even further. Statistically there's less of a chance they'll hit on us."

"Tell me that again," said Elliot, "when the tanks start rolling down Broadway."

Lorimer shrugged. "A show of force, at best. If anything, an occupying army would only increase countereconomic activity. There's no way a domestic army can be prevented from fraternizing during off hours without rioting themselves." At that instant, a couple sat down at the empty table next to theirs. Elliot and Lorimer nodded at each other, then got up to leave.

On their way out the door, they ran into a skinny man with a mustache on his way in; Elliot did a double take, then realized it was the clerk from the Rabelais Bookstore who had told him to beat it the previous week. Elliot intended to ignore him, but the man recognized Elliot and said, "You the kid who was in last week?" Elliot nodded. "Well, in case you still wanna see your friend, he got back."

Elliot froze an instant. All his doubts about Al returned. Still, his father had trusted him, and he was possibly a Cadre ally. Elliot asked. "He's in the bookstore now?"

The clerk shook his head. "He don't ever come in before four."

"Uh—thanks." The clerk continued in, and Elliot led Lorimer out.

"What was that all about?" she asked.

"A man I have to see. My father was using him as a stash."
Elliot checked his watch; it was one fifty. "We have a bit over
two hours. Might as well use the time to good advantage."

They crossed over to a discount drugstore where Elliot found
his hair dye and Lorimer a tube of shampoo. Approaching the
cashier, Elliot put the merchandise on the counter with a
eurofranc on top. The cashier, a pudgy matron, looked at Elliot
like a stern schoolteacher. "Young man, do you know the pen-
alty for offering illegal foreign money? Or accepting it?"

"I have a feeling you're going to tell me."

"Five years in federal prison and a one-hundred-thousand-
dollar fine."

"Well, I wouldn't like the prison term, but the fine sounds
like a bargain."

"Get out of here."

Elliot reached for his eurofranc. The cashier snatched it
away.

"I'm confiscating this for the police," she said.

Elliot shrugged. "Fair enough," he replied, taking the shampoo and hair dye. "I'm confiscating this merchandise as evi-
dence of violating the federal Food, Drug, and Cosmetic Act of
1938. Good day."

Elliot took Lorimer's arm, and they walked calmly out.

Lorimer asked, "What was that violation?"

"How should I know? It's a law we discussed in history. But
we'd better get out of here in case she decides to phone the
cops."

"The telephones are out, remember?"

Elliot grinned widely. "Who says we live in an unjust universe?"

After brief discussion, Elliot convinced Lorimer that they
should risk one more stop. He explained that it might be their
last chance for a while: if the government was again switch-

ing over to a new currency, there was the possibility they would close all stores temporarily as they had the previous time.

They stepped into a small Forty-second Street clothing shop, Elliot buying two shirts, briefs, socks, and Levis. Lorimer bought another pair of slacks and a turtleneck. There was no difficulty about eurofrancs with the proprietor of this store, an elderly German man who said he was a boy during the Weimar hyperinflation of 1923. Quite the contrary, there was enthusiastic bargaining and a seeming forgetfulness on the man's part to charge sales tax.

Afterward, to remain off the streets, Elliot and Lorimer slipped into a Forty-second Street movie house (payment by vendies) and watched an action-packed musical drama starring Dharmendra, Lion of the Indian Screen. Dharmendra had evolved, during the past few years, into a cult-film hero.

Elliot never found it necessary to use his hair dye.

At four fifteen, he and Lorimer entered the Rabelais Bookstore; once more it was without customers. Again Al was on the stool behind the counter. He looked up, seeing Elliot, and exclaimed, "You! But I thought—But how—?"

"Slow down, slow down," said Elliot. "You seem surprised to see me."

"Surprised? Kid, you couldn't've flattened me more if you come back from the dead. I thought you'd been busted for sure."

Al noticed Lorimer for the first time.

"It's okay," said Elliot. "She's with me. But why'd you think I was arrested?"

"That's what your old man told me, that your old lady, sister, and you—"

Elliot interrupted, shocked and delighted. "My father's alive? You've seen him? How did he get away from the feds?"

"Eh? I don't know what you're talkin' about," said Al. "Your old man was never busted. I just saw him a couple'a hours ago; I been doin' some legwork for him."

"But why didn't you let the Cadre know?"

"What? But how—"

Elliot twirled his gold ring once forward and once back. Al responded with twice forward and once back on his ring.

"Jesus Christ, I never seen such lousy communications," said Al. "Your old man didn't tell me you were an ally. He just said he wanted his business kept private so I didn't tell them anything."

"He didn't know," said Elliot, "because I'm a brand-new ally. But never mind that now. Where's my father?"

"He's been hidin' out at the New York Hilton all week."

Part Three

I think the most pitiable was a female Ghost.... This one seemed quite unaware of her phantasmal appearance. More than one of the Solid People tried to talk to her, and at first I was quite at a loss to understand her behaviour to them. She appeared to be contorting her all but invisible face and writhing her smokelike body in a quite meaningless fashion. At last I came to the conclusion—incredible as it seemed—that she supposed herself still capable of attracting them and was attempting to do so.   —C.S. LEWIS, *The Great Divorce*

Chapter 19

Shopping parcels notwithstanding, Elliot and Lorimer strode the three-quarter mile to the Hilton in close to fifteen minutes. They stopped at the hotel telephones, calling up the room number Al had given them, Elliot having decided that his father had a better chance of surviving his sudden appearance if given even momentary preparation. Losing his father a third time—especially from mere lack of social grace—was not a prospect he cared to face.

A tired voice answered on the fifth ring. "Yes?"

"Dad?"

A long silence followed. "What room did you want?"

"Dad, this is Ell. I'm calling from the lobby. Al told me where you were."

There was no exclamation, only another long pause. "Your mother and Denise—?"

Elliot hesitated only briefly. "They're not with me, Dad. Uh— I do have a friend with me, though. Is it okay?"

"Bring your friend up with you."

"We'll be right up."

After hanging up, Elliot told Lorimer, "He doesn't sound well."

"Are you sure you want me with you?" she asked.

"Now more than ever. Come on."

In five minutes they were at the room. Elliot almost did not recognize his father. His eyes had bags under them, making him look years older than his actual forty-eight, and though Dr. Vreeland was wearing a jacket, it needed pressing, as did the rest of his clothes. Elliot thought his father looked like a physician who had been serving in a plague. The hotel room did not look much better, the bed unmade, half a dozen coffee cups strewn around. There had been visitors: ashtrays were filled with cigarette butts.

Elliot and Lorimer went in, Dr. Vreeland closing the door. Father and son looked at each other briefly, then, for the first time since Elliot had been a small boy, they hugged each other. Elliot's father said, "You look older."

"You look a little battle-scarred yourself."

Dr. Vreeland smiled slightly, the tension broken.

Elliot took Lorimer's hand and guided her forward. "Dad, this is Lor."

"I'm very honored to meet you, Dr. Vreeland," she said. "I've learned a great deal from your books. Especially *Weimar, 1923*."

Elliot looked at her with surprise but said nothing.

Dr. Vreeland's surprise was equally great. "Your study is economic history? I would have thought you too young to be in graduate school."

"I'm afraid I haven't even started college yet."

"Then it is I who am honored to meet you," said Dr. Vreeland. *"Weimar, 1923* was my doctoral thesis, and I have been repeatedly assured by colleagues even more verbose than myself that it is just about the most thoroughly unreadable piece ever written."

Dr. Vreeland motioned them to sit around a coffee table in the corner, then apologized for the room's condition, explaining that he had not allowed a hotel maid in for two days. "When was the last time you slept?" Elliot asked him.

"Oh, I was catching a short nap when you called up. I was awake most of last night, and I'm expecting a visitor shortly— a business associate."

"Dad, what went wrong? When I got back to the apartment, everyone was gone—the suitcases were gone. I thought you were all waiting at the rendezvous point and was heading there when two cops—FBI, I think—showed up at our apartment looking for *me*. I gave them the slip, but not before I heard them say they had my family. I thought they'd gotten you all."

Dr. Vreeland shook his head. "I left the apartment with the luggage, as planned, wearing a disguise Denise had designed. Very naturalistic—even close up—but I looked like Mephistopheles, a silver-gray wig, false beard, and mustache."

Elliot smiled. "My sister has-always been somewhat melo-dramatic," he explained to Lorimer.

Dr. Vreeland nodded agreement, continuing, "I then drove to the airlines' office on Forty-second Street to pick up our tickets and clearances. By the way, as it turned out, your trip wasn't really necessary. I found time at six to check over with Dave Albaugh."

"Who?" Elliot asked.

"Ah, that's right. I never did tell you Al's name. Dr. Albaugh was one of my brightest graduate students at Columbia. A bril-liant thesis on the differences between Austrian and Chicago School approaches to—oh, never mind. I was back at Park Av-enue and Seventieth Street at six thirty, waiting there the next hour. How is it you didn't see me?"

"I got back to our apartment by ten of six and cut over to Lexington after escaping through the fire exit on my way out. Must've passed within a block of you."

Dr. Vreeland shook his head at the irony. "At seven thirty, after none of you had showed up, I returned up to our apart-ment and encountered two FBI agents. Probably the same two you saw."

Elliot whistled. "Lucky they didn't recognize you—disguised or not."

"I took the offensive," Elliot's father said. "I told them I was a neighbor—a friend of the family's—and wanted to know what exactly they were doing in what was now Cathryn Vreeland's apartment."

"And?"

"They said that they had been assigned to obtain an affida-

vit from your mother assuring the public that I had died naturally. That it was vital for national security that there be no
trouble about me at last Thursday's demonstrations. A good
cover story, and essentially true."

"I saw the article in Sunday's paper," Elliot said. He had a
sudden, horrid thought. "You don't think it took the FBI that
long to—get—the statement from Mom?"

"I don't think so. Your mother is a practical woman. She
would have given the agents the statement they wanted so we
could escape unhindered. Once safely out of the country, we
could say what we liked anyway. Nonetheless, I have since
learned a few data that explain what happened. The two agents
had a second assignment: to take your mother, sister, and you
into custody overnight—just long enough to make certain that
you did not appear at the rally in my stead, but released in
time to attend my funeral that afternoon. What evidently oc-
curred is that sometime early Wednesday evening the Bureau
learned that I was, in fact, alive—and decided to keep your
mother and Denise to blackmail me with. Either I continued
playing dead—or I would never see them again, one way or
another."

"But why wasn't the statement in Thursday morning's papers?"

Dr. Vreeland shrugged. "Confusion about how to counter
my strategy, I suppose. I think I know why the statement was
put in Sunday, though—to let me know that the very proof I
had manufactured to convince the world that I was dead was
to keep me that way. Again, one way or another."

"But there's no way they could do that. All you would have
to do is come forward and accuse them of the kidnaping—"

"To be called an expertly coached impostor, created by the
Administration's enemies."

"But with fingerprints—"

"Supplied by the FBI?" Dr. Vreeland asked. "The point is, by the time I had managed to prove my identity—assuming I had managed to keep out of a solitary-confinement cell or a state insane asylum—the best witnesses—my immediate family— would be dead."

"Not as long as they didn't have *me.*"

"But, you see, until a few minutes ago, I was convinced that they did. Though I don't see how they could have known that on Saturday."

"Well, anyway. What did you do after you left the agents at our apartment?"

"At about eight I drove back to Dave Albaugh's bookstore, where I arranged for him to act as my inquiry agent, then at nine I came here and checked in."

"That's three times in one night that I managed to miss you by *this* much," said Elliot, holding thumb and forefinger half an inch apart.

"What's this?"

Elliot completed his account of that Wednesday evening— his eight-thirty call to the Rabelais Bookstore and inability to reach Phillip Gross—ending up with his checking into the Hilton no more than ninety minutes after his father. "Next morning," he continued, "I went back to the Rabelais and was told that Al had 'gone south for the winter.'"

"Dave left temporary orders to evade questions. By the time you phoned, he had already locked up to begin initial inquiries for me, and he worked at it all night. If I'd had even the slightest inkling that you weren't also in FBI custody, I could have left messages for you at the Rabelais and a dozen other places."

"Well, never mind that now," said Elliot. "What do we—"

Elliot was interrupted by a knock at the door. "My visitor," his father said, rising to get it. "If both of you keep silent, I'll allow you to stay. I'm very near having Cathryn and Denise freed."

Dr. Vreeland opened the door and, even before his visitor entered, said, "Good news, we can proceed at once. You won't have to produce my son. He is—"

"Freeze!"

It was Lorimer's command. She had pulled her .32 caliber silenced automatic from her shoulder bag and was now in a businesslike, two-handed stance, aiming at the newcomer. The visitor, an erect, roughly handsome middle-aged man in a dark suit, only now saw her, and an expression of surprise—much milder than would be expected—appeared on his face. Dr. Vreeland had also frozen upon seeing the gun; his expression was closer to total fluster.

Elliot remained seated. He had been taken off guard at first but he understood when he recognized the visitor as a man he had just recently seen in the news. It was the director of the FBI, Lorimer's father.

"Inside," Lorimer ordered both men. "Keep your hands in the open."

The FBI director entered the room naturally, preceded by Dr. Vreeland; the room door swung shut. Lawrence Powers looked at his daughter and said, "Left foot farther forward, relax your right arm a bit. Haven't I taught you anything, Deanne?"

"You know her, Powers?" Dr. Vreeland asked.

"I never have," he replied, "even though she's my only child." Powers turned to his daughter. "If you're intent on committing patricide, Deanne, then do it. Otherwise, let Dr. Vreeland and me get down to our business."

Lorimer kept the pistol pointed at her father. Elliot told her sharply, "Don't."

She glanced at Elliot sidewise, then answered him tightly, "You wouldn't tell me that if you knew how lethal he is."

"Just *don't*."

Lorimer glanced at Elliot briefly again. Then she handed

over her gun to him.

The FBI director relaxed slightly. Elliot raised the pistol at him once more. "Not yet," he said, his voice shrill.

"Elliot," Dr. Vreeland said, "don't be a fool! He's come here to negotiate."

"I don't have any choice, Dad. Mr. Powers, please. With two fingers and slowly. Toss them onto the bed."

The FBI director shrugged and complied; presently, a service .45 and a .32 identical to Lorimer's lay on the double bed, ammunition for each safely in Elliot's pocket. As a final precaution, Lorimer held the gun on her father another few moments while Elliot frisked him. He found, in a jacket pocket, a shiny metal device the size and shape of a cigarette lighter, with a tiny red button.

Elliot held it up to Lorimer. "A microtransmitter?"

"A telephone key," the FBI director answered him, "for those who know how to use it. Which you don't."

Elliot considered it. Certainly the federal government would not jam telephone service to trusted employees. A device such as this perhaps could override blocks. "True," Elliot replied, pocketing the device.

He waved Powers, Lorimer, and his father over to the chairs around the coffee table, then sat himself on the bed with Lorimer's pistol on his lap. "Now you can talk," he said.

Chapter 20

On Saturday morning, February 24, when the FBI director had finally received from his New York field office the Vreeland "natural causes" affidavit obtained three days earlier, he would have found it quite convenient for Dr. Martin Vreeland and his entire, troublesome family to be out of the country. (He had sent the affidavit by private messenger over to the OPI—better late than never, he reasoned.) The following morning, Sunday, after a blistering twenty minutes in the Oval Office, Lawrence Powers knew that the President of the United States now considered Dr. Vreeland's goodwill far more valuable than his own.

It was not that the President had been piqued by Powers' loss of the master subversives file. As a matter of fact, the President was delighted that with loss of the file went any further possibility of Powers blackmailing him with respect to the President's agorist origins; presidential enemies would have loved the proof of a first congressional race financed with black-market profits and the blood of betrayed business partners. No. Dr. Vreeland himself had been transformed overnight from the President's second-most-dangerous enemy to his first—ironically, also, to his only chance for political survival. "And the survival of your goddamn Holy Bureau, too," the President had added.

What had performed such a feat of political alchemy on Dr. Vreeland was a telephone call, Saturday evening, that the Chancellor of EUCOMTO had made to the President of the United States. The Chancellor's eleven o'clock call from Paris (5 P.M. in Washington) informed the President that in a closed emergency session thirty minutes earlier, EUCOMTO had voted no longer to accept the American New Dollar. The Chancellor explained, as politely as possible under the circumstances, that the council had felt this necessary to protect European interests from the monetary consequences of American political instability.

"Instability?" the President had asked testily. "What do you think, that you're dealing with some banana republic?"

"Mr. President," the Chancellor had replied, "even bananas do not decay as quickly as the value of your currency these past few months."

The vote was final; the announcement would be made in Paris, 10 A.M. Monday,. at the opening of EUCOMTO's trading session.

The President had said, somewhat tentatively, that he assumed it was not merely courtesy that prompted the Chancellor's call.

The Chancellor had replied that he did not intend to mince words. He knew as well as the President what this action would do to the American economy in its current condition; most of Europe had gone through a nearly identical inflationary crisis fifteen years earlier. It meant an imminent collapse of the New Dollar, wildcat strikes not only in industry and the civil service but in the military as well, almost total financial chaos, and widespread civil insurrection that—without the military behind him—the President might never quell.

The President had said to go on.

Very well. A consortium of EUCOMTO banks was willing to lend the United States government enough gold to float a new hard currency. Obviously, a country as large as the United States still had a wealth of material and industrial resources to call upon. What it currently lacked was a stable atmosphere—political and economic—in which to guarantee the repayment of such a loan. Frankly, after the debacle of the last two American monies, European bankers did not trust the United States government not to pay off its debts in inflated currency—and they doubted that the American people were willing to be trusting again, either.

What the Europeans would require was a person to act as a top-level comptroller of the American government, with full, irrevocable power to guarantee to EUCOMTO American fiscal responsibility. Probably a new Cabinet-level post was called for, combining the functions of Treasury Secretary, director of the Office of Management and Budget, chairman of the Council of Economic Advisors, chairman of the Federal Reserve, and a number of lesser offices. Secretary of Economic Recovery, call it.

This person would have to be acceptable both to EUCOMTO and to American popular sentiment—a person in the past widely critical of the policies that had brought about the present Administration's current dilemma. And the only person whom the delegates of EUCOMTO had authorized the Chancellor to suggest was Dr. Martin Vreeland.

The President had paused a very long moment before he had ventured the thought that Dr. Martin Vreeland was dead. The Chancellor replied that if this is what the President had been told, then his own people were lying to him. The Chancellor had said that he himself had been in communication with Dr. Vreeland during the past week, and the latter was perfectly willing to discuss such a proposition with the President—the moment the FBI returned his family to him unharmed. And EUCOMTO was willing to act as go-between for further preliminary negotiations.

The President had said that he would call the Chancellor back the next afternoon, Washington time. After switching off, the President then told his appointments secretary to have Lawrence Powers in his office first thing the next morning.

Powers had not liked the tone in which the President spoke to him that morning. But he also knew that as long as the Administration needed Martin Vreeland's goodwill, and as long as that goodwill rested on getting Vreeland's wife and daughter (and his son, too—if he ever got his hands on him) safely out of Utopia, then Lawrence Powers could not be dealt out of the game.

This hand he was dealing.

Normally, it was unthinkable that two seventeen-year-olds would be privy to any piece of this information. When one of those seventeen-year-olds was holding a gun in a manner suggesting that he knew how to use it, the unthinkable was thought.

Elliot learned, during this discussion, that his father and the Administration had already outlined the basics of a deal; all that remained was to work out the bugs.

Point one. The Administration was ready to release Cathryn and Denise Vreeland to Dr. Vreeland. A major bone of contention had just been broken by Elliot's appearance: Dr. Vreeland had not believed the FBI director when he maintained that he did not have Elliot in custody.

Point two. Dr. Vreeland had agreed never to mention the arrest list, the capture of his wife and daughter, or the real reason for his death charade. Instead, his "death" was to be explained, in a joint statement, as a plan between Dr. Vreeland and the FBI to avoid an assassination plot on Dr. Vreeland by the Revolutionary Agorist Cadre while Dr. Vreeland was working to save the economy. It would be charged that the Cadre—learning of Dr. Vreeland's reformist solution—planned to kill him to disrupt his counterrevolutionary intentions.

Point three. As soon as Cathryn and Denise Vreeland were free, Dr Vreeland was to accompany the FBI director to the White House. Immediately following detailed agreement on the plan, Dr. Vreeland would appear with the President before a joint session of Congress to announce their emergency restoration of a hard-money, unregulated American economy, and to ask for immediate legislation to approve the EUCOMTO loan and Dr. Vreeland's appointment to the new Cabinet post.

This plan granted everything that Dr. Vreeland and Citizens for a Free Society had been demanding all along, and was politically feasible—because ruling American interests were pressed—for all parties.

All parties excepting, naturally, those damned revolutionaries of the Cadre. To Lawrence Powers they were just criminals—terrorists and racketeers—to be "dealt with." He even convinced Elliot that he was sincere in this view. To Dr. Vreeland, the Cadre were not criminals or terrorists but merely anarchists who had bet on revolution and would lose. Under different circumstances—had they advocated minimal rather than no government—Dr. Vreeland said he could even have worked with them, as he had worked with Al.

Lawrence Powers made the connection. "Dr. Vreeland, have you been having dealings with the Cadre?"

"Only one of its allies—clients—who once offered to sponsor me to them. A person of no importance to you whatever. "

The FBI director shrugged.

Elliot asked his father, "You don't care about what happens to the Cadre?"

"Losers always submit to victors' justice," Dr. Vreeland explained. "It is, sadly, a law of history. The best the Cadre can hope for is king's mercy."

"Now, son," Lawrence Powers said to Elliot, "I'm willing to forget this ever happened if you put that gun away and let your father and me proceed with getting your family released. Deanne, you took property of mine. I need it back. We have a lot to discuss when we get home. "

Lorimer lit a cigarette. Elliot could see by Powers's expression that this was an act of defiance. "Do you really think I'd go back with you?"

Powers remained calm. "Deanne, right now you're an outlaw. You've stolen valuable government property. There is no

way that even I can stop the chain of events that will occur if
you do not return it, but if you come home with me and give it
back, I'll see that nothing more comes of this."

Lorimer stood up. "Over your dead body."

Lawrence Powers winced, his daughter's words driving
home her decision more forcibly even than her pulling a gun
had done.

Elliot stood up also. "Dad, the two of us are leaving."

"You can't just leave them here," Lorimer told Elliot. "My
father will have both New York police and his agents after us
in minutes."

"Not without his passe-partout," Elliot answered, holding
up the telephone key, "and not without his ammunition."

"Aren't you forgetting something, Elliot?" Dr. Vreeland said.

Elliot looked over to his father.

"You gave me your word to accept my orders."

Elliot took a deep breath. "Don't hold me to that, now.
Please."

Dr. Vreeland studied his son for a moment. "All right. If you
must go, I won't stop you."

"But, Vreeland," Powers started. "Surely—"

"And you won't, either," Dr. Vreeland went on. "Not if you
want my cooperation."

Lawrence Powers lowered his head, then, a moment later,
raised it again. "I won't stop them."

Suddenly, Elliot remembered. He caught his father's glance
and hitched quickly at his belt. Powers, who was looking at
his daughter, did not notice.

Neither did he understand when, just before Elliot and
Lorimer left the hotel room, Dr. Vreeland told his son:

"It's yours now."

Even with cover of nightfall, Elliot and Lorimer wanted some
fast distance between that Hilton hotel room and themselves;

they settled for a quick march over to the Howard Johnson's Motor Lodge at Eighth Avenue. A hand-lettered sign on the booths proclaimed telephone service temporarily interrupted. Elliot claimed a booth anyway, Lorimer standing just outside to block the view of anyone wondering about the use of dead telephones.

As an experimental control, Elliot inserted a vendy, received a call tone, and punched in the Cadre number. A busy signal, as expected.

He retrieved and reinserted the vendy, got another call tone, then punched in the number as before. This time, however, he held the telephone key up to the handset mouthpiece and just after punching the number pressed its red button: the key emitted a series of audible, multifrequency tones. Nonetheless the substantive result was identical—another busy signal. "Try it before the number," Lorimer suggested.

Vendy, call tone, key tones, number. It worked; the number started ringing. The Cadre relay station answered as before, its tape requesting a recorded message in return. Elliot said, "'Queen takes pawn, Mate,'" then recorded his pay booth's number. "If I don't receive a callback within two minutes," Elliot continued, "I'll call again later with another message." He hung up. "Now we find out how sharp our friends really are."

They were sharp enough; Elliot broke a fingernail answering in the first instant of ringing.

A familiar voice said, "Joseph Rabinowitz?"

"Right," said Elliot. "Is this—?"

"Shut up," Chin cut in. You do recognize my voice, though? Answer only yes or no."

"Yes."

"Good, that saves time. Why didn't you come in as planned?"

"Come in? I don't know what you mean."

"You didn't get our message? We left it at your home early

this afternoon."

"Lor and I haven't been there since noon."

"All right," said Chin. "Listen carefully. There isn't much time. I don't know how you got telephone use—no, don't tell me now—but you've placed yourself in great danger. All permitted calls are relaying through the Federal Telecommunications System. Just stay right where you are. Don't argue. We know where that is—and we'll pick you up."

"How will I know—?"

"The usual way. Don't worry."

Chin hung up.

In under five minutes, a tough-looking giant wearing a pea jacket spotted Elliot and Lorimer near the telephones and flashed a ring banner. Elliot responded, the man approached. "I've got a hack in front. C'mon—and hurry."

The couple grabbed their parcels and followed the man—he said to call him Moose—through the lobby out to a battered wreck of a car standing at the curb, engine running, four-ways flashing. Elliot took one look at it and muttered to Lorimer, "What a piece of junk!"

"She may not look like much," Moose said, unlocking the doors "but she's got a million-dollar motor. I don't have time for old routines, though, so if you please, get in the goddam car."

Moose had slid into the front seat, Lorimer following Elliot into the back, when a pair of headlights pulled up behind. Lorimer first noticed them when the front passenger door opened the inside light revealing a black sedan with four passengers, one man climbing out. "Bureau," she advised Moose quietly, shutting her door to cut off their own light. "I recognize that one getting out. SAC—Special Agent in Charge, I mean—New York field office."

Elliot glanced back into the FBI sedan and turned white. "Get us out of here—fast."

Moose turned on headlights, easing the car into light up-town traffic. Suddenly, the SAC did an about-face back into his car. The sedan pulled out onto Eighth Avenue just behind them.

"They still might not be sure," said Moose.

"They're sure," Elliot said. "I don't know all the pieces yet, but they have to know. *She* saw me."

"What are you—"

"See the woman driving that sedan? I don't know what her real name is, but up until last week I knew her as Mrs. Tobias. She was my current-events teacher at school."

Moose glanced into the rearview mirror, first at the sedan, then at Elliot, and took the microphone from his transceiver, holding it low. "Tau to Omicron. Do you have me?"

"On visual," the radio responded. "We're tailing the sedan behind you."

"You've got it, Omicron. *Federales*, for sure. Lay cover for me at Fifty-fourth. Confirm, please."

"Copy. Burning at Fifty-fourth. Be ready."

Moose dropped his microphone, telling his passengers, "Get down when you hear the radio squawk. But not before."

The car was past Fifty-third Street.

"What are they going to burn?" Lorimer asked.

Moose did not answer; the car was nearing Fifty-fourth.

Suddenly, a green station wagon pulled alongside the FBI sedan. Moose's radio squawked. Elliot and Lorimer dropped their heads in time to see Eighth Avenue lit to daytime bril-liance.

Moose immediately floored the accelerator, fast pulling away from an FBI sedan with a temporarily blinded former school-teacher trying to pull over without crashing. The station wagon continued up Eighth Avenue at normal speed. Moose turned left onto Fifty-fifth Street.

After a few blocks, Moose slowed up a bit. "Magnesium," he finally answered Lorimer.

Chapter 21

Auld Lang Syne smelt of wet plaster and birchwood smoke.

After Moose had bid them good-bye at the West Side Heliport, Elliot and Lorimer were met by the peak-capped, sunglassed pilot of a private helicopter with corporate markings, examined for bugs, blindfolded by helmets as secure as chastity belts, and flown for just under an hour to parts unknown. Elliot, who loved any flying and had never been up in a helicopter, was heartbroken. A stomach-raising descent, the feel of terra firma as rotors slowed to silence, and a brief, sightless walk being pulled along through icy wind brought them inside again.

The odors of plaster and smoke were their first perceptions of this agorist underground, though they appreciated later ones more: the sound of a crackling log fire and its radiant warmth. When their blinders were finally removed, Elliot and Lorimer were inside a furniture-bare terminal, alone facing Chin's smiling face.

As they warmed chilled ears and fingers by the fireplace, Chin explained that though Auld Lang Syne had been built as a replacement for Aurora—scheduled for abandonment by June in any event—the raid had rushed things a bit. Nothing serious, of course, but damnably inconvenient. Personnel from Aurora were moved in and some final installations were being made, but the facility was not yet operational. Though, Chin added cryptically, it might never be necessary to open Auld Lang Syne at all.

Chin went on to give Elliot and Lorimer their first overview of Cadre activities. The Revolutionary Agorist Cadre, he said, comprised three main operating arms.

TacStrike was agorist guerrilla forces, elite veterans of civil wars, revolutions, and "national liberations" throughout the globe. It was nearly impossible to compare it with other forces except by implication. Cadre never fought openly, never claimed victories, and had no television series extolling their exploits. When they died, they died anonymously. Both the United States government and the Cadre had vested interests in keeping it generally unknown how strong the Cadre actually were and how far was their reach.

IntellSec was the agorist entry into the intelligence community, though without the restrictions that supposedly limited the FBI to domestic affairs, the DIA to military, and the CIA to foreign. Chin admitted that his first Cadre employment had been in Hong Kong for IntellSec.

TransComm, both the earliest and largest division, was responsible for providing Cadre allies with a wide range of transportation, courier, and communications services secure from invasion.

The network of Agorist undergrounds was TransComm-operated.

Normal trading-facility security procedures had not yet been set up. There were merely a few extra Cadre guards—armed with M-21's—on duty. Hammers and nails were in use only a few feet away from the rough-hewn security room that Chin led Elliot and Lorimer to. Commandant Welch was in charge.

Lorimer stepped forward. "I owe you an apology for Saturday," she told Welch. "I had no right pulling a gun on you, and was wrong when I called you a statist."

Elliot glanced over to her, shocked.

Welch seemed embarrassed. "Uh—you don't have to do that. I guess I had it coming. I haven't gotten it through my skull yet that I'm not a Chicago cop anymore."

Chin asked Lorimer, "You have no complaint now about this commandant's treatment of you?"

"Well," she said, "I still don't like being told where I can go and who with. But I suppose that's what I'd agreed to."

He faced Elliot. "No complaint."

"Very well." Chin turned to the commandant. "Mr. Welch, I'll withdraw my report and recommend that your fine be re-tuned. But for pity's sake let's not have an incident like this again. There's an old expression never heard anymore: 'The customer is always right.' Public relations demands we act upon it, even though it's abject nonsense."

"I understand. And thank you."

"All right. Let's bury the matter."

Chin produced a photo badge, handing it to Welch, who in-serted it into a desk console and pressed a button twice. A concealed wall panel slid open, revealing a corridor. After re-claiming his badge, Chin led Elliot and Lorimer several hun-dred feet to a steel door. He inserted his badge, and it slid open.

Beyond the door was the yet unfurnished anteroom to a suite of offices. Jack Guerdon was kneeling on the floor, installing a carpet.

Chin cleared his throat. Guerdon looked up, noting their presence and Chin's expression of disapproval. Clapping the dust off his hands, Guerdon stood up. "Now, Major Chin, you know it's the only relaxation I get."

"I wasn't criticizing, sir," Chin replied. "But there are oth-ers who ..."

Guerdon furrowed his brow slightly.

Chin shrugged resignedly. "Perhaps it's time for proper in-troductions?" he offered. Guerdon nodded. "Mr. Vreeland, Ms. Powers, may I present General Jack Guerdon, supreme com-mander of the Cadre's TacStrike forces."

For the second time upon meeting Guerdon, Elliot's eyes widened. "Uh—I thought you ran a construction company ...sir?"

Guerdon grinned. "I do. The general's job is only part time."

"The general is much too modest," said Chin. "First tour of

duty in Vietnam, 1965. Trained for and made the Green Be-
rets, three more tours of Indochinese duty, returning the last
time as a major—brevet, later confirmed. After the war, transferred to the Corps of Engineers, retiring as a full colonel.
Awarded the Purple Heart with bronze cluster, Bronze Star,
Silver Star, Legion of Merit—"

"That's quite enough, Major," Guerdon said in a low voice.

Chin looked sheepish. "Sorry, sir."

Lorimer dimpled slightly. "I hope you won't take this the
wrong way, General," she asked, "but do your men ever call
you Black Jack?"

Guerdon chuckled resonantly. "Some of them, no doubt
...but in the original moniker given to Pershing. Major, what
am I being called lately?"

"Sir?"

"Not the vulgar version, son."

Chin smiled slightly. "Well, I *have* heard one of the men
refer to you as One-Eyed Jack, sir."

Jack Guerdon snorted. "I must be too easy on them."

The four removed into an inner office that Guerdon had
commandeered, the only completely outfitted one in the suite,
and settled comfortably around a conference table with computer stations at each place. Before getting down to business,
Chin provided mugs of too-hot, too-bitter coffee from a stan-
dard-issue military urn.

Chin removed Elliot's telephone key from a pocket (it had
been confiscated by the pilot during the preflight search) and
handed it to Guerdon, who examined it briefly, then placed it
on the table. Elliot stirred dry creamer into his coffee, looking
at the two Cadre officers expectantly. Guerdon asked, "Would
you tell us where you got this?"

"Sure," Elliot said, hooking his thumb toward Lorimer.
"From her father."

Guerdon looked to Lorimer. She nodded.

"You don't have to worry, though," Elliot continued. "He didn't exactly give it to me of his own free will."

"I wouldn't have expected so," said Guerdon. "How did the opportunity arise?"

"It arose when Lor—Deanne, I mean—"

"I prefer Lor," said Lorimer.

"...when Lor got the drop on her father when he walked into my father's hotel room."

Guerdon's eyebrows rose.

Elliot nodded. "It gets rather involved, but what Lor and I agreed before that we should tell you is that my father is going to rise from the grave in a few days. This time as a friend of the Administration. What the Administration gets out of it is gold-backed money courtesy of a loan from EUCOMTO—with my father as the loan's cosignatory. What my father gets out of it are the promises of my mother and sister back ...and the job of U.S. economic czar. What you get out of it is the shaft."

"When you called us," Chin asked, "you were calling to tell us where they are so we could intervene?"

Elliot shook his head. "Not that it makes any difference. They're probably long gone by now."

"Then what were you calling us about?"

"I could ask you the same question."

"Let's not fence," Guerdon said. "I suspect we both want the same thing." He turned to Chin. "Major?"

Chin punched a series of codes into his computer station for a few moments. A document with FBI imprimatur appeared on each of their displays. "This was on the thirty-second roll of microfilm you gave us," he told Lorimer. "Examine it carefully, both of you."

On the display document—titled "For Further Investigation"—were hundreds of names, neatly printed out in alphabetical order. Elliot recognized many as belonging to students and faculty associated with Ansonia Preparatory School and sometimes their families.

Further down on the display was a somewhat shorter list marked "For Immediate Disposition." Among the names he recognized were his own—and those of his parents and sister—Phillip Gross, and his uncle, Benjamin Harper, and Ansonia's headmistress, Dr. Maureen Fischer.

"This is a partial list," Guerdon explained, "of those secretly to be arrested this past weekend and sent to the FBI prison code-named Utopia. Major?" Chin punched a new series in; another document, dated February 24, was displayed. "This one Ms. Powers obviously couldn't have brought us. We intercepted it through normal channels."

The document was a top-secret FBI dispatch to all field offices, informing them that Deanne Powers was to be arrested without warrant and transported to Utopia for interrogation. It was signed by Lawrence Powers.

Guerdon looked at Lorimer sympathetically. She shrugged and replied, "I'm not at all surprised."

"That first arrest list," Elliot asked. "What happened to them?"

"We managed to notify many ...and got them safely underground."

"Phillip Gross and his uncle?"

Guerdon shook his head sadly.

"They're both in Utopia?"

"Phillip is imprisoned there. Morris Gross is dead."

His second-worst fears about Phillip confirmed, Elliot was deeply saddened to have his worst confirmed about the vibrantly alive man who had befriended him. "They killed him?"

"He suicided." Guerdon paused an instant, then added, "As my TacStrike chief of staff, General Gross simply knew too much to allow himself to be captured."

"I see." Elliot stared down at his coffee for a few seconds, then looked up at Chin. "Why bring us here, now? The last you told me, you people were claiming a raid on that prison wasn't possible."

"'Removal not now possible,' I believe the phrase was," said Chin. "I programmed that myself last Saturday. But that was before we'd had a chance to inspect fully the microfilm Lorimer brought us."

Chin typed in still new codes. A moving sequence of documents—floor plans, written descriptions, and schematic diagrams—appeared on their displays. "This was on the forty-third roll of FBI microfilm," he continued. "The complete layout, specifications, codes, and operating procedures of the FBI prison."

"We are now ready to raid Utopia," said Guerdon. "We need the two of you to help us."

Elliot was slightly taken aback. Though he had fantasized the possibility of heroically rescuing his family from that prison, he had never taken the possibility of a chance seriously.

Lorimer took the announcement completely in her stride.

"Us?" asked Elliot. "Sure, I'd love a crack at it, but we're grass green, both of us. You must have better trained—"

"If it were merely a military operation," Guerdon interrupted, "we could have moved against the prison months ago. But a raid-in-force is precisely what Utopia is designed against. We need two people whose names are on the arrest list ...who are not already captured ...or dead ...who are allied with us ...who are not carrying secrets we can't afford to lose ...and who are unlikely to crack under fire."

"It all sounds great," Elliot said, "except for that last part."

"Don't run yourself down, son. I have seen psychometric profiles for each of you. Do you help us, or not?"

Elliot thought about it. Even if his mother and sister were to be freed anyway—a point he did not trust Powers on at all, and his main reason for calling the Cadre—Phillip was in there. Phillip, who, when asked for help, had simply said, "Of course.

What do you want me to do?"

The decision took only split seconds. "Sure," he answered offhandedly.

"Ms. Powers?"

"When do we leave?"

Elliot smiled at her and took her hand.

"Get a quick bite to eat," said Guerdon. "We'll be out of here the next hour."

In a private moment in the anteroom, while Chin and Guerdon were still conferring, Elliot asked Lorimer why she had volunteered. "Three reasons," she explained. "One. If I decide to make a career with the Cadre, this will look good on my application. Two. I can't think of anything that would make my father burn more. And three. I'm going along to make certain you don't get your ass shot off."

The commissary was not completely finished, but the kitchen was operational. While there were no allies other than Elliot and Lorimer in Auld Lang Syne, work crews and Cadre had almost filled the dining area. But at the moment they were not there only for the food.

Almost everyone in Auld Lang Syne at the time, approaching a hundred people—some with dinners, some without—was seated facing six temporary wallscreens.

The first screen displayed a computer-generated map of the United States, with almost ten thousand dotted red lights on it, clustering around densely populated areas but covering almost every human habitation in the country. Each dot represented a radio or television station.

The other five wallscreens were each carrying the signal of a major American network—television broadcasts (subject to censorship) of normal prime-time programming. Highest rated of the five programs, sandwiched in between a serial drama and a situation comedy, was *We, the Jury,* a program combining elements of an actual court trial, a game show, and an actual execution. (The rumors that producers had signed convicts willing to be executed for spinoffs were almost completely untrue.)

The commissary was humming with whispered conversations and a sense of rising expectancy as Chin led Elliot and Lorimer in. "What's going on?" Lorimer asked Chin.

"You'll see in a few minutes."

The three were near the end of the food line when a huge cheer went up in the chamber. Dozens of red lights on the electronic map had suddenly turned green, the lights changing like dominoes falling into each other, or as if the map was following the progress of an accelerated hurricane dancing across the country. Within a minute, there was not a single red light on the screen.

A second cheer went up as one of the wallscreens interrupted its broadcast—a symphony concert—with a notice reading: "MBS SPECIAL NEWS BULLETIN."

News? thought Elliot. *But no news was being permitted ...*

A man near the screens turned up the accompanying sound, "—rupt our regularly scheduled programming to bring you a special news bulletin. Reporting to you from our Mutual News Headquarters in New York is Phyllis Breskin."

A middle-aged but still-handsome newswoman appeared on the screen. "Good evening," she said in the industry's standard Oxonian tones. "Since early this morning, MBS News has been off the air in accordance with the official procedures of the Emergency Broadcast System. Our network, however, was instructed not to broadcast an Emergency Action Notification.

"A few moments ago, our Broadcast Command Center in New York received an official release allowing us to resume our normal news operations. We therefore bring you this special update ..."

Several of the other wallscreens were now carrying the news

bulletins of other networks.

A newsman on the Pacifica System was saying, "...morning at its trading session in Paris, the EUCOMTO announced that, in a closed session Saturday evening, it was voted to stop accepting the American New Dollar in exchange for eurofrancs. In making the announcement, Chancellor Deak stated that this had been necessary to protect European consumers from the effects of American political instability. He used, as an example, last Thursday's New York demonstration by Citizens for a Free Society that ended in a riot."

Elliot, in progress with his food tray to a table, barely managed to avoid spilling minestrone as he heard the results of the riot he had accidentally started. A history lesson from his junior year flashed through his mind, as he remembered the young Gavrilo Princip who, by the assassination of Archduke Francis Ferdinand and his consort, started the chain of events that had led to the First World War.

Another network newsman: "...prompt move to prevent this news from reaching the American public, where it was feared an immediate monetary collapse would trigger financial chaos, at 4:10 A.M. E.T., the President of the United States declared a state of national emergency, ordering all mass communications media to cease ..."

"The Emergency Broadcast System never sent out a release, did it?" Elliot asked Chin.

Chin shook his head.

"Wasn't that obvious?" Lorimer asked Elliot. "Everyone here was *waiting* for this."

They found an unoccupied table. "Then how did you manage—?" Elliot asked, setting down his tray.

Chin smiled. "Believe me," he replied, "you're not the only

person asking that at the moment."

Chapter 22

It was ice-cold on Mount Greylock.

A white-satin bedspread covered the mountainside, a star-broken midnight canopy over it. The air was crisp and clear. The snow—powder dry—made soft protests as four snowmobiles, one after another, left their tracks.

Three hours later, in the long-abandoned tourist lodge at the summit of the highest peak in Massachusetts, twenty six men and women of the Revolutionary Agorist Cadre, and two of their younger allies, were gathered around a roaring fireplace. The windows were opaqued. Next to a map stand—Elliot, Lorimer, and Chin on his other side—General "One-Eyed Jack" Guerdon briefed his Cadre.

It was the fifth and final briefing of a series started with contingency plans months ago that had weathered rehearsals, computer analyses, more rehearsals, and had only been given a final go-ahead hours before. The arrival of Lorimer's microfilm and the couple made the attempt on Utopia a tactically acceptable risk. Strategically, what had started as Contingency Plan D and was now Operation Bastille Day was considered by human mind and computer fail-operational.

"I know we've been through this three times already tonight," said Guerdon, "but this last time I'm hoping for any damn thing that pops into your head, no matter how silly. It may make the crucial difference for the prisoners.

"Designations again. Infiltration group—Major Chin, Elliot Vreeland, Deanne Powers—is *Judas Goat*. Hang-glider commandos—Captain Donizetti's group—is *Winged Victory*. The command 'copter—Captain Billis and crew, myself—is *Guardian Angel*. Transport helioplane—Captain McCarter and crew,

Dr. Schiller's medical team—is *Friendly Sky*. Laser technician group remaining on Greylock's summit—Lieutenant Evers in charge—is *Bigmouth*.

"At 0545 *Winged Victory* will drop near the relay tower, knock it out, then surround Command Shack Gamma. After receiving confirmation of this, *Judas Goat* will depart Nobody's Road, at 0600 breaching Utopia by SOP for entering prisoners. At signal from *Judas Goat*, *Winged Victory* will assault Gamma simultaneous to Goat's taking of Command Suite Beta—neutralizing all officers. *Judas Goat* will now establish microwave relay with *Guardian Angel*, then proceed to break into Monitor Booth Alpha. *Guardian Angel* will laser their video back here to *Bigmouth* for redundancy taping and relay to major television outlets as soon as the raid is completed." Guerdon turned to the laser technicians. "You should have their signal by 0615."

The technicians—Lieutenant Betty Evers, Sergeants Compton and Jones—nodded.

Guerdon spoke at large again. "When *Guardian Angel* receives video confirmation that Utopia is secure, we will immediately inform *Friendly Sky*, which will be guided down to Hoosac Lake by *Winged Victory*. "

Near the back, the helioplane commander raised his hand. "Captain McCarter?"

"I'm still concerned about landing conditions, General. The tank had a better weight distribution than I do, and I'm worried about that thirty inches of compacted snow on the ice."

"What's your fully passengered gross weight and landing estimates?" Guerdon asked.

"It's still forty tons. With the skis, we'll need a strip of about a thousand feet to land, twice that for takeoff."

"All right, don't risk a landing until you have to. I'll delay my signal until the last minute." Guerdon went on to the group: "With *Guardian Angel*'s assistance, *Judas Goat* will guide the two hundred prisoners to the landing strip, where *Friendly Sky* will treat any shock cases and airlift them out. With luck, we should all be heading home by 0720."

Guerdon recognized Lieutenant Evers, the twenty-four-year-old chief of the laser technicians. "General, wouldn't it be simpler to establish line-of-sight microwave relay between *Judas Goat* and my group? *Guardian Angel* could monitor on audio only."

Guerdon flipped back several maps and pointed to the stand. "This is Savage Hill. It's directly between Greylock and Utopia. To get line-of-sight we need two hundred feet of elevation, that Utopia doesn't have. *Guardian Angel* will provide that elevation—and then some."

"Distance of the transmission is about five and a half miles, General," she said.

"So?"

"We don't need laser for that distance, sir. Difficult to pinpoint when we could simply track modulated infrared from your engines."

"No doubt. But if *Bigmouth* is put out of action, I want the option of relaying my tapes directly through *O'Neill One*. Remember, from a strategic standpoint, our secondary tactical objective is more important than our primary tactical objective. We need to establish publicly that such prisons exist, and execute a graphic demonstration that we Cadre are not the terrorists and racketeers Lawrence Powers has been accusing us of being."

Another hand was raised, belonging to one of the commandos. "Lieutenant LaRue?"

"Can we still be damn sure about no ground resistance, sir? None?"

"Unless our data is out of date, we can be sure. The on-call garrison is a good three miles away, and knows nothing except to respond to an alarm. Once you put the relay tower out, we don't have to worry about reinforcements since Gamma and Beta both use it. Remember the theory behind this lockup. The security system relies almost totally on a few trusted men and electronic control. Mr. Powers wants as few witnesses to his private concentration camp as possible. The very design specifications for his fail-safe verify this. He would rather see all the prisoners—and his own men—in ashes than have proof of this get out. And, ultimately, this provides us with the Achilles' heel we need. Anything else?"

Hearing no response, Guerdon waited several moments before saying, "Very well. See if you can catch an hour's sleep. Dismissed."

At 0545 hours, 27 February, a lone, unmarked police sedan turned right at a red brick church house about six miles north of Pittsfield, Massachusetts, climbed a hill, and turned left onto a desolate country road, snow-plowed into banks on each side. A young Chinese man wearing a gray suit with tie drove the vehicle; behind him, separated by a soundproof glass partition, were a young man and woman handcuffed to each other.

It was while they were standing still at Nobody's Road that Elliot asked Lorimer if she were scared.

Lorimer nodded. "You?"

"Shitless."

Lorimer smiled slightly. "I wish I had a cigarette."

"Listen, Lor," Elliot went on. "This is probably a crazy time to get into it, this late and everything, but you're not going to have any—well—problems in there, are you?"

Lorimer regarded him scornfully. "You should know me better than that by now. I'm not the fainting type. Why, are you?"

"No, you're not following me." Elliot adjusted his handcuff to chafe slightly less. "Let me try it from another angle. If I hadn't stopped you, would you really have shot your father?"

"Oh, yes," she said simply.

"Because he drove your mother to suicide?"

She shook her head. "Look, you think you can become cold-blooded when you have to. You're an amateur compared to me, and it's a trait I inherited from my father. How did he seem to you, in the hotel?"

"Controlled. Cool. Rational."

"He's *always* that way," Lorimer said, "and he always has been. I can't ever remember seeing him furious or ecstatic or releasing any strong emotion."

"Now I'm not following you."

"Don't you know any psychology at all? A human being can't bottle up emotions forever. There has to be an outlet. My father's is pretty much out of Machiavelli. He likes to give orders. When a man like this gets his hands on a police organization, the only sensible thing to do is kill him before he kills others."

"And what's your outlet?" Elliot asked her.

Lorimer did not answer.

Chin received a radio signal that *Winged Victory* had knocked out the communications relay tower and was now positioned around Gamma.

A few minutes later, the sedan pulled up to the electrified main entrance gate to Utopia.

A quarter-century earlier, in more prosperous times, the property had been a private summer camp where urban children—mostly from New York—escaped their nagging parents for eight weeks of hiking, boating, and ceramic-ashtray making; in winter, it had been a ski camp. And it was on these grounds, over two holiday weekends one fall and one spring, that small groups of libertarian investors had gathered to discuss a then-infant science of countereconomics.

Now, through an eminent domain that had taken the property from later owners for a federal highway that was never built, the property had passed into less innocent hands.

A video camera mounted on a post at the entrance swiveled around to examine the car. Chin flashed headlights twice, then once again. The gate opened for him by remote control.

Chin drove onto the grounds.

Utopia was built upon a sweeping landscape now covered with picture-postcard snowdrifts, here and there illuminated by floodlights. Video cameras followed the sedan's progress as it drove a snowdozed dirt road that wound, eventually, down to Hoosac Lake. A half-mile short of the lake, close to a large, flat-topped building semi-underground on a hill, Chin pulled into a small parking lot and cut his engine.

Taking an attache case and a drawn pistol with him, Chin opened the sedan's rear door, leading his two prisoners out by their handcuffs. He began pulling them toward the fifty-yard-distant building, in their last few seconds of privacy telling them quietly, "Remember, once you're in the holding cell, you must remain absolutely still—no matter what—until I get you. Don't even think about moving."

Elliot and Lorimer nodded.

At the entrance to the main building, an armored door peeking out of the hillside, Chin held his gun to Elliot's back while a video camera watched them. A few moments later, over an intercom, a voice asked:

"Who sent you?"

"The Old Boys," Chin replied

"What did they tell you?"

"To keep my palms dry."

The armored door slid open, and the three went in.

The vestibule to utopia comprised a jail cell reminiscent of a small town—two chain-held cots on the wall, a seatless toilet—a door (to the Monitor Booth) that would have looked at home on a vault, and (on the side opposite the cell) the suite belonging to the officer on duty. This last was the only part of the prison interior not usually monitored by the Alpha Booth;

instead it was cross-monitored with Command Shack Gamma, where five other officers—one on duty, four off—were stationed. The two on-duty monitor guards had a similar relief arrangement, but there was no cross-monitoring with the off-duty guard shack, a half-mile away.

It was precisely 6 A.M. by a digital wall clock when the OD left his office to meet Chin and the two prisoners in the vestibule. He was a stocky man in his forties, well muscled with a slight potbelly, and looked exactly like an accountant, which is how he had started his career. The OD extended his hand to Chin in greeting. "I don't think we've met," he said. "Sydney Westbrook, late of the Boston office."

"Special Agent Chin, just out of San Francisco." Chin tucked his attaché case under his left arm, transferred his pistol left, and with his right took the proffered hand briefly. "Where do you want them?"

"Who are they?"

"This one is Elliot Vreeland and—"

"Vreeland?" Westbrook interrupted. "Jesus, I wish the chief would make up his mind. They just came for the other two not an hour ago."

Startled, Elliot involuntarily asked, "My mother and sister aren't here?"

"Shut up, punk," Chin cut in, "you'll speak when you're spoken to!"

Westbrook shrugged, telling Chin, "Don't wear yourself out. He'll find out anyway." He told Elliot, "That's right." Powers had kept his bargain. Westbrook looked over to Lorimer. "Who's this one?"

"The chief's little girl."

"Really? I saw her on the list but didn't think the chief would have the heart to go through with it. But you know the chief. He won't allow anyone to imply that he would show favoritism."

"Yeah. Like I said, where do you want them?"

"Right over here, for a few minutes."

Westbrook led Chin and his prisoners over to the holding cell and unlocked it. Chin removed Elliot and Lorimer's handcuffs. Lorimer went in immediately, but Elliot, precued, hesitated a moment. Chin shoved him in roughly—a little too roughly, more than Elliot was expecting. He fell against the cot. Lorimer looked as if she was about to spit at Chin, but held back. Elliot was never entirely sure that she was only acting.

As the OD locked the couple in, Chin asked him, "You wouldn't have some coffee on, would you? I'm half frozen."

"Sure," he replied, "A fresh pot in my office." Westbrook motioned Chin to follow: Chin holstered his gun and did. "So," the OD continued, "how's Frisco this time of year?"

"Please," said Chin, sounding genuinely annoyed. "That's SF—if you must shorten it—not Frisco. A hell of a lot warmer than here, I'll tell you."

Continuing to make meaningful comments about the weather, Chin followed Westbrook into his office while Elliot and Lorimer took positions on their cots, leaning back against the wall in a relaxed, braced manner, suggesting dead tiredness to anyone watching on video. Neither one moved a muscle.

As soon as Chin and Westbrook were completely inside the OD's office and monitored only by the other command center, Chin dropped his attaché case onto a chair, triggered a pulse from a small transmitter connected to its spring latches, and removed a plasti-sealed handkerchief from the case. Westbrook was heading to the coffee maker. Chin delayed a few moments until he saw, on the OD's cross monitor to Command Shack Gamma, that the other officers were swooning from the knockout gas Donizetti and his men were introducing there. Then, breaking the seal with one hand, Chin silently edged up on the OD's back and grabbed him with the other hand, pressing the chloroform-soaked handkerchief against Westbrook's mouth and nose. The OD struggled, trying to shout, but Chin outclassed him. After some seconds, Westbrook, unconscious, stopped struggling. Beta was secured.

Donizetti showed his head in the command monitor a half-minute later and gave Chin a thumbs-up; Chin returned the thumb signal with an "Okay" sign. Gamma was neutralized, also. Donizetti and his commandos would now head down to the lake to guide *Friendly Sky* in.

The most critical stage of Bastille Day had been completed.

Chapter 23

There were two rooms in the OD's suite: a front office and a rear one.

The first contained the OD's monitors—both the cross-monitor to the remote Command Shack and the slave monitors that would reproduce whatever the Alpha monitors were looking at. There was still another monitor that would allow the OD to look in on the Alpha guards themselves.

The second office contained a large freezer and a semiautomatic microwave food-processing system, and was sometimes used by officers and monitor guards as a break room when off shift. Chin dragged Westbrook to this later office, positioned him on a couch, and carefully injected a sleeping serum into his arm. Westbrook would be out of action for at least the next twelve hours and would have a considerable amount of explaining to do, as would his counterparts, when he awakened.

Chin returned to the front office.

On the Alpha-room monitor, Chin could see two men seated in a small booth, themselves facing several rows of video screens. These were the two guards whom Chin soon had to knock out; not only did they control the Sequence Prime destruct mechanism—which they were under orders to implement as soon as prison security was irrevocably threatened—but they also controlled knockout gas, concussion grenades, and remote-control machine guns at frequent points inside and outside the compound. But at the moment, they were out of Chin's reach, sealed into their booth separated from the vestibule by the vaultlike door. The only way into the prisoner compound was through a similar door, also in the guard booth.

On the other monitors, Chin could see views of the prisoner

compound, Elliot and Lorimer's cell, the vestibule, and various points outside. By their nature as repeaters, Chin knew that the guards were not watching the OD's office. It was obvious that juniors were not invited—except in an emergency—to oversee the actions of their senior. Even in areas of security, rank had its privileges.

The guards, however, were not Chin's immediate concern.

Placing his attaché case on the OD's desk, Chin removed his computer, tools to strip shielded cable, a set of his own cables with alligator clips at one end and receptor plugs at the other, a pair of goggles, and a hand laser torch. Plugging the laser into a wall socket and putting on the goggles, Chin began work cutting into the wall below the monitors.

Five minutes later he had exposed what he had expected to find: shielded cables to the video circuits. Putting the laser aside, Chin placed his computer on a chair next to the wall, stripped cables inside the wall, and attached alligator clips to the cables, plugging the receptors into his computer.

He checked the Alpha monitor: one guard lit a cigarette while the other played solitaire. Nothing happened on any of their screens. Chin could see Elliot and Lorimer, still motionless in their cell.

Typing a short program into the computer, Chin started its disc into motion, as he did, there was a brief flicker on several of the screens. The guards did not notice. Chin sighed. This was the only visible signal that might have given him away.

The computer would now, automatically, decode the digital information taken from the video system, record two minutes from each camera, then replay that signal to the guards' monitors infinitely with three areas excepted: from those cameras monitoring the prison compound, the inactive camera in the OD's office, and cameras monitoring the roadside front gate. Chin was now free to operate throughout the vestibule and outside its door, but this was not the only video trick he had to perform.

Returning to his attaché case, Chin removed two microwave transmitters. The first was a short-range job with a small horn antenna; the other—a small dish on telescoping tripod—would pick up the first transmitter's signal and relay it.

Chin plugged the first transmitter into his computer, aimed the horn to the main door, and flipped the device on; a small red light showed it operating. Stepping into the back office again briefly, Chin fetched keys from the unconscious OD, returning front. He picked up the dish transmitter and continued through to the vestibule where he crossed to Elliot and Lorimer's cell.

The digital clock now read 6:13.

As he approached the two, Chin placed a finger to his lips and motioned them to the cell door. After he unlocked the cell, they briefly joined him in the vestibule. Chin whispered, "You have seventeen minutes."

Lorimer nodded. Elliot whispered, "Good luck." Chin pointed them to the OD's suite, patted each of them on the shoulder, then departed with his transmitter to the front exit.

Inside the front office, on the Alpha monitor, Elliot and Lorimer glanced at the guards in their booth, still—respectively—smoking and playing solitaire as, on another monitor, a videotaped Elliot and Lorimer still sat motionless in their cell.

As he watched a cycle of various views within the prisoner compound, Elliot reflected that if one could tell an architect by his work, then Lawrence Powers emerged with a cynical sense of humor, for his utopia—by a purely dictionary definition—met the major qualifications.

Within bedroom accommodations fully up to commercial standards—and those of the Cadre themselves—two hundred anarchists and three babies slept under pale blue lighting. Each room had a full private bath, internal telephone, holosonic cassette machine, and videodisc player. The furnishings were luxurious, to say the least.

With video monitors seeing into all corners, there was no reason to restrict the prisoners' privacy from each other, nor their access to each other when they tired of privacy. Internal facilities included a library, game rooms, lounges, gymnasium, and medical center. (Several physicians were in residence as prisoners themselves.) The only external restriction was imposed by the timing of meals. The prisoners' food was commercial frozen dinners, microwave heated by the OD's food processor and passed in by the officer three times daily through an exchange chute from the front office; empties and refuse were passed out by the prisoners through the same chute. In addition, hot and cold beverages and cold snacks were available twenty-four hours a day in the dining area.

Responsibility for the prisoners' well-being, beyond the facilities provided, was left totally up to them alone. There was no physical contact between prisoners and keepers, not for punishment or any other reason, but the existence of the guards gave the prisoners an outside enemy on whom they could vent their frustrations with impunity. Neither did the prisoners have any knowledge of Sequence Prime or very much reason to fear for their safety. They knew that if Lawrence Powers had wanted them dead, they would have been dead already.

Internal sanitation, comfort, rules, recreation, and dispute settlement were left to the devices of the prisoners. Within the confines of their world—literally in the middle of "no place"—they were free to live their lives as best they were able, propertyless, with the necessities of living provided free of charge.

Assuming one placed no price on personal liberty.

Elliot tried to locate Phillip on the monitor, but the cycle went by without catching a glimpse of him. But, he reflected, all this meant was that he liked to bury himself among pillow and blankets. Lorimer nudged Elliot silently, pointing to the

Alpha monitor where the guard was playing solitaire.

He had just played out.

High above Utopia, *Guardian Angel* hovered.

Up front was the helicopter pilot, Captain Billis, Jack Guerdon beside him; in the rear were Sergeant Stokowski and the communications technician, Sergeant David Workman. All wore headsets.

It was at 0616 that Sergeant Workman reported he had *Judas Goat*'s signal on his monitor. "Roger," Guerdon replied over headset. "Start recording and set up your laser link with *Bigmouth*."

On the Mount Greylock summit, outside the abandoned television relay station, a temporary laser antenna had been erected. Inside, a few minutes after Guerdon's order to Workman, Sergeant Compton reported to his lieutenant that they, too, were now receiving the signal. "Record and put it on monitor, Compton." Evers replied. "Jones," she continued, "let *Guardian Angel* know we have it."

A few seconds later, the first image appeared on the Greylock monitor. It was the digitized signal from the video cameras in Utopia, showing, when each signal was decoded, various views of the main prisoner compound, the prisoners asleep in a pale, blue light.... "Guardian Angel, a perfect signal," Sergeant Jones transmitted.

On the helicopter, Workman relayed this information to Guerdon. "Stokowski," he ordered in response, "let them know downstairs that we're punching it through."

Below, in the cold, twilight air, Chin stood just outside the armored front door to the main building, the microwave transmitter—tripod legs extended, dish facing the sky—beside him. Chin blew briefly onto his hands and rubbed them together. Suddenly, three pinpoint flashes appeared above him. Blowing on his hands one last time, Chin returned inside.

It was 6:23.

The monitor guards, themselves monitored, even now sat facing inactive screens as Elliot and Lorimer, quite active in the OD's rear office, prepared two hundred breakfasts: plastic trays filled with farina, scrambled eggs with bacon strips, a sweet roll, and a sealed container with non-melting straw that held coffee. It was a frozen breakfast sold—when in stock—at any supermarket.

Chin popped into the office, gave his two allies a thumbs-up, then grabbed the laser torch and his attaché case, returning to the vestibule.

Twenty-five at a time, Lorimer removed trays from the deep freeze with the OD's gloves, inserted them into the processor, and set a two-minute heating cycle. At the other end of the cycle, Elliot removed trays bearable to the touch—but just—with naked hands, quickly stacking them onto a wheeled breakfast cart with multileveled shelves.

At 6:30, when Elliot and Lorimer rolled the breakfast cart into the front office, Chin was at work on the door from the vestibule to the monitor booth, using the torch to etch a pattern on one section of the door, and molding plastic explosive into it. Elliot and Lorimer began stacking breakfast trays into the transfer chute, delivering them to the dining area where they would be available—still warm, for the next forty-five minutes—to prisoners who chose to rise for breakfast.

Suddenly, the door to the monitor booth opened, knocking Chin sprawling forward. Elliot and Lorimer froze behind the door. "Hey, Sid," a voice called out. "How about letting Mike and me get a couple of those breakfast—" And one of the guards stuck his head out of the door, spotting Chin and his handiwork. "Oh, shit," he said.

Though both men were startled, each started reaching for his gun. Chin did not quite make it. The FBI man drew his pistol first and fired twice at Chin, hitting him in the abdomen and right arm.

Chin went down. The guard slammed the armored door shut.

Elliot and Lorimer rushed over to Chin. The interoffice telephone began buzzing in the OD's office. "Try to stall them," Chin told Elliot hoarsely. "I need just five more minutes. Lorimer, I'll need your hands."

"What about your—" Elliot started.

"Don't argue," Chin rasped. "Move. *Move!*"

Elliot ran off to the office. Unknown to him, Chin quickly lapsed into unconsciousness.

Nervously, Elliot picked up the telephone, watching his antagonists on the Alpha monitor. The other monitors still showed the entire complex—including the vestibule—inactive. They had not seen Lorimer or him. The monitor still showed them motionless in their cell. Elliot decided to try a desperate gambit. "Yeah?" he said hoarsely.

"Sid?" the guard asked. "What the hell is going on out there? Are you all right? Who is that I shot?"

"Eh? I'm fine," Elliot said. "It must be your imagination. The entire board's quiet. Go back to sleep."

"But I *shot* someone out there. He started drawing a gun."

"You opened up the door? Asleep or not, that's strictly against orders."

This last, being of course the guards' first standing order, was true, but Elliot's heart sank, as he saw from expressions the two guards exchanged, that they knew something was wrong. "All right, who the hell is this?" the guard asked.

Elliot tried to bluff it through. "This is Westbrook. What is this? If you think you can try pushing this off on me—"

But the gambit had failed. Queen takes pawn, Mate ...only this time he was the pawn. Elliot looked to the repeater monitors and saw himself, standing with the telephone, in the OD's office. The guards could see him now. "I asked who this is," the guard asked once more.

Elliot took a deep breath and tried to think what to do. He knew that a wrong answer could mean the lives of the prisoners, Lorimer, Phillip, Chin ...himself. He knew that at any moment knockout gas or a concussion grenade could be used on him by the guards.

He wished his father were here to advise him.

"You've got five seconds to answer me," the guard said. "Five ...four ...three—"

"All right, okay," Elliot stopped him. "I'm from the Revolutionary Agorist Cadre."

"How many of you are here? Where are the rest?"

They were still seeing taped replays on their monitors, still blind to what Lorimer was up to in the vestibule. *Stall*, Chin had said.

"There's no one else," Elliot replied. "Only us two."

"You're lying."

The guard waited until it became apparent that Elliot would not answer, then said, "Boy, you just made the worst mistake of your life." He turned to the other guard. "Implement Sequence Prime." He started to hang up.

"Wait!" Elliot shouted, panic triggering an idea.

"Make it quick," the guard said.

"A straight offer," Elliot said. "You can both walk out of here rich men." Elliot started spinning out words quickly, extemporizing. "I have twelve Mexican fifty-peso gold pieces for each of you. That's about forty-six hundred eurofrancs apiece. With the blues not being accepted by EUCOMTO anymore, gold will be the only money around. It'll be the only thing, practically, that people will accept."

The guard maintained a cold silence as Elliot wondered whether his on-the-spot economics lesson had hit home.

"What's the matter?" Elliot asked. "You don't believe me? I have the gold right here, in my belt."

"Yeah," the guard said. "I suppose I believe you. I know you brownies are loaded."

"Then you'll do business?"

"Nah," said the guard. "The chief wouldn't like that."

"The chief?" Elliot said. "Your chief doesn't care whether you live or die. There's something about the setup here they never told you. If you kill the prisoners, you're dead, too. Sequence Prime destroys this entire complex. Powers doesn't want any witnesses."

"Don't you think we already know that?" the FBI man said softly.

"Then why kill yourself? Is Powers holding your families somewhere? Are you serving a life sentence?"

"You still don't understand, do you?" the guard said. "The chief would be in this booth himself, if he had the choice. Loyalty works both ways, kid. It works both ways."

The guard named Mike turned to the first guard and said, "We're cut off. The Command Shack is out, and so is the alarm."

The guard pondered this a moment, then smiled at Elliot. "Listen, boy, this place is going up in about two minutes, and there's nothing you can do about it. But you can do me a favor and be a real hero at the same time."

Perhaps this was the stall he had been looking for, Elliot considered. "What is it?"

"There are three babies inside the compound. Cute little tykes, remind me of my own at that age. I'll feel a whole lot better if you take them out with you. And don't try blackmailing me. If you don't take them out with you, they'll die too."

Elliot thought then, and would always think, that this twisted attempt at humanitarianism was the final, logical result of all he had seen in the past few days. A man—trapped in an execution chamber by virtue of loyalty to a false idol—was willing to kill himself and two hundred others for what he believed. His willingness to protect the future only underscored his ghastly mistake.

But he would have to open the door. "I'll take them," Elliot said.

"Okay, I'll wake the parents."

"No, don't do that," Elliot said. "You'll panic them."

He had reached a decision. His own loyalty was demanding a payment.

"You have a prisoner in there named Phillip Gross, right?"

After a moment, the guard replied. "I'll get him."

Elliot returned to the Monitor Room door and found Lorimer stroking Chin's forehead. "He's unconscious?"

"He's dead," Lorimer said.

Elliot knelt down, checking Chin's neck for a pulse. There was none. Elliot felt cold and sick. He tried pulling himself together. "Did you get anywhere on the door?"

Lorimer shook her head. "It has to be in a certain pattern or it won't work. He died before he could tell me."

"Maybe we could try anyway?"

"It'll explode this whole place if it's tampered with," Lorimer said emotionlessly.

Elliot tried slowing down his heart. There went his surprise advantage. He bent down and picked up Chin's gun. "Okay, Lor, listen to me. That door is going to open in a minute. More than anything else, I've got to try getting a friend of mine out. But there are three babies in there, and you've got to get them out of here with you. Can you do that for me?"

"But—"

"Can you do that for me?"

Lorimer stood up and nodded. "I *do* love you, Ell," she said.

Elliot stroked her hair. "I love you, too."

He did not say that he would not expect to live long enough to enjoy it.

Elliot stood, poised for his assault. He stood there well over a minute. Then he realized that he would not get his chance.

The door would not have to open.

An alarm on the exchange chute to the compound signaled refuse on its way out. Elliot listened dumbly for a few moments, then understood what it meant.

The first infant was already in it, crying its eyes out. All that's left is the future, he thought, handing the three-month-old boy to Lorimer. The second was a girl, perhaps only five weeks old. The third, another boy, looked to be six months old.

Elliot carrying two, Lorimer holding the third, they made a dash out to the now daylit parking lot where *Guardian Angel* spotted Lorimer's waving and began alighting to meet them.

Utopia began exploding. No, that wasn't right, Elliot thought. It had never existed and never would.

They were far enough away not to be hit by the blast; the explosion was efficient, its rubble being contained in the immediate area.

As Stokowski and Workman took them aboard, Guerdon shouted into the radio for *Friendly Sky* to abort, repeat, *abort* its landing.

The last survivor in, *Guardian Angel* mournfully rose into the morning sky.

It was a few minutes later, as Sergeant Workman replayed Utopia's final transmission on his monitor, that Elliot saw Phillip Gross spelling out "laissez faire" with his ring after he had passed the last infant out.

Chapter 24

The revolution came the same day.

At a little past noon, they were awakened by persistent knocking at their apartment door. After a few series of knocks, a sleep-deprived Elliot unwrapped himself from Lorimer, pulled on undershorts, and managed to pad into the living room. He opened the door a crack. It was Mr. Ferrer with a sealed envelope for him. Elliot took the envelope and thanked him.

Elliot broke the seal. Inside was a note reading:

> Merce Rampart wishes to meet both of you today.
> Please be at my Ansonia office at 2 P.M. Important.
> *Benjamin Harper*

Elliot read the note twice, then returned to his bedroom and handed it to Lorimer.

An hour later, showered and dressed, Elliot and Lorimer ate a quick brunch while, on television, a pair of network anchors brought them up to date. The EUCOMTO rejection of the New Dollar—fueled by news of the Utopia prison atrocity—had brought about the feared chaos.

The Federal Reserve Board had ordered all affiliated banks closed "for duration of the emergency." The Securities and Exchange Commission had suspended all trading—also "for the duration." The FBI had been disbanded, and the President had ordered the arrest of Lawrence Powers. The President, backed up by Congress, had declared martial law.

It mattered little. Lawrence Powers had gone into hiding. Three quarters of enlisted military personnel from all services had begun wildcat strikes, two thirds of the strikers deserting bases and heading home. The Revolutionary Agorist Cadre had surfaced, with no effective opposition. The objective conditions for a revolution having arisen, the revolution was in progress.

For some, business went on as usual. A filmed commercial came up on the television. The same TV-series actor and actress whom Elliot had seen in a public-service announcement were now dressed in conservative attire walking staidly through a bank, camera dollying backward before them. Elgar's fourth "Pomp and Circumstance" march began rising slowly in the background.

The actor began sincerely, "Fellow Americans. We at AnarchoBank are doing everything we can to end this emergency. Most of you right now are without any money; no money means no trade, no business."

"Our immediate aim," said the actress, "is to get a new money *into your hands*. Within forty-eight hours, we will have fully operational offices serving major financial and employment centers to begin exchanging AnarchoBank gold coins and gold certificates for a number of readily available commodities, and making short-term loans to those who cannot—"

"We'd better leave the dishes till we get back," Lorimer said to Elliot.

"The First Anarchist Bank and Trust Company," concluded the actor. "A New Dawn in Banking."

Yellow cabs were back on the street, though not from any fleet Elliot recognized. He flagged down a Checker with a black flag painted on the door, displaying in white letters the logo for "BLACK BANNER TAXI." On the door, under the logo, was a rate chart:

AU 2 cents 1ST 1/3 MILE
AU 1 cent EACH 1/3 mile thereafter
AU 1 cent = € .10, 1 US SILVER DIME, 1 QUARTER VENDY

After Lorimer had climbed in, Elliot followed, telling the driver to take them to Ansonia's address. The driver flipped on his meter, then picked up the microphone. "This is Black Banner Twenty-Eight. Copy me, Egotripper?"

"Dispatch to Twenty-Eight. Proceed."

"In transit to Park West and Seventieth."

"Affirmative, two-eight. Pick up at that location available."

"I'll take it, Egotripper. Bee-Bee Twenty-Eight, off."

"Sounds like a good day," Lorimer commented to the driver.

"Nonstop," he replied. "I've been up to Park West and Seventieth half a dozen times already today, Well, might as well enjoy it while it lasts."

"Why shouldn't it last?"

"Are you kiddin'? Within a week every fleet in this city'll be back on the street. Price wars you wouldn't believe. Then when the subways and busses are movin' again—"

"Who'll run them?" Elliot asked. "The city's bankrupt. There's no official money. Who'll pay the transit workers?"

"Don't ask me," the cabbie said. "All I know is there's a fortune in equipment just layin' around, and someone's damn well gonna make some money with it."

Between Sixty-ninth and Seventieth streets—the block containing Ansonia Preparatory School—a contingent of New York City Police, still in blue uniforms but now with red Cadre "SECURITY" brassards on their arms, had barricaded off traffic to that part of Central Park West.

It was not a homesteading action, but merely a temporary expedient. Along the street, in line waiting to get underground and out of the cold, were about two thousand persons late of the United States military. Most were—as full-page newspaper advertisements had specified—in uniforms with insignia removed, personal weapons slung over their shoulders, duffel bags at their feet. They had been promised a union-approved contract, billet and food provided, with weekly payment in gold at rates—depending on position—between four grams a week for infantry and fifteen grams for an engineer.

There were no taxes or other deductions.

On a flagpole extending over the street from number ninety was hanging a black flag. It was raised to half-staff.

Elliot and Lorimer passed by a now-unbricked entrance to the perpetually unfinished Central Park Shuttle, bypassing the long military lineup going downstairs past a new sign.

AURORA COMMAND
REVOLUTIONARY AGORIST CADRE

The two were challenged at the school entrance by armed Cadre guards. Elliot told them who they were and that they were expected. One guard checked an appointment clipboard and nodded. They were fifteen minutes early.

The couple was unceremoniously escorted into the assistant headmaster's office on the first floor, but the assistant headmaster was not occupying it. They took seats, Elliot rising a few minutes later when Mr. Harper entered. "Elliot …Ms. Powers," he said, shaking hands with each of them. "We have a few minutes to chat before our meeting is scheduled to begin."

Elliot and Harper sat down. Elliot nodded slowly and said, "So Ansonia was a Cadre front all along."

Harper allowed himself a half-smile. "Well, a front in the sense that it concealed Cadre lodgings above the school with Aurora built into the subway tunnel below, but Ansonia itself never propagandized agorist ideas. That would have been the last thing we wanted. Any front—to be effective—must misdirect attention away from its actual purpose. So we maintained a policy of ideological neutrality. At most we refrained from the standard 'civic' indoctrinations. And, perhaps, we placed a little more emphasis than is usual on logic and clear definition—always dangerous heresies, wouldn't you agree?"

Elliot nodded.

"As a policy, also, Dr. Fischer and I did not hire any Cadre allies as teachers. Even without a party line, there is always too much danger of the kind of intellectual inbreeding fatal to academic inquiry. So, at most we tried to weed out those professing a clearly statist philosophy. We were not always successful."

"Mrs. Tobias," said Elliot.

Harper nodded. "Not that she gave us any clues at first. I doubt that when the FBI assigned her here that they even suspected our Cadre affiliation."

"Then why—?"

"It was *you* she was to watch."

Elliot stared at Harper intensely.

"She was assigned to get information about your family that the Administration could use against your father."

"The microfilm?" Lorimer asked.

Harper nodded. "In the course of her work here," he continued, "with little bits of information put together from her reports, the FBI slowly stumbled across the conclusion that Ansonia was a Cadre front."

"But if they knew about Ansonia, why didn't they raid it?"

"You forget, you yourself were evacuated from Aurora during the course of that raid—this past Saturday at 6:30 P.M., exactly as planned in the microfile Ms. Powers gave us on Friday. Mrs. Tobias's resignation last Wednesday morning—using as an excuse a difference over policy—was the FBI withdrawing its operative preparatory to the raid."

"Why did they wait until the weekend?"

"For the simple reason that Aurora did not operate during the week. There would have been no traders to arrest."

Harper turned to Lorimer. "Ansonia will be resuming classes next Monday," he told her. "We can have your records transferred here if you'd like to graduate with us."

Lorimer looked startled. "Why, I'd love to."

"Good," said Harper. "I'll expect both of you Monday, 9 A.M., sharp."

He looked at his watch and stood up. "Shall we proceed?"

Chapter 25

Mr. Harper led the couple to a door Elliot had always thought concealed a janitor's closet. Inserting a key, Harper opened it. There was an elevator waiting. It was the same elevator Elliot and Lorimer had been experimenting with when challenged by the Cadre Guard. They got on, Mr. Harper inserting his key into the control panel.

Lorimer had Elliot look at the panel. "Wait a second," he said. "This elevator shows ten floors, and this building only *has* five stories."

Mr. Harper smiled slightly.

Elliot looked indignant. "'Maximum security floors' indeed."

When the elevator doors opened again, they were on Aurora's Terminal floor, Harper explaining that this was in the building's cellar. He led the two to the security alcove, inserted a photo badge into a console on the empty desk, and pressed a key twice. A concealed wall panel in the alcove slid open, revealing a second corridor. Elliot-realized that aside from a reversal of direction, the plan was the same used in Auld Lang Syne.

After reclaiming his badge, Harper preceded Elliot and Lorimer the several hundred feet to the steel door. Upon the insertion of his badge, it slid open. Elliot looked past the threshold. "Dad?"

Beyond the door was an anteroom to a suite of offices, identical to the one in Auld Lang Syne, only completely outfitted. Inside were Dr. Vreeland, lack Guerdon, and Ansonia's headmistress, Dr. Fischer.

Elliot saw only his father at first. "How did you get here?" he asked. "Are Mom and Denise with you? They weren't in Utopia."

Dr. Vreeland looked at his son gravely. "They're not with me. I don't know where they are.... aside from my assumption that they're still in federal custody. As for how I got here, Dave Albaugh acted as go-between."

"But why—?"

Harper touched Elliot on the arm. "That's what this is all about."

Elliot looked over, seeing Jack Guerdon and Dr. Fischer. He exchanged nods with Guerdon first and said, "When is the service?"

"Nine thirty, tomorrow morning," Guerdon replied. "You'll be expected to say the eulogy for Phillip, as I will for Chin."

Elliot nodded, then turned to his headmistress. "Hello, Dr. Fischer," he said wearily.

"Elliot," she replied gently. "I'm sorry the circumstances of this meeting are no happier than our last." She turned to Lorimer. "I assume you are Ms. Powers?"

Lorimer nodded.

"Well, everyone's present," Harper said. "About time we got down to business?"

"I thought Merce Rampart was supposed to be here?" asked Elliot.

Dr. Fischer led them into the conference room. "Merce Rampart is already here," she said, taking a chair at the head of the table. "Shall we begin?"

After pouring coffee for those who wished it, then for herself, Dr. Merce Rampart turned to Elliot's father. "Dr. Vreeland, you are the only person ever allowed into Aurora without first allying with us. Everyone else at this conference is contractually obligated to keep our secrets. But when you leave here, we will have no way—short of methods we never employ—to assure your silence. Yet we *must* be assured of it if we are freely to discuss our possible cooperation."

"You have my word," said Dr. Vreeland. "What I hear will not leave this room."

"Thank you, Professor. As I believe you already know, we will be holding our first news conference in about an hour. This will be the first time our organization has ever formally gone on the record. We wish you to attend us, announcing at the conference that your supposed death was a defense against the government aggression toward your family, and that your wife and daughter were kidnaped by them to blackmail you into cooperation."

"You know the risk I took in coming here," Dr. Vreeland said, tapping his fingertips together professorially. "It is likely that simply through my refusal to follow through on my agreement with the Administration, I have already condemned my wife and daughter to death. Must I make certain of it by publicly embracing you as well?"

"If that is how you feel, Dr. Vreeland, then why—?"

"You know why," Dr. Vreeland said angrily. "I cannot honor a contract with murderers ...no matter what the personal cost."

"I would have expected no less of you," Dr. Rampart answered. "But the cost may not include your wife's and daughter's lives. In a kidnaping, whether or not the ransom is paid—in this case your cooperation being the ransom—has little to do with the kidnapers' future behavior, which is based on their view of *current* self-interest."

Lorimer nodded. "Bureau statistics show almost the same chance for a kidnaper to release the victim whether or not the ransom is paid."

"And you believe," said Dr. Vreeland, "that publicly revealing the kidnaping would shift the Administration's interest to releasing Cathryn and Denise?"

"Yes," said Dr. Rampart, "if there's any modicum of sense left in their camp. This Administration is in the most precarious political balance of any Administration in this country's history. While it is wholly unlikely that they can save their rule, they might wish to save their necks. There is a spirit of bloodlust in the air."

"Dr. Vreeland," said Guerdon, "this revolution has been, all along, a war of propaganda and counterpropaganda. The Utopia prison atrocity has just given the government the worst publicity possible. Whichever group—or groups—offers the public order in such chaotic times will gain support—perhaps the critical balance. I doubt the government will wish to appear lawless at this time. In the past, the government has preferred to bargain with the barrel of a gun. With the military strikes, they have just lost the gun. If they now wish to seek the support of human beings, they will now have to utilize the civilized methods of human beings. Whatever chances your wife and daughter have at this point rest with our ability to pressure the rulers into realizing this. And whatever else we may think of them, I do not think they are less analytical than we are."

"Even if this is so," Dr. Vreeland said, "why should I appear at your press conference, aligning myself with your Cadre?"

"May I be so impolite as to point out," Harper said, "that through your son's association with this school you are already—in the Administration's view—aligned with the Cadre. The difference between a radical and a revolutionary is an esoteric one at best, understood by those involved in the factionalism and few others. Don't expect the differences in our philosophy to be understood by Lawrence Powers. So long as you advocated reforming the State, instead of advocating abolition as we do, you were tolerated—perhaps even considered counterrevolutionary. In fact, without your support of the moderates in Citizens for a Free Society, the government might have fallen months ago. Remain silent, and the Administration will fall,anyway ...perhaps deciding to take your wife and daughter with them as revenge. Publicly align yourself with us and accuse them of the kidnaping ...and they might back down."

At that moment, the door slid open, a gray-haired man in Cadre uniform entering. Elliot recognized him as the man on the screen who had announced the G-raid alert. He walked up to Merce Rampart and said, "We found two."

She nodded. "May I introduce our chief of security, Ron Daylutan? Dr. Vreeland, his son Elliot, and Ms. Powers."

"Pleased to meet you."

"Descriptions?" Dr. Rampart asked.

"Very professional work. Would have blown half the building. My guess is that it's a present from the CIA—their style of work."

"Any possibility there are more?"

Daylutan shook his head. "I'll bet my life on it."

She smiled. "You have."

"Uh—I'll check again."

The security chief left, the door sliding shut after him.

"Damned terrorists," said Guerdon. "I don't know what this country's coming to."

"I don't understand," said Elliot. "Why would the CIA bother at this point? Aren't they as finished as the rest of the government? No tax revenues, no official currency to pay employees with."

Mr. Harper shook his head. "I'm afraid we're not so lucky. They are very much alive and will remain so for quite some time, though somewhat less potent, of course. In addition to private business interests both here and abroad that the CIA owns, no doubt it will continue receiving backing from those most dependent on the State for privileges."

Merce Rampart turned to Dr. Vreeland. "Well, Professor?"

Dr. Vreeland drummed on the table. "I must know where you stand," he said, "what your plans are. Are you writing a constitution? Do you plan to hold general elections? Will you impose a 'temporary benevolent dictatorship'?—oh, a most anarchistic one, I'm sure. What's your foreign policy?"

"It is the policy of the Revolutionary Agorist Cadre to deal with foreigners," said Dr. Rampart. "Assuming they also wish to deal with us. Your other questions assume we are—or intend to become—a government. But we are agorists: propertarian anarchists. Our prosperity to date has come by following agoric principles and we envision even further prosperity when agoric principles are generally adopted. Why would we abandon market principles we have found efficacious in favor of hegemonic ones that have led society after society into ruin?"

"I have no wish to argue elementary libertarianism," Dr. Vreeland said. "Whether or not you call yourselves a government, you are a large organization of ideological components, raising a military, and seem to have a natural monopoly on the prime functions traditionally performed by governments."

"I'm afraid our board of directors is nowhere as optimistic on that point as you. We expect *severe* competition—immediately from agencies such as the CIA, later from protection syndicates, independent militias, trade unions, and counterrevolutionary movements, each wielding as much force as we will."

"And what will keep these groups from each other's throats?"

"What keeps anything as innately aggressive as governments from warring, except a realistic appraisal for conquest and the eventual realization by the ruling parties—usually fragmented—that they have more to gain by peaceful commerce than expensive wars? Why play negative sum games when positive sum games are available? But even when these groups do fight, I doubt it will prove as chaotic and damaging as the wars states engage in. Without territorial identification, war levies, and conscription, masses of people will no longer be dragged into every single conflict. We can afford nothing less in this age of potential total holocaust."

"Yes," said Dr. Vreeland, "but how long will your Cadre—this agora of yours—survive?"

Merce Rampart sat back in her chair and smiled.

"I haven't the faintest idea," she said.

Chapter 26

As soon as Dr. Merce Rampart and Dr. Martin Vreeland, closely followed by Jack Guerdon and Elliot, entered the school cafeteria—now jammed to capacity with media representatives—the photo strobes began flashing rapidly. The four took seats at a front table facing the reporters, television cameras, and hot lights. Neither the hot lights nor photo strobes were technologically necessary for good color reproduction; they were present just so everyone would know the event was important. Considerable rumbling arose as they entered—Dr. Vreeland's face was as well known as Dr. Rampart's was not—and Merce Rampart began waiting for strobes and noise to die down, so she could begin.

Mr. Harper guided Lorimer to a seat in the rear, an empty seat in front of it so she could see well. After a brief discussion with Jack Guerdon, Merce Rampart had suggested Lorimer keep a low profile in case she wished to apply for Cadre status.

"Good afternoon, ladies and gentlemen," Dr. Rampart started, her voice echoing widely. "Welcome to the premier news conference of the Revolutionary Agorist Cadre. I am chairwoman of the Cadre Board of Directors, Merce Rampart."

More rumbling and photo-flashing began as widely held opinions about Merce Rampart's identity were shattered.

"If I may present those seated with me," she continued over the din, "on my right is General Jack Guerdon, commander of our guerrilla forces ...and I was able to see that you recognized a man we thought was no longer with us, on my left the esteemed Nobel laureate in economics, Dr. Martin Vreeland, with his son Elliot."

There was heavy applause.

"If you don't mind," she continued, "I'll pass on making a statement pertaining to our goals and ideas, referring you to the folios handed out earlier. After statements from General Guerdon, Dr. Vreeland, and Elliot, I'll open up the conference to questions. General?"

Guerdon cleared his throat. "I'll start with our intelligence on the military situation in the nation. You already know the extent of the military strikes that have been occurring since reveille this morning. What you may not know—since there has been no official confirmation of the rumors—is that simultaneous to these strikes, officers at about 20 percent of military installations—almost half at Marine bases—began immediate executions of strikers."

It was almost a minute before it was quiet enough for Guerdon to continue.

"Reports have it," he went on, "that 68 percent of officers pressing such executions have themselves been assassinated, the remainder successfully fleeing. Strikers are in present control of about a fifth of military communications, ground and air transport, naval vessels, ammunition dumps, and fuel depots, another two fifths being sabotaged. The computer networks of the Tactical Air Command are hopelessly fouled. The Strategic Air Command seems unique in that its personnel have refused to leave the government without nuclear retaliatory capability.

"Sympathy strikes paralyze the National Guards in thirty-three states. Few reservists have successfully been called up. And the most remarkable thing about all this revolutionary activity," said Guerdon, "is that we've had nothing to do with it."

There was considerable mixed reaction—noise, angry shouts, and laughter—from the press.

"Now," Guerdon continued. "Our own operations and plans. First. We claim credit for the release of communications facilities last night, liberating them from statist control. Second. Cadre forces are available to communities and businesses needing help against looting and vandalism. Third. The Revolutionary Agorist Cadre became a nuclear power today, having expended four one-hundred-kiloton devices."

Audible shock waves coursed throughout the hall.

"Only one," Guerdon continued loudly, "was detonated, however—and that was in the Pacific, harmlessly, so that it could be recorded that we have nuclear capability. The other three devices were mere shells, without plutonium, planted at remote military sites within Russia, China, and EUCOMTO, where civilian populations would have had time to protect themselves. We provided detailed directions on these devices' locations to those powers' security agencies, and presumably they have found them by now.

"We will not, of course, reveal how the devices were planted. But I think the point is clear. I am *not* expecting any foreign military intervention into American affairs."

Guerdon paused to let the full impact sink in, then went on. "Domestically, we are recruiting only a small standing army— fifty-five thousand total—the first ten thousand being Cadre already called up. Forty-five thousand enlisted personnel—the cream from all services—will be hired into our three Cadre branches. Our forces will, of course, engage only in defensive actions in favor of our clients and their property. Anyone with complaints against us need only file an action with the arbiters we are submitted to.

"Most importantly, we will offer a quarter-year salary—up front, in gold—to any serviceman or woman who signs with us as a reservist, then goes home. This policy will solve half a dozen problems at once, not the least of which is need for quick injection of noninflationary capital into the economy."

Guerdon nodded to the chairwoman that he was finished.

"Thank you, General," she said. "Dr. Vreeland?"

Dr. Vreeland gazed out into the audience. "Most of you," he began, "have no doubt been wondering why I am sitting here if I am dead." He waited out the laughter. "My first duty is to explain to you that my death charade was part of a cover story I planted hoping to arrange an escape out of the country for my family.

"I had a report that the Vreeland name was on the FBI list of persons to be secretly arrested. It was my intention to avoid those arrests." Dr. Vreeland took a breath. "My plan did not work. My wife and daughter were imprisoned in the death-trap raided this morning, by luck or divinity taken out just before the extermination. But I still do not know where they are ...or even if they are still alive ...only that they have not been returned to me. I'll let you draw your own conclusions as to the motives of their kidnapers.

"Let me close by saying that at the time of the arrests, neither myself nor any member of my family considered ourselves subversive. I would say, at this juncture, that I would now embrace that term heartily."

After shattering applause had died out, Dr. Rampart turned to Elliot.

Elliot started to speak, found his throat dry, and sipped a glass of water. "Uh—there's not much I can add to that," he finally got out. "You've all seen the tapes of what happened in Cheshire. I was there. I lost my best friend there, a student from this school." He paused to swallow. "His last act was handing out three infants, the only prisoners who survived. All I can say is, it's up to you the sort of world they have when they grow up. If this is a revolution, then let's not fuck it all up this time." He paused a moment. "Uh—I guess that's all."

"Thank you, Elliot," Dr. Rampart said. "I'll open the floor to questions at this time." She recognized Frieda Sandwell, who identified herself as representing ABC Television. "Dr. Rampart, inasmuch as you seem at this moment to have won your revolution, would you tell us what your Cadre intends doing with millions of civil servants?"

"We don't intend 'doing' anything with or to them," she replied. "Though I regard government workers as being among the worst victims of statism—forced by destruction of market opportunities into sterile bureaucracies—the Cadre have limited resources and cannot restore overnight an economy it took the government a century to destroy. Nonetheless, we can suggest an approach by which government workers can solve their own unemployment problems."

Sarcastically, Freida Sandwell asked, "Would you enlighten us?"

"Surely," Dr. Rampart answered, taking the question at face value. "With the exception of those government workers who perform no marketable service—tax collectors, regulators, and so on—we are urging them to declare their agencies independent from the government, and to organize themselves into free workers' syndicates. Shares of stock could be issued to employees and pensioners by whatever method seems fair, and the resultant joint-stock companies could then hire professional managers to place the operation on a profitable footing. I can envision this for postal workers, municipal services, libraries, universities, and public schools, et cetera. As for those civil servants whose jobs are unmarketable, I suggest that most have skills in accounting, administration, computers, law, and so forth, that readily could be adapted to market demand. There's the idea. It's now up to those with the necessary interests to use it or come up with something better."

Dr. Rampart recognized Carey Sanford of *Liberation*. "Is the Revolutionary Agorist Cadre a friend or foe of the corporate capitalists?"

"A foe. Agorist theory recognizes that most of the evils attributed to capitalism were true of it—but caused by its historic role of private industry working hand in hand with governments. An extreme form of this is fascism."

"But isn't the Cadre itself a corporation?"

"Oh, my, no. We are a joint-stock company with all profits automatically reinvested to maximize operating capital—a deferred-profit venture, if you will. Corporations are creatures of the State, created by it and having two privileges that protect them from market pressures. First, corporate liability for damages to others is automatically limited by fiat; and second, responsibility is shifted away from individuals to a fictional entity. Each of the Cadre assumes full responsibility for his or her actions, though liabilities may be insured." She saw another hand. "Yes?"

"Alan O'Neill, *Time* magazine. Who'll run the highways?"

"Why ask me? I suggest you take it up with the American Automobile Association."

Amidst laughter, Dr. Rampart recognized Halpern Sinclair of the *Washington Post.* "Dr. Vreeland. Does your presence here today indicate merely an alliance-of-convenience with the Revolutionary Agorist Cadre, or have you secretly been a member all along?"

"Neither one, Mr. Sinclair. Though I only came into direct contact with the Cadre this morning, I would not be sitting here were I not in agreement with the principles I have been assured the Cadre stand for."

As Dr. Rampart recognized Waldo Hinckle of *US News & World Report*, who asked Guerdon a question regarding the costs of his military expansion, a reporter who had arrived late sat down on the seat in front of Lorimer, blocking her vision. She began looking around for another seat, and found one in the second row, getting up to head for it.

Guerdon filled a pipe with nonaromatic burley. "If all two million U.S. military personnel signed on with us as reservists," he said, "it would cost us a bit over one and a half billion eurofrancs this year. Add in another half billion for TacStrike—

the other divisions are financially self-supporting—and our military budget this year would be somewhere around two billion eurofrancs, taking into account ..."

A dark-suited photographer with long hair and a beard moved from his third row seat out to the aisle.

"I hadn't realized your organization was that well-heeled," Waldo Hinckle said.

"Mr. Hinckle," said Dr. Rampart, "Cadre allies did well over sixty billion eurofrancs' worth of business last year, of which the Cadre took in just under seven billion eurofrancs in payment for services rendered. I would think that the approximately 12 percent overhead we represent—"

The bearded photographer reached into his camera, pulling out a .32 caliber automatic pistol.

Lorimer was up to the fourth row.

The gunman raised his automatic pistol toward Dr. Vreeland.

Elliot was the first to see the photographer raise the gun at his father. Everything that happened in the next second and a half seemed in slow motion to him. He reached into his holster and pulled out his own pistol. It did not seem that he, himself, was doing it.

"—was not unreasonable, considering—" Dr. Rampart saw the gunman and stopped short.

The assassin now had his automatic pistol pointed directly at Dr. Vreeland. He shouted, "Death to traitors!"

Elliot now had his revolver out but did not have it fully raised.

Lorimer walked into the assassin's visual range—not in front of the gun, but simply within his range of peripheral sight. The assassin noticed her and seemed thrown off stride, distracted by her presence.

Dr. Vreeland looked up, seeing that it was his own chest the gun was being aimed at.

Somebody screamed.

Elliot had automatically gone into a precisely correct Weaver stance—left foot slightly forward, right hand—its arm slightly bent—aiming the gun, left hand holding the right fist to steady it ...and during that mere instant when the assassin was distracted by Lorimer, Elliot fired once at his head.

The .38 bullet from Elliot's revolver struck the assassin's head, knocking off a wig and tearing a chunk out of his skull. A final muscle spasm knocked him back against the chairs, and from there to the aisle floor.

The image of his daughter standing over him was the last thing the assassin saw before he died.

There were more screams. Several people threw themselves onto the floor.

Lorimer averted her eyes, then started pushing her way through the crowd to Elliot. Along the way, she casually grabbed the camera of a news photographer who had snapped a picture of the body, and smashed it to the floor.

Cadre guards were now pulling reporters and other photographers away from the dead man—blood seeping slowly from his head—cordoning off the death scene.

Lorimer finally reached Elliot, who was standing at the table, being steadied by Dr. Rampart and his father. With a strange tone in her voice that he had not heard before, she told him:

"Thank you. You've just killed my father."

Elliot gasped.

Then Lorimer reeled a moment and began throwing up onto the floor.

Chapter 27

The President of the United States ordered all political prisoners released immediately.

At eight thirty the morning of Friday, March 2, Elliot Vreeland, his father, and Lorimer stood at a plate-glass observation window at Metropolis Airport, New York, watching a domestic-route jetliner taxiing into its berth.

The President's order had been delayed three days, awaiting the resumption of traffic routing by former government personnel who had formed the North American Air Controllers Syndicate.

A few minutes later, passengers began deplaning through a portable tunnel. Among the passengers were Cathryn and Denise Vreeland.

Son and father saw mother and sister at about the same time they saw them also, and the two parties began rushing toward each other, waving madly.

Hugging. Kissing. More hugging.

"Are you all right? Did they hurt you?"

"We're fine, just fine."

Everybody was just fine.

Elliot introduced Lorimer to his mother and sister. He had a feeling that Lorimer and Denise would get along splendidly.

The five of them began walking through the long, fluorescent tunnel to the parking lot, exchanging information and stories.

"No, they didn't hurt us at all," Mrs. Vreeland explained. "We were given VIP treatment from the moment the FBI arrested us ..."

"It was so horrible when we heard about what happened Tuesday," Denise said. "We'd all gotten very close, even just being together a few days. I got a chance to know your friend Phillip, and there was this one girl my own age, Barbara ..."

"I had a pretty bad time of it right after the press conference," Lorimer told Mrs. Vreeland in answer to her question. "Dr. Taylor put me on sedatives until Wednesday night..."

The family emerged from the passenger terminal and walked to Dr. Vreeland's rented car.

"...have engaged me as a liaison between the Cadre and EUCOMTO," Dr. Vreeland said, as they drove back to Manhattan. "EUCOMTO announced recognition of the Cadre as the 'legitimate government of the United States,' and Dr. Rampart refused the status. We'd set it up in advance, of course, as a publicity device ..."

"Lor and I signed a lease on our apartment until school is out," Elliot told his mother. "Dr. Fischer wants Lor to get her bachelor's before she signs on with IntellSec, and if there's a college that's put a pre-law program back together by September, then I ..."

"...CNN outbid the other news services for my sketches of the prison," Cathryn Vreeland said.

"...the police and firefighters unions ordered their members to remain on the job after the arson at Rockefeller Center," Dr. Vreeland explained. "NoState Insurance is working out the retainer so it can start offering its general protection policies..."

They drove past Pennsylvania Station.

On a tall flagpole, two banners flew at half staff, commemorating the dead of Utopia. Elliot pointed them out as they passed.

Each had a revolutionary tradition. Throughout their histories, both had been misunderstood, misrepresented and betrayed.

The black flag was raised again this day.

Once more flew the revolutionary "Don't Tread on Me" flag.

A yellow taxi passed Dr. Vreeland, the *tzigane* honking his horn and swearing.

Things were looking up for a change.

On Monday, Elliot turned in his thousand words to Mr. Harper, detailing why the capitalist system had, after all, been self-destructing.

Lorimer turned in two thousand words in rebuttal.

The End

Are We *Alongside Night*?
A Talk the Los Angeles Libertarian Supper Club
December 10, 1979
by J. Neil Schulman

An abridged version of this talk appeared as an afterword in the 1982 Ace paperback edition.—JNS

Let me take you back six years, and three thousand miles east, to the time and place seeds were planted that eventually grew into this skinny little book. For all intents and purposes, you are looking at those six years, when I hold this book up. You are looking at an obsession worse than heroin to a heroin dependent, worse than a dragon to a knight, worse than Hamlet's ghost to Hamlet, Junior. You've all heard C.S. Lewis's line—or some variant of it—about the man who lives for others: you can tell the others by their hunted look. That's the look I got used to from close friends whenever I saw them during the writing of this book...they knew I had another two-and-a-half pages written...and they weren't getting away alive without reading them.

If this presentation seems a little lopsided at times, it's because those six years are all crowded together, screaming to get out, and I'm not in any condition to adjudicate among them.

So what you're getting is a sort of recollective pot luck.

Okay. We're back six years, in late 1973, when I was a young libertarian writer living in New York City. Nixon was president, the economy was going to the dogs, and a fellow named Harry Browne was going around telling people that Armageddon was on the way—you'd better have your gold, silver, and Swiss Francs—and a well-stocked bunker to put them in.

We were going to have a wheelbarrow hyperinflation, by

God—even Murray Rothbard said so—and anyone who didn't prepare for it was just plain dense. Just look at the price of gold...Jesus, over a hundred dollars an ounce! You can't count on the banks—even the safety deposit boxes; they might be confiscated by the government—and there was going to be rampant strikes, looting, vandalism, food riots, New York would be a disaster area...

And damned if that didn't sound like a pretty good idea for a story.

Something like this. A guy who's read Harry Browne and has made all the right preparations is somehow still stuck in New York City when the *merde* hits the *ventilateur*...pardon my French. This guy has his fallout shelter—excuse me, *retreat*—all stocked and ready to go in upper New York State, but he keeps his gold, silver, and Swiss Francs in a private lock box on the other side of Manhattan. And before he can go to his retreat, he has to fight his way across town, fending off youth gangs, and food rioters, and traffic is jammed, he can't get a cabdriver to take his money, the buses are on strike...and I figured the idea was worth about four thousand words and a couple of hundred inflated bucks.

I made some notes on the story but never got excited enough about the idea to bother writing it.

We jump ahead, now, to February, 1974, when Harry Browne's new book, *You Can Profit From a Monetary Crisis*, is being released by Macmillan. I manage to wangle myself an invitation to a press luncheon Macmillan is putting on in honor of Browne, and during the question period I ask Browne something related to Austrian economics...I haven't the slightest idea what it was. Anyway, at the end of the luncheon, Browne's literary agent, Oscar Collier, comes up to me, hands me his card, and tells me that if I ever decide to do a book, to get in touch with him... and the next thing I know, I'm pitching him the idea I had as a short story and telling him that I'm thinking of doing a novel. By the end of the conversation, we had a sort of understanding that I'd write three chapters and an outline, and he'd give a shot at selling it if they were any good.

Well, about a month later, I gave him the chapters and outline, and Oscar agreed to submit them...which is a statement about Oscar's ability to develop writers, because looking back now at those first attempted chapters...they're terrible. Overwritten, wordy, overly detailed. But I should also mention, on Oscar's behalf, that the chapters that open my novel are the same chapters...after judicious editing that Oscar prompted me into.

Oscar made a number of submissions of the chapters and outline, which was to be a novel called *Ice And Ashes*. I later changed the title when a science fiction novel named *Ice And Iron* by Wilson Tucker was released. But not to digress too much, here, the project didn't sell, so I put the project aside for a while, at that point five chapters and an outline.

Then Sam started spreading the gospel of countereconomics, as we all headed into the depression of 1974—as Murray Rothbard calls it—and I organized a couple of fairly successful conferences on countereconomics called CounterCon. For those of you who have read the novel already, you'll understand when I mention that these conferences were held at Camp Mohawk, in the Berkshires, a children's and ski camp owned by relatives of mine, and that Camp Mohawk is the location of the Utopia prison in my story.

And to jump ahead once again, we're now up to summer of 1975, when Sam and I and a few others moved out here to California. On the way across Sam and I outlined a book called *Counter Economics*—which he is still going to write one of these days—and as another digression that book can be found on the library shelves of Aurora in my novel, so Sam is committed to writing it so my prophecy will come true. But this digression also has a point: when I decided to resume writing my novel, when I'd gotten settled out here, I redid the outline to include the update in libertarian theory that my experience with countereconomics represented.

The rest of this story involves too many personal details to get into here about finishing the book in May 1976, rewrites, and a sale of the book to Berkley Book's science fiction paperback line—a deal that was broken off later—and changes in agents because Oscar Collier was out of the agent business...but the bottom line is that it took around eighteen rejections, eight rewrites, and five years to produce this little book. Remember that the next time you go into a bookstore and plunk down a few bucks for a book. That's what some poor shmuck of a writer had to go through to give you a few diverting hours.

Does this sound like self pity? [Big grin] I sure hope so.

Okay. Now I'm supposed to talk here tonight about a few specifics related to the topic. Let's see. *Romantic Manifesto*, arbitration, countereconomics, hyperinflation, what the world of *Alongside Night* looks like, where my ideas come from... Schenectady...that's Harlan Ellison's joke, by the way...How they developed and were dramatized...how publisher interest was developed...and the likelihood of the scenario coming true. [Deep breath] Well, you might as well get comfortable, we're going to be here until next Thursday. I'll tell you what. I'll hit the high points and we can catch what I miss during the question period.

The question that I'm supposed to be addressing tonight is: Are we Alongside Night? I came up with that title in kind of the same way that Rand once asked in an essay; "Is Atlas Shrugging?" to address the question of how much of the events of her novel were coming true. So when I ask, Are We *Alongside Night*?, I'm asking; how much of the scenario of my novel is already coming to pass...and how much can we realistically expect?

Now this has an assumption in it that I have to make explicit and examine. Why should I ask—why should anyone care—whether a fictional scenario—a story—will come true or not? Does its likelihood of coming true make it more entertaining, or give it more artistic value? Does *Lucifer's Hammer* become more entertaining when a comet is about to hit earth? Was *Atlas Shrugged* a better novel when the lights of New York went out in 1965? Does one have to abuse oneself in the Holland Tunnel to enjoy *Portnoy's Complaint*?

No, of course not. A work of fiction finds it validity not in how well it records—or even projects—reality, but in terms of isolating universal experience in terms of metaphors.

So what I was trying to do with *Alongside Night* was not precisely prophecy. And, though it may be prophetic—since I painted in broad strokes based on long term trends that are almost impossible not to see—it can still be perfectly valid even if none of the specific events it portrays ever come to pass.

What was I trying to do, then? Well, let me sneak up on that from a rather oblique direction.

And here's where I sneak in the *The Romantic Manifesto*. That book, for any of you who haven't read it, is a collection of essays by Ayn Rand stating her artistic credo...the artistic methodology she used in writing *The Fountainhead* and *Atlas Shrugged*.

And, since in her introduction to that book, she states that "There is no romantic movement today. If there is to be one in the art of the future, this book will have helped it come into being" let me state for the record that I consider myself part of the romantic movement in fiction today, based on Rand's criteria as stated in that book.

Now, what Rand was concerned with was portraying things and characters: as they might be and ought to be. And she is very detailed and explicit about how this is supposed to be done. To restrict myself to the fiction writer, we're supposed to abstract essential details from the subject being portrayed, then—by a process of deductive logic—put together a model that has the universality of an abstraction but looks like a concrete. In a character, for example, I would mention only those traits that relate to the essential nature of the kind of person that character is.

The theme of a story—the central proposition—comes about in the same way: a thesis one wants to demonstrate. And the plot is a dramatized series of interconnected events that demonstrate that theme. In terms of theme, plot, characterization, one selects only the essential. Art is a "selective re-creation of reality" and what is selected is metaphysically important merely by its fact of being included. If it weren't important, the artist wouldn't have put it in; if it's not important, it shouldn't be mentioned in the first place.

Rand uses this analogy: "If one saw, in real life, a beautiful woman wearing an exquisite evening gown, with a cold sore on her lips, the blemish would be nothing but a minor affliction, and one would ignore it. But a painting of such a woman would be a corrupt, obscenely vicious attack on man, on beauty, on all values, and one would experience a feeling of immense disgust and indignation at the artist."

Now, if Rand were the only writer I considered to be worth a damn, I would have taken that credo and what I would have written—like so many so-called Objectivist writers—would have been imitations of Rand's style. But that wasn't the case. I have been a lifelong admirer of Robert Heinlein, for his science fiction, C.S. Lewis for his fantasy, and J.D. Salinger for his slick mainstream writing. And all four writers have a good deal in common, though they span the range of philosophy. All four are moralists—though their moral codes differ widely— all four write to what Rand would call "an objective psychoepistemology" ...which is another way of saying that they give you the details and let you imagine your own pictures...and all four consider themselves entertainers of a sort, as well as having serious things to say.

So armed with *Romantic Manifesto*, and four different writers whose writing I admired, I set out to write my own story.

And I found that by working from Rand's basic premises—without attempting to imitate her style—I had some major disagreements with the execution of those principles.

For example. Rand says her goal was the portrayal of an ideal man, first in Howard Roark, later in the heroes of *Atlas Shrugged*.

And she defines the essential characteristic of a man as rationality. So when she portrays John Galt, she portrays a man who is *always* rational. He always is right on top of it. If he has any weakness of flaw, Rand doesn't mention it...and therefore it is metaphysically insignificant. He is, by definition and portrayal ideal and perfect.

He is also her least convincing character.

Now this in itself is not a condemnation; Rand could easily argue—and has—that anyone who objected to Galt on that basis would be declaring his own depravity...the desire to see a flaw in Galt is the desire to see perfection itself destroyed.

If one is writing epic myth, then it is perfectly okay to portray gods and goddesses. There is even a usefulness for such models: they give us a standard against which to measure our own behavior.

But human frailty *is* metaphysically significant. It exists in all of us, even our geniuses and heroes. And they are not made less of because of their flaws; they are made greater by it. All three of the other writers I mentioned understand this; Rand does not. But Heinlein in particular taught me this lesson. Who is more brave: the man who fearlessly charges into battle, or the man who is so afraid that he wets his pants...as he charges in anyway?

John Galt stacks up pretty well as a god. His generator even throws lightning bolts of a sort...enough to knock down an air-plane, anyway. But as the portrayal of an ideal man, he falls completely flat...because if he has any weaknesses which he has had to conquer, we are never shown them.

If John Galt had some weakness—some fear—that Mr. Thompson could have used against him when he had Galt pris-oner, which Galt had to overcome within himself, then Galt would have been more essentially true to the nature of Man, and the meaning of *Atlas Shrugged* would have been amplified.

Now, remember that woman in the evening gown with the cold sore?

Literature is not static, like a painting; it is fluid, dynamic. What a fiction writer can do that the painter can not is to por-tray the beautiful woman *with* the cold sore, and demonstrate that she regards it "as nothing but a minor affliction" that should be ignored...exactly as one would in real life. Then, the meaning becomes even clearer.

By the way, Rand's favorite writer, Victor Hugo, did just this in *The Hunchback of Notre Dame*. The most important thing about Quasimodo is not that he is a hunchback, but that he is a human being *in spite* of being a hunchback.

Okay, now to tie this up.

The naturalist writer—as Rand talks about it in *Romantic Manifesto*—is interested in portraying things as they are. Rand is interested in showing things "as they might be and ought to be."

And what I was interested in doing in *Alongside Night* was showing how things are likely to be, and what we have to do if we don't want them to be like that. Or to put this in concrete terms: the setting of my story is the crisis that Harry Browne described...only we were ready for it.

I chose as my viewpoint character Elliot Vreeland, the sev-enteen-year old son of a world famous libertarian economist...his father, Martin Vreeland, is a combination of

Murray Rothbard, Milton Friedman, Wilhelm Roepke, and a few others. But the main character is Elliot, not his father; the things that are seen are from Elliot's vantage point, within the framework of his understanding.

Now, why did I do this? I certainly didn't make things easy on myself. If I wanted to portray an armed uprising, a soldier would have made a better viewpoint character. If I wanted to show a business collapse, an industrialist would have been at the thick of it. Political turmoil could have best been seen by a government official on the inside, as Ben Stein did in his inflation scenario, *On The Brink*, or Erdman did with an international banker in *Crash of 79*...incidentally, both these books came out after I'd finished my own first draft.

So I had to go through a good deal of trouble, in terms of plot twists, to get my seventeen-year old into a position where he could see any of the causes of what was happening. Now why did I do it this way?

Well, being the son of an economist, he's had some exposure to what's going on, so he won't be a complete ignoramus. But being young, nobody—not even the most ardent Objectivist—could expect him to be a John Galt...to have at his command the resources of a John Galt. He would be vulnerable to the tremendous forces bulleting his world, and so if I cut him off from the only really powerful person he knows—his father—then he's on his own, and he has to learn to cope with the world without very many resources at his command.

In other words, he's in much the same position any of us would be in having to deal with economics catastrophe...assuming we aren't living like a hermit in a retreat somewhere.

Throughout my story, Elliot Vreeland is pushed along by circumstances beyond his control, and very often the only choice he has is who he can trust and who he can't trust. He has to decide—by loyalty, by friendship, by what people say and what people do—who are the good guys and who are the bad guys. His decisions aren't made on an ideological basis, but on a personal basis...which is how most people make the choices about their lives.

In essence, his only weapon is his own moral discretion.

And so he is in precisely the position, in my novel, that most people are today when confronted with libertarians. They don't understand all our fancy theories; all they care about is whether or not we can be trusted. They're not interested in hearing about how perfect we are and how terrific our ideas are. They got a bellyful of that from the communists and the socialists and the utopians and the technocrats and the fascists, and each of them had the Answer...only it never seemed to work. It doesn't make any difference that what we're talking about *would* work...we have not *proved* it yet, and so we're in the same position as all these others. And don't tell me how our ideas are historically self-evident; if they were self-evident, we'd be living in a libertarian world today.

So what I did in my story was to show them a guy who has to make the same choice. He has to know who he can trust when all these things start coming down.

And here's the important part: the libertarians in my story aren't libertarians because they spout all the theories, and demonstrate and go to Supper Club, and read *New Libertarian Strategy*. They're libertarians because they're living their lives in accordance with libertarian principles. They have something concrete to offer: safe areas, free trade zones, communication and transportation immune from the State, ways to beat the system. Not words, but action. Not promises, but results.

And that's precisely what will have to happen before we can deal with this nightmare that we're "alongside."

Shall I get to concretes?

Hyperinflation? I can't say for sure that it's coming, but inflation is going to be around for a while, probably in double digit and quite possibly in triple digit. And if you don't think that's a volatile situation, ask yourself if we'd be involved in this mess in Iran if David Rockefeller and Jimmy Carter didn't want to get our minds off the economic problems right here.

You might also ask yourself if any of the Iranian students holding the hostages are as young as seventeen.

The counter-economy? It's here right now. *U.S. News and World Report* from October 22nd—seven weeks ago. The I.R.S. already has a quarter of the American economy listed in the underground economy...half a trillion dollars a year. Twenty million Americans. And if those twenty million can't be gotten to with the message that what they're doing is, in fact, libertarianism in practice, then you can kiss the future of freedom goodbye: the statists will pull another hat trick and we'll have another new "ism" to contend with.

It may already be too late on that score: those twenty million may already have libertarians pegged as a group of minor politicians trying to muscle in on the big boys. And to them, politicians are the enemy.

Arbitration? It's so common it's probably the only reason the U.S. court system hasn't collapsed under its own weight. You know how long it takes to get onto a court docket? And how much business bypasses the whole mess through the American Arbitration Association and other groups like the Better Business bureau and Fair Ballot Association? Neither do I; but it's in the millions of whatever you're counting.

Private protection? A huge industry. Alternate money? Gold is skyrocketing at the same rate that prices are in general. Decadence and chaos? Did you hear about *The Who* concert a few days ago?[1]

All the elements are already here. The revolution is already in progress. It's simply a matter people identifying who the revolutionaries are...and for the most part, the revolutionaries don't even know they're the revolutionaries.

You see, we don't have a John Galt leading us. We can contemplate him as a literary character—and maybe learn something by doing it—but the function he performs in *Atlas
Shrugged* isn't being performed in the real world.

There's only us. So if we want to achieve great things—our
dream of a free society—we have to do it in spite of our own
weaknesses, and fears, and mistakes.

But, maybe we don't really need a John Galt after all. As
libertarians, we know about the efficacy of free trade. When
people trade, they parley everyone else's production, and
achieve what they could not achieve acting alone, as
individuals.

The great socialist utopia has been here all along: it's the
marketplace. Or—as the ancient Greeks called it—and I picked
up from Sam who picked it up from 1960's libertarian activ-
ists—the *agora.*

In *The Romantic Manifesto*, Rand states that she writes solely
for the enjoyment of living, for a while, in a universe that is
"as it might be and ought to be." Her intent is not the didactic
one of teaching people how they should do things, but for the
feeling of the experience of having them done. A psychologi-
cal breather...soul food.

Rand used the analogy that it is not the purpose of a novel to
teach its readers how to live anymore than it is the function of
an airplane to teach its passengers the principles of aerody-
namics.

But *Atlas Shrugged*—and *Alongside Night*, for that matter—
is not a world, but a book. You can't live in it. It is a portrait,
not the thing itself—the map, not the territory. And when you
come to page 1168 in *Atlas Shrugged*, the story is finished and
you're stuck back in this mess which we have to live in.

So I set out, like Rand, to portray things "as they might be
and ought to be" but not as an end in itself, the way it is for
her.

You see, if things "might be and ought to be," then I won't be satisfied until they *are.*

My intent with *Alongside Night* was to show, by dramatic example, the major preconditions for the achievement of the free society.

My theme: freedom works.

My context: the political economic mess that the theories of Austria economics say must end in collapse...the sort of economic collapse that historically had led to a Man on Horseback taking over. Napoleon after the 1790s' hyperinflation in France; Hitler after the crack-up in 1923 Weimar Germany.

My plot: the events leading up to and culminating in the collapse of the American economy, and the arising of the underground economy given conscious identity by libertarian revolutionaries.

And that's where you all come in. On one level, I wrote my book as an adventure story—self-contained, self-satisfying, enjoyable whether or not it can actually happen.

On another level, I wrote it for you...as a teaching aid. All of us have argued endlessly, trying to tell others how libertarian ideas would work in practice and how we can achieve them. What I set out to do was give some of the fundamental necessities—the preconditions—in a form that makes it obvious what we're talking about.

Now, some of these topics are best handled in the question period. Let me just run through some of them and you can hit me about them if you're interested.

The idea of the General Submissions to Arbitration as a precondition to a civilized society.

Technology as a neutral element in the set...neither pro-state nor anti-state.[2]

A centralized libertarian Cadre as a danger to liberty.

The necessity for a separation of courts and protection agencies.

Is the Revolutionary Agorist Cadre, in my novel, a libertarian protection agency or a government?

You see, I'm leaving these sorts of things out of my formal presentation, because they are the sorts of things that libertarians are going to have to debate among themselves. When you get to Page 131[3] of *Alongside Night*, and close the book, you'll have read a road map to a libertarian society...but you're going to have to do the driving yourself. All I was able to give you was shadows of the libertarian story that each of you can write.

Thank you.

Footnote 1: On December 4, 1979, eleven concert-goers were trampled to death to get through the open doors at a general-admission concert by The Who in Cincinnati.

Footnote 2: Was I pessimistic about Agorist technology not giving the revolution a decisive advantage, or did I simply not want to recapitulate Heinlein's *The Moon Is A Harsh Mistress,* where one self-aware supercomputer makes the entire revolution possible? See J. Kent Hastings' afterword "Pulling Alongside Night" for a detailed, contemporary discussion of this question.

Footnote 3: Page 255, this edition.

How Far *Alongside Night*?
by Samuel Edward Konkin III

This afterword first appeared in the 1987 Avon paperback edition.—JNS

Samuel Edward Konkin III is the Father of Agorism, the economic philosophy that inspired the Revolutionary Agorist Cadre in Alongside Night. As editor of the longest-lasting "purist" libertarian magazine, New Libertarian, *and executive director of the new countereconomic think tank,* The Agorist Institute, *Konkin is attempting in real life what Merce Rampart has accomplished, so far, only in my imagination.—JNS*

Two thousand dollars for a taxi ride across Manhattan? Underground shopping centers where the stores accept payment only in gold? The Almighty Dollar so worthless that even the United States Army won't take it anymore?

Surely this sort of paranoid fantasy went out with the seventies?

Certainly, in the eighties of Reaganomics, low inflation, and tax "reform," we don't have to worry about this economic scenario anymore.

Or do we?

To answer that question, we need a quick look at economic history.

In 1910, an economist named Ludwig von Mises had his doctoral thesis published in his native Austro-Hungarian Empire. It eventually appeared in English under the title *The Theory of Money and Credit.*

On the face of it, this does not sound like the most important event of the twentieth century, but it may very well be to the science of economics what the publication of Einstein's General Theory of Relativity was to the science of physics.

Mises set forth principles that explained the Roaring Twenties and—two decades before Black Thursday—the inevitability of the following economic collapse that would lead to the Great Depression. Mises also provided the only set of economic principles that could explain the "stagflation" of the late 1970s. Other economic theories stated that this mixture of inflation and recession could not exist and floundered when it did.

Mises was no Nostradamus. Financial analysts and entrepreneurs followed his "Austrian" theory in the teeth of Friedman's and Keynes's hatred of that "barbarous yellow metal" as gold was about to be legalized. They saw the price per ounce skyrocket to $800, settle down to $300, and begin a steady upward climb. His prophecy proved to be a valid scientific prediction and...on the money. When a set of general principles is found, over the long term, to be able to make valid predictions in a certain field of knowledge, that field has qualified as a science.

In a nutshell, Mises's theory ran that if government inflated the money supply, it would generate a boom. Since supply follows demand, investments are made to provide luxury goods and services for the boom time. But the inflationary money is only "temporarily real." Price levels go up everywhere, people find they can't buy as much as they thought they could, cut back on their consumption, and the demand drops, usually below previous levels, because of squandered real goods. Luxury goods sit on store shelves, which causes businesses to cut back. Capital is wasted, workers are in the wrong jobs. Luxury goods are sold off below cost in going-out-of-business sales, and workers are laid off.

This period of poor business and high unemployment is called a depression.

Injecting money into the economy is like injecting heroin

into the body. A "high" results, but it's temporary, and a bigger dose is needed for the next "high." Eventually, this leads to overdose. If the government doesn't go cold turkey and leave the money supply alone, the people come to expect a total inflationary wipeout, dumping their money as fast as they get it (or faster). Nobody wants it. Everyone knows it's not real. Inflation has gone runaway, and this is known as hyperinflation or crack-up boom.

What an economy looks like in the last stages of the overdose is portrayed in *Alongside Night*.

Historically, this has happened repeatedly: in the American Revolutionary War, in the French Revolution, in the U.S. Civil War, in Germany in 1923, in China in 1949, in Brazil in 1964, and so on. Currency collapses either started revolutions or pushed them over the top. That's as far as Mises's economic predictions went.

In the late 1960s, Mises's economics spread through the radical movements. Radical libertarians, having outright rejected or abandoned Marx as demonstrably false, not only latched onto Mises but took notice of an effect that conservative "Austrians" feared and spoke of only in hushed tones: the economic theory predicted, more or less accidentally, the collapse of an economy and hence political revolution.

But what a place for a radical to start. The government, by its own stupidity, was going to bring about a revolution. In the early 1970s, it certainly looked like it. The radical libertarians stood on the shoulders of the giant Ludwig von Mises. And in 1972, a young student radical named J. Neil Schulman clambered up there with the rest of us.

In 1973, the United States of America, through the Federal Reserve Board, appeared to have lost control of inflation. The libertarian Right was turning to survivalism and heading for the hills—these are the "brownies" of *Alongside Night*. We of the libertarian Left looked forward to the insurrection following economic collapse as a rare opportunity. The socialists had smoked pipe dreams of American proletariat arising for a century; now they were down to ashes. The libertarian free-market Left saw Mises's infallible indicators predicting the stripping of everyone, including the middle class, of their wealth: wiping out their bank accounts, annihilating small businesses and workers' wages. Now *this* is what would finally bring comfortable, complacent Americans into the streets. But when?

In 1973, Ludwig von Mises died. Austrians, neo-Austrians, Left and Right Austrians outbid each other with predictions of the righteous monetary thunderbolt of the market at last bringing justice to the statists (and profits galore for those who went "long" on gold and silver). No one but Mises was sufficiently respected to judge, and he was gone. The cautious Austrians claimed that predicting the timing of real-world events was one of those things Man Was Not Meant To Know. But the rest of us remembered Mises's success and plunged ahead.

Judging from events such as Nixon's imposition of wage and price controls (a truly fascist concept), I foresaw a wave of repression as early as 1975 as inflation went runaway.

Neil was relatively cautious and decided to play it safe, setting his portrayal of the economic collapse of America at least several decades away.

Alongside Night is terribly accurate. *Whenever* the American crack-up boom happens, few libertarians would disagree with his outline of the scenarios. But Neil went one step farther than most of the libertarians of the time. He integrated the new science of countereconomics and the economic philosophy of Agorism, which I had only begun to develop in 1974.

Agorism is the view that, regardless of whether or not it is sanctioned by the state, free trade conducted morally is still moral. Crack dealers, midwives, porn pushers, truckers using CB to outrace Smokey, coyotes, and tax evaders are to be regarded as truly free-market businesspersons and moralists; law-and regulation-abiding types are seen as wimps; and tax-subsidized, loan-guaranteed corporate heads are seen as a bunch of fascists.

Agorism is the only philosophy that explains why, in an East German alley, a hooker and a bible smuggler ducking into the same doorway to avoid the police not only won't turn each other in but are also *both* acting right and proper.

Sure, *if* it ever happens, *Alongside Night* is right. In other words, it is "hard" science fiction by virtue of its use of a theoretical science to predict real-world events. But how likely is it, when we live in (what appear to be) noninflationary times?

In 1975, the legalization of gold acted as a safety valve on the economy. And with the Vietnam War over, the government's pressure for spending money it didn't have (additional taxation through inflation) was gone, at least temporarily. The government of the United States of America took some of its medicine and we headed into a depression instead of hyperinflation.

In the early Reagan years, the inflation continued—but completely anticipated. It even became *lower* than anticipated because of bankruptcies, liquidation sales, and unemployment. Unions are still collapsing as an aftershock but, brag the Reaganites, at least we brought down inflation.

The mechanics of what happened are still fairly complex and controversial even among Austrian economists, but it is clear that the Reagan administration "bit the bullet" by lowering the rate of inflation and accepting the depression. The money supply was fine-tuned so that the fall in prices resulting from the depression was matched by the continued increase in the money supply: that is, canceling out most of the price increase usually resulting from inflation.

But the quick fix has run its course. The American dollar edges downward in world currency markets and drags along foreign banks and currencies that accept American inflation as an export—so far. Gold continues relentlessly upward in price long term. And still the federal budgets and their deficits, now past two trillion, grow higher and higher.

The fundamental principles of Austrian economics remain in place. And what they predict is still valid. Either the United States will give up monetization of its debt and live humbly with what it can extract from taxation alone, or the scenario of *Alongside Night* will come to pass.

When the next clamor for massive government spending arises, whether for a Greater Society or Star Wars defenses, the money will have to roll from the presses, the consumers will be caught, the inflation will be anticipated ever higher, and the hyperinflation scenario will be in place again. But with one difference: the last inflation spree left a permanent part of the economy underground, not just pimps and pushers but *straight* businessmen and their workers who left the "aboveground" economy for the countereconomy. When the feds inflate, they confiscate from a smaller base, and as they inflate, they push more and more entrepreneurs Agorist-ward—and have less and less tax base and fewer and fewer victims.

With fewer people accepting the same amount of money, it buys less. That is, it inflates—even without the government doing it. The people going countereconomic take the decision out of the hands of the state and force a crack-up. But this time it's only the statists themselves upon whom the consequences are visited. And that is the scenario of that profoundly moral novel of justice finally served, *Alongside Night*.

When? You decide, dear reader; but you are now well armed to see the signs and know what actions to take. Thanks to Ludwig von Mises, a small band of rational revolutionary students, and J. Neil Schulman, artist.

Interested readers may find out more about agorism at the *Agorist Institute* Website at http://www.agorist.org/.

Pulling *Alongside Night:*
The Enabling Technology is Here
by J. Kent Hastings

J. Neil Schulman is a prophet.

Two weeks after his twenty-third birthday, on May 1, 1976, J. Neil Schulman finished the first draft of *Alongside Night*, a novel that accurately discerned the outline of 1999 reality. He finished the final draft in 1978, for publication on October 16, 1979.

Alongside Night describes things that weren't around in the '70s but arrived later, or are becoming commonplace now. "Citizens for a Free Society" could be the populist/libertarian source group for today's Patriot movement. The "TacStrike" division of the novel's Revolutionary Agorist Cadre could be recruited from today's militias, revolutionaries, and mercenaries, while today's cypherpunks could form the basis for the novel's "IntelSec."

In the future of *Alongside Night* as in our own 1999—but *not* in the 1970's when it was written—panhandlers and the homeless are omnipresent due to economic hardship, professional youth gangs roam the streets of New York freely while big-time drug and people smuggling are ubiquitous; videophones are hitting the consumer market and computers are in use everywhere.

Schulman's "First Anarchist Bank and Trust Company," a Swiss bank subsidiary, uses accounts denominated in gold, linked offshore—a dream of today's cypherpunks. He predicts re-prohibition of gold, with TV actors warning "that just one little ounce of gold bullion can put you away in a federal penitentiary for up to twenty years."

Transportation to one of Schulman's "Agorist Undergrounds"

shields against all transmissions to prevent discovery of location aboveground, including heartbeat detectors in use now by the Immigration and Naturalization Service at the Mexican border. Weapons, cameras, recorders, transmitters, and radioactive materials are checked in transit.

Security at the A.U. uses non-lethal weapons. Guards disarm guests upon arrival, then return their guns on their way to the trading floor. One shop is called "The Gun Nut," and "Lowell-Pierre Engineering" sells nukes. Rental per-square-foot calculates any risk of a government "G-Raid" against the costs of security measures.

Cadre General Jack Guerdon, also the builder of some A.U.s including "Aurora," explains how the location of a large complex could be kept secret from the construction workers:

"They were recruited from construction sites all over the world, were transported here secretly, worked only inside, and never knew where they were. If you think security is tight now, you should have been here during construction; a mosquito couldn't have gotten in or out."

Thinking about it now, robots with telepresence may achieve the same security, with even less risk, since only Cadre equipment would be inside.

TransComm's smuggling of contraband predicted marijuana traffic expanding into the sort of operation done in the 1980s by the cocaine cartels, small airports and all.

Aurora's trading floor offers non-prescription drugs, marijuana, cocaine, heroin, and LSD sold in defiance of DEA and FDA regulations, but with voluntary warning labels.

Dialogue in *Alongside Night* decries smoking prohibition at the time of the story. In California today, you aren't allowed to smoke in restaurants, workplaces, airports or other public buildings. The U.S. FDA classified nicotine a drug this year, so it's just a formality to prohibit delivery systems (cigarettes, cigars, and pipes) nationwide as well.

Classroom video intercoms exist in the novel, even before consumer VCRs were a hot item. One of *Alongside Night*'s characters, Chin, uses a video capable laptop in a sequence written years before IBM introduced the first PC, and more years before anything you could call a laptop.

Consumer electronics? "Aurora's library had a fair collection of books, videodiscs, and holosonic music cassettes"—years before DAT, DVD or MP3 were introduced.

All trading and billing is done by computer with access controls, a projection made before most banks even had ATMs, much less telephone bill-paying.

Elliot chooses a pass phrase like today's PGP requires, and the Cadre contract assures authorized disclosure only. Aurora's hotel room keys are computerized in the novel, but it wasn't like that at hotels in the 1970s. Also in Aurora, computer terminals are in each hotel room.

The electronic contract used by the Cadre in *Alongside Night* is imitated today by digital forms used millions of times daily on the World Wide Web, including Schulman's own site http://www.pulpless.com/.

Schulman wrote the first chapters of the book in 1974, describing his fictional economist "Martin Vreeland," winner of the Nobel prize for economics—two years before Milton Friedman actually won his in 1976. And while Schulman did fail to predict the collapse of the Soviet Union, his description of the almost casual fall of the United States government over the two week timespan in his novel parallels the bloodless coup attempt against Gorbachev in 1992, which completed the fall of the Soviet Union.

Neil predicted Chinese Norinco handguns and rifles being imported into the United States: Elliot Vreeland carries a ".38 caliber Peking revolver." Such imports were legalized after *Alongside Night* was written and, after becoming popular items, imports of Chinese firearms into the U.S. are now banned again.

The Cadre are armed, but not on an aggressive revenge mission against the feds, as a "drive-by" with a non-lethal, temporarily-blinding magnesium flash, used to evade an FBI sedan, demonstrates.

Foreigners with hard currency buy relatively cheap U.S. assets in *Alongside Night*, before Rockefeller Center or major portions of the entertainment industry were bought by Japanese conglomerates. Schulman predicts the "mall-ization" of America because of fear of crime on city streets, and police replaced with private patrols such as "Fifth Avenue Merchant Alliance Security (FAMAS)."

"Air Quebec" indicates Schulman's prediction of Quebec secession, which may happen after a fifty-fifty split in the recent election to test the issue. The secession of Texas doesn't seem as far-fetched these days as it did in 1976. Just think of the Montana legislators who introduced a bill to secede a couple of years ago.

Schulman's novel is set during the final two weeks of a catastrophic "wheelbarrow" inflation. Confiscatory taxes have forced people out of aboveground jobs and into either working "off the books," or unemployed on the dole. Gresham's Law has Americans using blue "New Dollars": "More than anything else, it resembled *Monopoly* money"; and fixed-value coins disappear so fast for their metallic value that vending-machine tokens fixed daily to the price of the "eurofranc" are just about the only real money in circulation.

The President complains about the U.S. being treated like a banana republic by the "European Common Market Treaty Organization, a combination of the European Common Market and a U.S.-less NATO," the U.S. having been kicked out for no longer being able to afford keeping overseas troop commitments. The Chancellor of EUCOMTO informs the White House, "Mr. President, even bananas do not decay as quickly as the value of your currency these past few months." In the 1970's, the European Union was not yet negotiated and NATO was still almost entirely controlled by the United States.

In *Alongside Night*, political dissidents are arrested on secret warrants, and the FBI gulag they're stuck in (codenamed "Utopia") is blown up by the feds as a cover-up. Of course, nothing like that could ever happen in real life, right?

Schulman's account of a Federal Renovation Zone rebuilding Times Square in N.Y. predicts today's sweeping federalization of lands, opposed by the sagebrush rebellion.

Future conflict between militias and the feds seems inevitable today since both sides see the other as a fatal threat and neither side is backing down. An "Oracle" headline in *Alongside Night*: "FBI Chief Powers attributes last night's firebombings of bureau offices to outlaw 'Revolutionary Agorist Cadre.'" The recent FBI raids in Colorado and West Virginia against militia groups supposedly planning terrorism—not to mention Waco and Ruby Ridge—demonstrates that anti-federal sentiment isn't laughed off as harmless anymore.

The FBI chief in the novel keeps copies of "confidential" enemies lists at home, long before Filegate. In the 1970's when J. Neil Schulman wrote his novel, the general image of the FBI was Efrem Zimbalist, Jr., on *The FBI*. Today's FBI is better characterized by the paranoia of *The X-Files*, where higher-ups are usually in complicity with dark forces.

The Emergency Broadcast System in *Alongside Night* extends even to telephones—using the phone system during the crackdown requires authorized beepers—while radio and TV programming simulates normality while the government collapses. Today's FBI digital wiretap law will provide capability for millions of simultaneous wiretaps. The major broadcast networks have accepted official explanations uncritically of everything from who started the fire at Waco, who knew about the bombs placed in Oklahoma City before the explosion, to the cause of the explosion that destroyed TWA Flight 800.

In *Alongside Night*, we learn that a *New York Times* front-page story headlined "Vreeland Widow Assures Public Husband Died Naturally" is disinformation. Echoes of Vince Foster and the Arkancides?

An "Oracle" headline in *Alongside Night* predicts military dissent: "TEAMSTER PRESIDENT WARNS POSSIBILITY OF ARMED FORCES WILDCAT STRIKES IF PENTAGON DOES NOT MEET DEMANDS..." And when—due to a busted budget—an absence of government paychecks combines with the latest government scandal, a two-century-old superpower collapses like a house of cards.

Where did a prediction of revolution in the U.S. come from, if not the fevered dreams of a militant paranoid? Young Schulman, a student of Austrian economics, just "followed the money," determining who would earn it and who would control it.

During the 1970s, hippies dropped out and moved to communes, while tax and sagebrush rebels fought to keep the government out of their pockets and off their lands. California's Proposition 13 and the election of U.S. President Ronald Reagan were the results of the establishment co-opting anti-government positions.

Despite this, the current political situation in the U.S. is more volatile than ever. Job security doesn't exist for anybody, so leftists are forming new parties out of disgust with the Democrats, while right-wingers who believe Republicans indistinguishable join militias.

But perhaps the most revolutionary development is the Internet and the World Wide Web, which threaten government currency controls, tax collection, and media restrictions.

Alongside Night predicted revolutionary cadres organizing to resist and replace the State with an "agorist" society. Agorism, according to Samuel Edward Konkin III, who coined the term, is the integration of both libertarian theory and counter-economic practice, neither inactive "library libertarians" prattling on with their idle complaints, nor simple criminals preying on society.

Agorists insist on both civil and economic liberties for all individuals, encourage efficient restitution for contract and rights violations, yet oppose a monopoly of coercion from even a limited "minarchist" State.

From Konkin's *New Libertarian Manifesto*: "Coercion is immoral, inefficient and unnecessary for human life and fulfilment." This is not pacifism because defensive violence is not coercion. Coercion is the *initiation* of violence or its threat. You can't morally start a fight, but you can finish one. ... "When the State unleashes its final wave of supression—and is successfully resisted—this is the definition of *Revolution*."

Most citizens go along with the government, whether "right or wrong," to preserve order, defend freedom, and more recently to assist the poor and protect the environment. When it becomes obvious that the government is actually hostile to these purposes, many of its subjects will no longer feel guilty about joining the radical opposition.

A rich, slave-owning, dead European white male cracker named Thomas Jefferson (sorry, he's not "the Sage of Monticello" anymore), wrote similar things about King George III in the *Declaration of Independence*.

I'm sure T.J.'s writings would be found in Aurora's library, along with the following titles, most of which are specified in *Alongside Night*. Productive workers will "withdraw their sanction," according to Ayn Rand's 1957 *magnum opus*, *Atlas Shrugged*, and this will lead to "the collapse of the Looter's State." Rand also described an underground "Galt's Gulch" of black market revolutionaries in her classic novel. Murray Rothbard hinted at stateless defense in *Man, Economy, and State* (1962). Robert Heinlein portrayed a stateless legal system and revolution in *The Moon Is A Harsh Mistress* (1966). Rothbard describes stateless defense services fully in *Power and Market* (1970), echoing Gustavus De Molinari's 1849 essay "The Production of Security."

Molinari was an economist in the original French *laissez-faire* school of Frederick Bastiat. Molinari concluded that justice and defense were goods like any other, best provided in a competitive market rather than political monopoly. Konkin's *New Libertarian Manifesto* (published in 1980, based on a talk given in February 1974 which influenced *Alongside Night*) inspired the creation of The Agorist Institute, "symbolically founded on the last day of 1984," now with a web site at http://www.agorist.org/.

That's all fine for free-market supporters, but wouldn't "progressive" groups try to impose their own one-party dictatorships? What's in it for the masses?

Despite their famous friendship with Newt Gingrich, Alvin and Heidi Toffler are active in labor and ecology circles. They point out that telecommuting is 29 times more efficient than physical commuting in private cars. If 12% telecommuted, the 75 million barrels of gasoline saved would completely eliminate the need for foreign oil and future Gulf Wars. Real estate now used for office space could be used for local housing. The Tofflers believe traditional factors of production such as land, labor, and capital are being dwarfed by the growing importance of information. Information is inexhaustible, it can be shared but still kept.

Widely copied software brings more user suggestions and faster improvements. It puts scarcity economics on its ear. Expensive bulky production methods are being "ephemeralized" (to use a term coined by Bucky Fuller), replaced by flexible cheap computers to satisfy local consumer tastes. More people can afford access to computer resources, with less damage to the environment.

Telecommuting is safer than driving, which currently kills a Vietnam War's worth of fatalities each year, without requiring "strategic" resources like fuel and rare metals to fight over. Silicon comes from sand, which is plentiful. Because programs like PGP protect users from both evil hackers and a fascist global police state, traditional leftists embrace the new technology, and even build their own web sites.

Karl Marx wrote of objective and subjective conditions being necessary for Revolution. "Objective" in this case means the physical ability to overthrow the current regime. "Subjective" means the desire and mass support to do it.

The 1960s arguably provided the subjective conditions: an unpopular war, a vicious police crackdown on agitators, and hundreds of thousands of protesters marching in the streets. But these conditions weren't perfect. The economy was still robust, not yet weighed down with the debts racked up in the 1970's by the Wars On Poverty and Vietnam, and no stagflation and oil crisis yet. The objective conditions were bad. Individuals and small groups could not do much mischief without being overwhelmed by Chicago police or National Guard troops thrown against them.

Today, a single troublemaker can afford to sign up for Internet service under a pseudonym and use anonymous remailers to post messages in widely read "newsgroup" conferences, distributed to hundreds of countries without identification.

The Rulers and the Court Opinion Makers won't let their ill-gotten monopolies collapse without a fight. Every day we hear about the Four Horsemen of the Infocalypse: Terrorists, Pedophiles, Money-Launderers, and Drug Smugglers. Defenders of privacy and free speech on the Internet get smeared for "fighting law enforcement" just like the Revolutionary Agorist Cadre in *Alongside Night*.

Restrictions on the Internet are likely to be passed for "crime and security" reasons and to hold users "accountable." Civil libertarians complain that such pornographically-explicit words as "breast" are being filtered by online services fearing prosecution, with the "unintended consequence" of forcing breast cancer survivors to choose euphemisms like "tit".

Critics of data censorship say these restrictions are like trying to stop the wind from crossing a border. For example, when France (in anti-*laissez-faire* fashion) blocked some newsgroups, an ISP in the United States made them available to French users via the World Wide Web.

Next there's the problem of how to make a living underground. Schulman watched Anthony L. Hargis found a "bank that isn't a bank" in 1975, with "transfer orders" instead of checks, denominated in mass units of gold. ALH&Co. survives to this day, despite IRS inspections, hassles with the Post Office and local authorities, and ever-tighter banking restrictions against "money-laundering."

Hargis explicitly forbids (by voluntary contract) his account holders from selling drugs, which suggests how proprietary communities can choose to be drug-free within a future agorist society. Hargis is sincere in this restriction, not just playing clean to fool the authorities. Unfortunately, Hargis is not enthusiastic about encryption or the Internet. "Honest Citizens have nothing to hide."

Rarely does the weed of government research bear anything but the bitter fruits of mass destruction, disinformation, and bureaucratic disruption of innocent people's lives. Exceptions may include public-key cryptography, spread-spectrum radio and the Internet Protocol.

Programmers such as Pretty Good Privacy (PGP)'s Philip R. Zimmermann are using the government sponsored RSA algorithm to thwart the efforts of every State's security agent. In Myanmar (formerly Burma), where PGP is used by rebels fighting dictatorship, the mere possession of a network-capable computer will bring a lengthy prison sentence.

In 1995, David Chaum announced the availability of untraceable digital cash ("Ecash"), denominated in U.S. Dollars (Federal Reserve Units, or "frauds" as Hargis would call them) from Mark Twain Bank in St. Louis, MO. This service has ended and Digicash is bankrupt, but banks in Europe still use the technology and newcomers offer improved, more practical systems.

Ecash can be withdrawn, deposited, and spent without fee anywhere on the Internet. The only charge is when exchanging Ecash for a particular currency. Chaum lives in Amsterdam, the location of the "secret annex" in *The Diary of Anne Frank.*

During World War II, the Nazis seized the government records in Amsterdam before partisans could burn them, and used them to track down and kill Jews, including members of Chaum's own family. Perhaps this explains his desire for computer privacy.

In 1985, David Chaum described his invention in an article as "Security Without Identification: Transaction Systems To Make 'Big Brother' Obsolete." Ecash protects privacy yet thwarts deadbeat counterfeiters. Similarly, software filters against "spam" and other unwanted messages obviate a State crackdown against anonymity.

Chaum's Digicash company now serves a number of banks in different countries, and provides the "electronic wallet" software for use by their account holders. With Ecash, items may be purchased without identifying the buyer, even if the banks and merchants exchange information, but the seller may be disclosed if the buyer wishes to publicly dispute a purchase. As it exists, privacy is compromised because of bank disclosure requirements, but it isn't hard to imagine underground banks with unofficial ecash (as opposed to proprietary Ecash), using their own currency or gold.

Respecting your right to be secure in the privacy of your own home would let you advertise, send catalogs, take orders, send processed data or tele-operate machinery (in other words, do your *work*), then send invoices, collect ecash payments, and deposit your unreported earnings scot-free in offshore accounts. Using ecash and encrypted remailers, there would be no way for tax collectors to tell if you made $100 last year or $100,000,000.

If measures such as mandatory internal passports and routine checkpoints can't restrict who can work or determine accurate income taxes due, they'll have to employ ubiquitous surveillance—a totalitarian system will be the only way to protect the privileges of the tax eaters. Although necessary for the future survival of the State, a crackdown will provoke resistance. Private communications bypass official propaganda, as the Committees of Correspondence did during the American Revolution.

They'll be forced to bug your house. Don't worry, the automatic image-processing 24-hour cameras will be labeled "for your protection." Worse than Orwell's *1984*, they won't need humans to look through them, they'll identify everyone and trace their movements with blessed convenience.

Couldn't they just tap the phones? Sure, but with encrypted data to and from an Internet Service Provider they wouldn't get much. Couldn't they require back-door "escrowed" keys and outlaw strong encryption? Not good enough, they need *constant* monitoring (not just with a court order) to find suspects

Scofflaws might send innocent looking images and sound files with steganographically hidden data using methods designed to thwart detection and disruption. Now any data collected about you can be shared with the FBI, U.S. Customs, DEA, IRS, Postal inspectors, and the Secret Service because the Financial Crimes Enforcement Network (FinCEN), located down the street from the CIA in Vienna, Virginia pools the data. I guess anything goes to stop crime and protect the children, right?

In *Alongside Night*, temporary relays and infrared modulation of engine heat disguises communication signals. With enhancement of spread-spectrum radios recently introduced, a channel wouldn't be defined by a single radio frequency, but by a "spreading code" of frequency hops with staggered dwell times, so that jammers and eavesdroppers won't be able to predict where, and for how long, the carrier will go next.

A hybrid with the direct sequence technique would mix each bit of the message with several pseudo-random "chip" bits, to spread the signal at each hop. A transmitted reference in one band, of purely random thermal noise in a resistor for example, can be compared to the reference mixed with a message in another, so that the authorized receiver correlates the two to recover the message.

Low-powered microwave, lasers, unreported underground cables, antennas disguised as flag poles and many other methods would insure that the email got through during a blackout.

Today, when "rightsizing" has made a temporary placement firm the largest employer in the U.S., and the President's own budget projects a federal tax rate of 84%, not including state, county, city and other local taxes, we can count on greater numbers swelling the ranks of radical movements in the face of a hostile establishment.

"Dr. Merce Rampart," the woman leading Schulman's Cadre, offers advice to dislocated personnel in the "New Dawn" of a proprietary anarchist revolution:

"With the exception of those government workers who perform no marketable service—tax collectors, regulators, and so on—we are urging them to declare their agencies independent from the government, and to organize themselves into free workers' syndicates. Shares of stock could be issued to employees and pensioners by whatever method seems fair, and the resultant joint-stock companies could then hire pro-

fessional managers to place the operation on a profitable footing. I can envision this for postal workers, municipal services,
libraries, universities, and public schools, et cetera. As for those
civil servants whose jobs are unmarketable, I suggest that most
have skills in accounting, administration, computers, law, and
so forth, that readily could be adapted to market demand. That's
the idea. It's now up to those with the necessary interests to
use it or come up with something better."

In the 1980's, after *Alongside Night* was published, this idea
became popular among libertarian-leaning conservatives. It's
called privatization.

Alongside Night shows us a world where such ideas aren't
merely a smokescreen for greater efficiency in the service of
an ever more encompassing State.

Remarks Upon Acceptance into the Prometheus Hall of Fame for *Alongside Night*,

Noreascon III World Science Fiction Convention, September 2, 1989, Sheraton Boston Hotel
by J. Neil Schulman

This is an important award.

No, it doesn't have half a million dollars attached to it like the Nobel Prize.

No, we aren't being broadcast into half the living rooms on Earth like the Academy Awards.

No, the winner of this award will not have his picture in *The New York Times* tomorrow.

This award does not even have the prestige with the general public to ensure that a work winning it will remain in print.

This is nonetheless an important award. It may well be the most important award being given out on this planet today.

The year in which this award is being given out is the year of Tienanmen Square ... where the world saw a freedom movement assassinated with guns, gas, and clubs ... and one lone freedom fighter hold back a tank with nothing more than courage.

The year in which this award is being given out is also the year that, almost fifty years to the day from its invasion by a foreign power, the people of Poland found themselves free from domination by foreign powers.

The year in which this award is being given out is the year that the United States government, finding itself without a foreign power of any magnitude to oppose it, decided to begin expanding its empire over the continent to its south, because

292 Alongside Night

while the War on Drugs may not be much of a war, it's the only war we've got.

We live in a world in which freedom of any sort is a precarious and expensive commodity. The victories by the forces of darkness are the lead stories in every newscast, on the front pages of every news publication. I find that about 75% of what is labeled news on the evening newscast is government propaganda, not even rewritten enough to disguise its purpose.

Those who choose to see the world as it is, and write about how it might be and ought to be, are a small but hardy band. I am *proud* to be in a room with Prometheus laureates Victor Koman and Brad Linaweaver. When our oppressors no longer write the books on literary history, these names will *shine*.

I am *proud* to win an award whose previous winners include George Orwell, Robert Heinlein, Ayn Rand, Robert Anton Wilson and Roger Shea, C.M. Kornbluth, and Ray Bradbury. When our oppressors no longer write the books on literary history, these names will *shine*.

I am proud that my book was chosen out of as prestigious a collection of works as Zamyatin's *We*, Rand's *We the Living*, Kesey's *One Flew Over the Cuckoo's Nest*, LeGuin's *The Dispossessed*. When our oppressors no longer write the books on literary history, these names will *shine*.

Great oaks from little acorns grow. The literature of liberty contains the seeds of our liberation. The war to liberate the human race will not be won only with guns. Guns can only kill people; they can't kill ideas. The war will also be won with an idea. It is a wrong idea that enslaves us: the idea that human beings can't be trusted with their own lives. It is a right idea that will free us: that if we do not begin trusting each other, no one else will.

Each of the books that has won either the Prometheus Award or has been inducted into the Prometheus Hall of Fame is a weapon in the War to Liberate the Human Race. It may not be the last War the human race must fight, but if we do not win it, we will not survive to fight any others.

This is an important award because it is the only award that *recognizes* we are engaged in a War of Liberation, that recognizes what the price of losing this war is, that camped behind enemy lines calls the honor roll of the soldiers who dedicate their lives to victory.

I stand here because my name has been called. And someday ... some *day* ... the War for Freedom will be won and the names on that honor roll will *shine*.

I thank you all very much.

God Here and Now?
An Introduction to Gloamingerism
Church of the Human God
Reverend Virgil Moore

This is the septagram, the symbol of the Gloamingers. It symbolizes the divergent paths to be traveled over the seven continents, leading to the *one God*, Who shall be revealed through *one Question*.

GOD IS NOT IN HIS HEAVEN!

The religions of the past 5000 years are all wrong! *They* are responsible for the suffering and pain you see around you. **IT'S TRUE!**

The major religions of the world (and all of the minor ones—*with one exception*)—preach that God is an omnipotent, omniscient, supernatural being. They demand that you accept this, *without proof, without knowledge*. They demand that you accept an all-powerful, all seeing God *strictly on faith.*

But if God is so powerful, why does He not wipe out all pain and agony? Books like the Bible and the Baghavad Ghita are filled with excuses, none of which satisfy the minds of those who think through things before accepting them. The "explanations" only CONFUSE and DRIVE OUT the logical thinkers, leaving the religion to those who believe without requiring proof—*the faithistic followers.*

THE FATAL FLAW

The **ONE MISTAKE** made by *every* major faith is the belief that God, whether He is called Christ or Jehovah or Allah or Krishna, is a supernatural being.

THIS TERRIBLE MISTAKE leads to holy wars, inquisitions. plunder, and murder. For if someone is your enemy, against you and your religion, he is **ANTI-GOD**—something evil to be disposed of.

THIS IS WHY human *agony* and *suffering* exist. **BECAUSE ALL OTHER RELIGIONS HAVE BEEN LOOKING FOR GOD IN THE WRONG PLACE!**

The wonderful truth is that **GOD EXISTS!** Not in some imaginary Heaven or Nirvana or Valhalla, but **HERE! ON EARTH! RIGHT NOW!**

There is one religion, *which is not a faith*, which exists to aid those who seek an answer to the problems of our time.

THE ANSWER IS that God is on Earth *at this very moment*. And He (or She!) is every bit as human as you or I. **THAT** is the secret.

GOD is *not* all powerful or all-knowing. He may be a little stronger, a little smarter than some people, but He is an ordinary human just the same.

THEN WHAT MAKES HIM GOD? We have seen that the old religions' definition of a supernatural God is flawed in that God allows evil to exist even though He could stop it. *They are wrong*. Evil exists because God cannot take care of all of it at once! But, far more tragically, God Himself may not know He exists!

THIS is the tragedy of our time! God is somewhere in the world today. You may have seen Him on the street and not have noticed Him. But, for the **FINAL, CATACLYSMIC BATTLE** between good and evil to take place, **GOD MUST BE FOUND AND MADE AWARE OF HIS EXISTENCE!**

This is the mission of the *Gloamingers*. Gloamingers, the children of the **CHURCH OF THE HUMAN GOD** , are dedicated utterly and wholeheartedly to finding God and, through Him, Salvation.

THE SECT OF THE GLOAMINGERS

Gloamingerism is the belief that **GOD EXISTS** right now, on Earth, and that *you* can find Him if you try.

GOD CAN BE FOUND! But only in one way. God can be anyone, male or female, young or old, of any race or color, in any part of the world. There are almost six billion people on the Earth today. The search will not be easy.

GOD WILL REVEAL HIMSELF, though, when He is asked the Question face to face by another person.

THE QUESTION, when asked, will force God, *by His very nature*, to reveal Himself to the questioner, whether He knows He is God or not! The Question must be worded, in English, at least, in this exact way:

"If Thou art God, I offer myself and, in exchange, ask proof."

Ask the Question of the next person you meet! **GOD WALKS THE EARTH TODAY!** Now! He may reveal Himself to you!

IT IS TRUE that we can live without God, that our happiness is of our own making and comes not entirely from Him. You can live without God, but would you want to?

WHEN THE LAST APOCALYPTIC STRUGGLE AGAINST EVIL BEGINS—AS IT MUST—GOD SHALL NEED ALL THE HELP HE CAN GET FROM HIS CHILDREN. AND YOU CANNOT HELP GOD UNTIL YOU FIND HIM!

This booklet is the work of one who is searching for GOD. Your donation will not be refused.

The Last, True Hope
by Bishop Alam Kimar Whyte

DO YOU SEE the suffering about you and wonder why it exists?

DO YOU HEAR the cries of the poor, the hungry, and wonder why it is so?

DO YOU FEEL that the answers and solutions given by other religions are wrong?

IT'S TRUE! Christianity, Judaism, Buddhism, Islamism, and all of the other religions are wrong. They are the forces responsible for the suffering and the pain they supposedly wish to prevent. How is this so?

All of the ancient religions, and all of the modern religions *with one exception* suffer from the fatal flaw of believing that God—whatever His or Her name may be, whether it be Christ or Jehovah or YHVH or Allah or Krishna—is an omnipotent, omnipresent, omniscient, supernatural being.

THIS TERRIBLE MISTAKE leads to holy wars, to inquisitions, to plunder, and to murder. If this God is so powerful, why has He not shown Himself to us? The Bible is full of excuses and polylogistic games to confuse the reader, to confound the doubtful and to leave within the religion only those who choose to accept God *on faith*, without proof.

WITH SUCH BELIEVERS, the major religions of the world have been able to trample the doubtful beneath their sandals, to seize power over others and ravish the Earth. All they have to do is to label their enemies **ANTI-GOD** and all that remains is to dispose of them. In this horrible manner have the establishment religions (and so many of the aspiring new ones) lain waste to this planet. God's planet.

BUT THERE IS HOPE! There is one religion, *which is not* *a faith*, that exists to aid those seeking an answer to the problems of our time. An answer, and an explanation. The explanation is so gloriously simple that the legitimacy and the honesty of all other religions is called into *extreme doubt* by it.

GOD EXISTS! Oh yes, nobody can doubt that. But He is not all-powerful and all-knowing. He is as **HUMAN** and as **ORDINARY** as you or I. **THAT** is the secret!

GOD IS HERE. Right now. On earth. There can be no doubt as to that. The signs of a **CATACLYSMIC STRUGGLE** between Good and Evil are completely apparent!

THE REASON for misery and pain and death is that *God is not omnipotent.* He is only one man (or perhaps one *woman*). Perhaps He is a little more powerful than many of us, perhaps He is a little smarter. But He is a Man nonetheless! You may have even seen Him and not noticed Him! Even God Himself may not know who He is! *This is the tragedy!* **GOD MAY NOT KNOW HE EXISTS!**

THIS IS OUR MISSION—to find God and, in finding Him or Her, find our salvation! God cannot cure *all* suffering. Nor is God the fountainhead all joy. You can live your life without God. But would you want to? God will grow in power, it is true, but so will Evil (whatever its name). If God is a mere human as you or I, then He needs all the help He can get.

THE FIRST CHURCH OF THE HUMAN GOD is dedicated utterly and wholeheartedly to the search for God, the man. The beginning of a **NEW WORLD** is almost with us. The old religions will try to hold us back by having us search for a God in the wrong place. **GOD IS HERE—RIGHT NOW! WE MUST FIND HIM AND HELP HIM, OR ALL IS LOST!**

About J. Neil Schulman

J. Neil Schulman is the author of two Prometheus award-winning novels, *Alongside Night* and *The Rainbow Cadenza*, short fiction, nonfiction, and screenwritings, including the CBS *Twilight Zone* episode "Profile in Silver."

His first nonfiction book was *Stopping Power: Why 70 Million Americans Own Guns*, of which Charlton Heston said, "Mr. Schulman's book is the most cogent explanation of the gun issue I have yet read. He presents the assault on the Second Amendment in frighteningly clear terms. Even the extremists who would ban firearms will learn from his lucid prose."

Stopping Power was published in hardcover in June, 1994, by Synapse-Centurion, and sold out its first printing of 8,500 copies. It was quoted from by witnesses on both sides in the March, 1995 hearings on firearms before Congress's House Subcommittee on Crime. An updated edition with new material is being released by Pulpless.Com, Inc., in Spring, 1999.

Schulman's next book, *Self Control Not Gun Control,* picked up where *Stopping Power* left off with an exploration of the uses and abuses of both personal and political power.

Dr. Walter E. Williams, talk show host, newspaper columnist, and Chairman of the Department of Economics at George Mason University, says of *Self Control Not Gun Control*, "Schulman interestingly and insightfully raises a number of liberty-related issues that we ignore at the nation's peril. His ideas are precisely those that helped make our country the destination of those seeking liberty. The book's title says it all: personal responsibility, not laws and prohibitions, is the mark of a civil society."

Schulman's most-recent book is *The Robert Heinlein Interview and Other Heinleiniana*, just released by Pulpless.Com, Inc., which Virginia Heinlein calls "a book that should be on the shelves of everyone interested in science fiction."

Schulman has been published in the *Los Angeles Times* and other national newspapers, as well as *National Review, New Libertarian, Reason, Liberty,* and other magazines. His *L.A. Times* article "If Gun Laws Work, Why Are We Afraid?" won the James Madison Award from the Second Amendment Foundation; and in November, 1995, the 500,000-member Citizens Committee for the Right to Keep and Bear Arms awarded Schulman its Gun Rights Defender prize. Schulman's books have been praised by Nobel laureate Milton Friedman, Anthony Burgess, Robert A. Heinlein, Colin Wilson, and many other prominent individuals. His short story "The Repossessed" was the lead story in *Adventures in the Twilight Zone,* edited by Carol Serling; and his short story "Day of Atonement" appeared in the shared-world anthology *Free Space* edited by Brad Linaweaver and Ed Kramer, a Tor hardcover published in July, 1997.

Schulman is a popular speaker on a variety of topics, and a frequent talk show guest for such hosts as Dennis Prager, Michael Jackson, Oliver North, and Barry Farber. He was on ABC's *World News Tonight* as an expert on defensive use of firearms during the 1992 Los Angeles riots, and was chosen to debate Los Angeles County Sheriff Sherman Block on UPN Channel 13 News Los Angeles on the topic of the repeal of the federal "assault weapons" ban.

J. Neil Schulman is a pioneer in electronic publishing, having founded in 1987 the first company to distribute books by bestselling authors for download by modem. He is currently Chairman and Publisher of Pulpless.Com, Inc., which operates the Pulpless.Com web site—"Pulpless Fiction & Nonfiction, too!"—on the World Wide Web at www.pulpless.com, and his personal web site is at www.pulpless.com/jneil/. His internet address is jneil@pulpless.com.

All of Mr. Schulman's books are available for download from these web sites.

CPSIA information can be obtained at www.ICGtesting.com
Printed in the USA
LVOW132049271112

309047LV00008B/1241/P